TWICE DEAD

BOOK TWO IN THE TAYLOR MADISON MYSTERY SERIES

ELIZABETH DEARL

Hard Shell Word Factory

This book is for Joe, who never stops believing

My thanks to Sergeant Joe Hollingsworth
for providing forensic detail, and to Keron and Jesse
for allowing me to use your names.

eBook ISBN: 0-7599-3303-0
Published April 2005

Trade Paperback
ISBN: 0-7599-3307-3
Published May 2005

Hard Shell Word Factory
PO Box 161
Amherst Jct. WI 54407
books@hardshell.com
www.hardshell.com

Chapter One

A SLIVER OF dawn peeked through the gap in my bedroom curtains. As it fell across my closed eyelids, attempting to coax me from contented slumber, I buried my face in the pillow and snuggled deeper into the covers. After spending the majority of my twenty-eight years in Houston's near-tropical climate, I still wasn't accustomed to the chill of a West Texas autumn and struggled with the adjustment to weather that actually changed with the seasons. Though I looked forward to witnessing Perdue's first snowfall, I was less enthused at the notion of learning to drive in the slick white stuff.

The man beside me stirred, pulled me to him. I nuzzled his neck sleepily, reveling in his warmth.

Warmth. Man. Man in my bed. Dawn.

I sat bolt upright. "Oh, shit, Cal, we fell asleep! Get up. Hurry, it's morning!"

He grinned, reaching for me. "Bribe me."

I pushed him away and scrambled out of the bed, grabbing my robe. "Stop joking, damn it."

"Who's joking? C'mere." He held out inviting arms and I nearly weakened. But only nearly.

"Get up," I insisted. "Half the town is awake and having breakfast by now. Do you want to get caught?"

He sat up and rubbed his face. "Taylor, I wish you wouldn't phrase it like that. Neither of us is sneaking around on a spouse, we're both of legal age, and we're even of opposite sexes."

"None of which would prevent this from becoming a town scandal if it got out," I reminded him as I snatched up my brush and began tugging tangles from my hair. "The sheriff's election is less than a month away. Do you really think the puritans of Perdue, Texas will vote for someone openly indulging in sex without benefit of wedlock?"

He shrugged, the muscles in his shoulders rippling seductively. I turned away before the sight could tempt me, but I couldn't escape his voice.

"I guess we could get married, just to make them happy," he said.

I clenched my teeth. "We don't have time for jokes. You know very well that every tongue in town will be wagging by noon if you're seen leaving my house at this time of day."

"So it seems to me the problem will be solved if I don't leave."

"Cal Arnette, if you're not out of that bed in ten seconds..."

"You'll come in and get me?" he suggested hopefully.

I stalked out of the room and into the kitchen, where I expended a little frustration on the old, tin coffeepot. It made satisfying clanging noises against the sink as I slammed it down to fill it with water. I longed to replace it with a Mr. Coffee drip machine, but it still seemed somehow disrespectful to get rid of the late sheriff's personal belongings. The thought irritated me. This was, after all, my house now.

And I had been the one to solve the murder of Sheriff Miles Crawford—had, in fact, been the only one convinced that his death had been something other than an accidental snakebite. His killer was dead, Crawford's death revenged. There was no reason for his ghost to linger—unless you counted the fact that he had been my biological father. I had not learned that myself until after his death. Perhaps he was trying to get to know me.

"If that's the case," I said aloud, striking a wooden match to light a burner on the ancient gas stove, "you might as well find out I happen to enjoy modern conveniences."

"Who are you talking to?"

I turned, burning my fingers on the match. Cal watched me from the doorway, his eyebrows cocked quizzically. He was still in his underwear, the white cotton boxers contrasting nicely with bronze skin. Cal's mother was of Mexican descent, his father French, and the combination of their genes had produced a lovely hunk of man.

He padded over to me, dark hair loose about his shoulders, not yet tied back into the ponytail he wore when in uniform.

"Why aren't you dressed?" I demanded, foiling his efforts to kiss my neck.

"Uh-uh. You have to answer my question before I answer yours. Who were you talking to?"

"Myself. Now answer mine." I pushed him firmly away, and popped bread into the toaster.

"You'd shove a man out on the street before he's had his morning coffee? Cruel, Taylor." He examined the tin pot, which was only now beginning to make perking sounds. "Why don't you break down and buy yourself a Mr. Coffee? Didn't you just get a healthy advance on that new novel?"

"Quit changing the subject. You have to get out of here."

"Too late," he said smugly, digging through my refrigerator for a jar of jelly. "Dorothy's front drapes were twitchin' up a storm when I fetched the newspaper off the porch."

I dropped the egg I had been about to break into a skillet. "You went out on my porch dressed like that? Undressed like that?"

Cal tsked and bent to clean up the mess with a wad of paper towel. "Cat's out of the bag, I guess." I could hear the hidden laughter in his voice.

"The whole litter's out of the bag if Dorothy Stenson spotted you. Oh, hell." I sat down heavily in a kitchen chair and watched him butter a slice of toast. "I thought you wanted to be sheriff."

"I do. Don't you have any strawberry preserves? I hate grape jelly."

"No." Infuriating man. "Cal, what are we going to do? Maybe if I talk to Dorothy, she'll keep it to herself, do you think? Oh, gad, that's a stupid notion. Cal, what on earth are you doing? Cal?" He had scooped me up into his arms and was heading out of the kitchen.

"Long as we're caught anyway," he drawled into my ear, "might as well make the most of it."

His lips stopped any protest I might have made. And I have to admit that by the time we reached the bedroom I had long since stopped trying to protest.

WHEN I AWOKE for the second time that day, my bedside alarm clock read nine-thirty. Cal was gone, as were his clothes. I staggered back into the kitchen and found all traces of our interrupted breakfast cleared away, the burner under the coffee set to low. I poured myself a tepid cup and took it into the backyard.

The morning had warmed a bit, so I was comfortable in my robe and fuzzy slippers. Someone in the neighborhood was burning leaves, and the aroma took me back to early childhood, before all the environmental rules and regulations made leaf-burning a crime on the same par as assault and battery. No one would dare to burn leaves in Houston these days, but one of the charms of a small town like Perdue was that people tended to follow their own rules. Personally, I'd take burning leaves over muggings and drive-by shootings any old day.

I left the door propped open so the house could benefit from the sweet smelling breeze and perched on the top step, lighting a cigarette, my first of the day. I was trying to cut down, but refused to give up the one that went with my morning coffee.

A tiny, cold nose nudged my hand and I pulled Hazel into my lap, covering her shivering body with a flap of my robe. "Well, good morning, princess."

I doubted ferrets really hibernated during the winter, but I had seen little of her since the first cold snap. She had scouted out all the warmest nooks and crannies in the house, and spent most of her time lately curled up into a snoring ball of fur.

"Want some breakfast? C'mon."

I was out of cat food. Again. "You eat like a Saint Bernard," I grumbled as I scrambled an egg and scraped it into her bowl. She gobbled it, then licked her long whiskers and looked at me hopefully.

"Oh, no, you don't. One egg is plenty. I'm not hankering to own a forty-pound ferret, thank you." I stopped. Hankering? Had I actually said "hankering?" Cal's West Texas speech patterns were clearly contagious.

I spent a couple of hours editing the chapter I had finished the night before, then took a bone warming shower and climbed into a sweat suit. A trip to the grocery store was in order, for people food as well as ferret food.

Unless I was willing to make the fifty-mile trip to Lubbock, Posey's was my only choice. Located on Perdue's main drag, Posey's Grocery combined country store whimsy with its owner's sharp business savvy, and stocked everything from pickles in a wooden barrel to Lean Cuisine in the freezer case.

A little bell rang as I opened the door and the elderly man behind the counter paused to dribble tobacco juice into a Styrofoam cup before greeting me with a stained smile.

"Why, Miss Madison. Good to see you!"

"Hi, Arnold." I glanced around, but the two of us were alone in the big room. "What are you doing here? Where's Bo?" My heart gave an uneasy flutter. I had never known Bonita Posey to miss a day at her beloved store. And she was, after all, an old woman.

Arnold chuckled, dispelling my gloomy thoughts. "Just took herself a day off is all. Asked me to look after things." He preened, as well he might. I felt sure it was an honor to be compared with guarding the royal jewels.

Taking a wicker basket, I prowled the store for needed items as he continued talking. Arnold would never be accused of telling half a story.

"What's this?" I interrupted him, discovering a pile of unlabeled zip-locked bags in the freezer section. They contained chunks of some kind of meat, perhaps fish or chicken.

"Just some rattlesnake meat," he replied. "Hester Miggs always freezes a bunch to sell in the off-season, in case folks get to cravin' it."

"Uck." I dropped the bag in a hurry. I'd tasted snake meat during my first visit to Perdue's annual Rattlesnake Festival, but not by choice—no one had bothered to tell me what it was until after I'd put it into my mouth. "When will Bo be back?"

"Dunno. She didn't say. Funny thing. I've minded the place for her before, if she wanted to go somewhere. Vegas, usually. She goes a few times every year...always loses. Not that she has to worry about money." He spat into his cup. "But this is the first time I recall that she up and decided on the spur of the moment to take a day off. Called me at five a.m. "

"Really," I murmured, only half-listening as I read the directions on a frozen pizza. I missed pizza most of all, hot and fresh and delivered to my door. Domino's would most likely not be tempted by the prospect of opening a franchise in Perdue, Texas. Pity.

"I think it's the day," he confided, lowering his voice as if the other non-existent customers might overhear.

"Hmmm?" I looked at him. "What day?"

"You know, the...anniversary, I guess you'd call it, though that seems an awful happy word for somethin' so bad."

He had lost me. "Anniversary of what?"

"Guess she just couldn't take it anymore," he went on. "Said she was gonna clean out that house and then have it torn down. Shoulda done it years ago, if you ask me."

I shook my head, but the words refused to fall into logical order. "Arnold, I have no idea what you're talking about. What house?"

The bell above the door jingled and a woman shivered her way in. "Cold enough to freeze the tail off a hog," she said. "How-do, Arnold. Where's Bo?"

Arnold started his spiel from square one, but oddly enough made no reference to "the day." The woman bought a can of baking powder and departed.

I put my loaded basket on the counter and met his eyes. "What day is it, Arnold?"

"Why, Tuesday, I reckon. Isn't it?" Obviously, he was regretting his earlier ramblings. Before I could persist, he dropped his gaze, began ringing up my purchases on the antique cash register and threw in a subject that made my ears prick up. "Say, though, if you need any furniture for that little house of yours, you might want to run out to Bo's and take a look. She said she'd sell what she could and donate the rest to charity."

My confusion cleared a little. "She's having a yard sale? Why didn't you say so in the first place?" I had spent most of my life economizing. Use it up, wear it out, make it do—the credo during the Great Depression was still a useful one to live by if you existed on the verge of bankruptcy. Garage sales, yard sales and rummage sales had furnished my Houston apartment, as well as providing most of my college wardrobe. Thanks to three published mystery novels, I was hopefully past the skimping stage of my life, but the magic words yard sale still made my blood rush a little faster.

I paid for the groceries and hustled the bags into the passenger seat of my old Volkswagen, so excited that I had started the engine and pulled out of the parking lot before I realized I had never been to Bo's house and had no idea where it was. I glanced into the rearview mirror and winked at myself. A problem easily solved.

The sheriff's office was only a couple of blocks away. Cal was fiddling with the thermostat when I opened the door, and I could immediately understand why. As cold as it was outside, the front office felt like a meat locker. I said as much.

Cal scowled. "Thanks for stating the obvious, Taylor. That really helps."

"Don't snarl at the woman who's come to take you away from all this."

He gave the thermostat one last whack, then crossed the room to take me into his arms. "Tahiti? Bermuda? Say the word, lady, and I'll type up my resignation."

"Would you settle for lunch?"

"Sure. Your place?"

I loved that leer, but tried to keep my goal in mind. "Not today. Is it okay if we take your car?"

He looked puzzled. "A car? Aren't we going to Lucy's?" Lucy's Café, Perdue's only restaurant, was directly across the street from the courthouse.

"Nope. I had something else in mind." Shamelessly, I gave him my best attempt at a come-hither look.

It worked. Before I knew it, we were seated in his patrol car, the heater blasting away.

"Seems a little chilly for necking in the back seat, but I'm game if you are."

"Mmmm." I returned his kiss before pushing him gently away. "Maybe later. Right now, I need a ride out to Bonita Posey's house."

Cal was still shaking his head fifteen minutes later as he turned off the highway onto a gravel road. "Lunch, she said. More, her eyes said. I'm a sucker, that's what I am."

"Quit griping," I said. "I fed you lunch from my own bag of groceries."

"A peanut butter sandwich," he mumbled. "I hate peanut butter."

"I'll make it up to you." I peered out the window, but all I could see in any direction was empty land. "I had no idea she lived so far out in the boonies. Thanks again, Cal. I never would've found this place on my own."

"I could've just drawn you a map." I had neglected to bring drinks, and he was still tonguing peanut butter off the roof of his mouth.

"But your car has more trunk space than mine," I pointed out. "Of course, if I end up buying a chair or a table or something big I'll need to borrow a pickup, I guess."

Cal rolled his eyes.

We rounded a curve and a two-story farmhouse, tucked into a grove of large pecan trees, appeared on the horizon. "What a pretty house! Surely that's not what she's planning to tear down."

"What?"

I repeated Arnold's explanation of Bo's activities as we pulled to a stop, red dust flying up from the dirt driveway.

"I doubt Bo's planning to bulldoze her home," Cal said. "Arnold must've misunderstood."

"I guess so." We followed paving stones to the front door and I knocked. No one answered.

"Don't think she's here," Cal said after a few minutes.

"She has to be." I shaded my eyes and peered through a front window, but heavy draperies blocked my view. "Come on."

Cal followed me around to the back of the house. I rounded the corner and came to an abrupt halt, catching my breath. "Wow."

"Yeah. Impressive, isn't it?"

A carefully tended garden stretched into the distance. Bare, recently turned earth in some patches, thriving green in others, it seemed to go on forever. I'm not a botanist, but I recognized some of the leaves: winter cabbage, carrots, sweet potatoes. The vegetables shared space with fall-blooming flowers—lilies and bronze chrysanthemums big enough to choke and elephant.)and lilies and bronze chrysanthemums big enough to choke an elephant. And roses, roses everywhere in a blaze of color against the gray sky. No frost had yet materialized to kill them back. I knew how much work roses took in their own right. Surely an eighty-two-year-old woman didn't tend this by herself.

Before I could ask Cal, a movement in the distance caught my eye. "There she is!"

Cal squinted. "Oh, yeah, I forgot about that little house. That must be what Arnold was talking about. Don't know why she'd want to get rid of it, though. Looks like a nice place to me. She ought to rent it out." The small, white house crouched at the opposite end of the gigantic garden, and Bo stood at the entrance, vigorously shaking out a dusty cloth.

I set off in her direction, ignoring Cal's suggestion we take the car. By the time I reached the smaller house, though, I was wishing I had listened to him. The distance proved greater than it had seemed, and I was frozen solid when I knocked at the half-open door.

Bo appeared immediately. She stared. "Taylor? What in hell are you doing here?"

Not the friendliest greeting I'd ever heard, but I was too cold to care. I pushed past her, but the temperature inside the little house was no warmer. I noticed then that Bo was wearing a down-filled jacket and thick gloves.

"I probably should've called first," I apologized. "But when Arnold told me that you were planning a yard sale, I couldn't resist getting the first peek." I was already scanning the stacks of boxes and piles of furniture, my sale radar set on locate. "Wow, is that coat tree real brass?"

She sighed, leaning against a wooden crate. "I might've known the old fart would go blabbing my business all over town. Shoulda just told him I was off to Vegas."

Her tone finally penetrated my distracted fog and I tore my gaze away from a curio cabinet—real cherry, I'd be willing to bet—to peer at her more closely. She looked older, somehow, her usually rosy cheeks pale, her wrinkles more pronounced.

"I really am sorry, Bo," I said, sincerely this time. "If I'm intruding, I'll wait and come back when you have the actual sale. I can help, if you want," I added, offering an olive branch.

She took it. "Pay me no mind, Taylor. I shouldn't have snapped your head off like that. You're welcome to stay and look around, really. It's just the day, I guess. I've been in a rotten mood since my feet hit the floor this morning."

There it was again. "The day." I was still trying to figure out a way to question her without sounding like a busybody when Cal came tramping in.

"Enjoy your stroll?" he asked dryly. "Howdy, Bo."

She nodded shortly. "Cal. Arnold strikes again, I see."

Cal raised an eyebrow at me and I shook my head. "Cal just gave me a ride, Bo. I don't think anyone else is coming."

"Glad to hear it." She pursed her lips thoughtfully. "Not such a bad thing after all. Cal can help me lug some of the heavier stuff outside while you look around."

It wasn't a request. Cal grinned and grabbed a large box. Like everyone else in Perdue, he jumped when Bo barked. Besides being one of the two county commissioners, she collected secrets the way some women collect recipes, and delighted in the fact she held most of the town residents "by the short hairs," as she put it.

While Cal toted and Bo supervised, I wended my way through what had to be several decades' worth of accumulated treasures, trash and junk. There was no apparent order. It reminded me of a childhood friend's attic. Tina and I had spent many a rainy Saturday exploring the possessions of three generations, peeling away layers little by little, the books and clothes and furniture getting older and older the further we dug. Tina, not surprisingly, went on to become an archeologist.

I lusted after a six-foot tall bookcase with glass doors, sneezed my way through a waist-high stack of yellowed magazines, mostly the *Saturday Evening Post* and *National Geographic*, and ran my fingers along the intricate carving of twining vines that decorated the lid of a trunk big enough to serve as a child's coffin.

At the very rear of the big room, I found—*it*.

"Oh, my God," I whispered reverently, kneeling before it.

Solid mahogany, and a swipe with my thumb was all it took to reveal the gleaming beauty that lay hidden but undimmed beneath a thick layer of dust. Stacks of cardboard boxes hid the desktop, but the drawers were mine to explore. Tarnished brass rings dangled enticingly, and I glanced over my shoulder with a twinge of guilt before pulling the first one. I needed to see if the drawers still opened smoothly, but I didn't want Bo to think I was snooping. Not to worry. I could hear her chatting with Cal, but the mounds of junk hid them from my sight. And me from theirs.

The first drawer contained nothing but a cobweb, and I closed it hurriedly in case the web's architect was still in residence. The second drawer, deeper than the first (perfect for holding paper supplies and manuscript pages) was empty as well. Only the long middle drawer that stretched across the kneehole was anything but bare, and all it held was an old Bible.

I stood up, my excitement fading in the face of harsh reality. It didn't take the expertise of an antique dealer to know the desk was worth a fortune. And though I was more financially comfortable than I had ever been in my life, it was way out of my price range. But oh, to have such a desk! I could already picture my computer sitting regally atop the polished wood, my second bedroom cleared of unpacked boxes left over from my move to Perdue and set up as a real office. The desk would center nicely below the large window, affording me a view of my beloved backyard, the sun shining through the leaves of the maple tree...

Stop it, I told myself firmly. *You want a desk? Buy one at K-Mart. Particle board will hold a computer just as well as mahogany, won't it?*

I gave the desk one last, loving stroke and squeezed my way back to the front of the house, not bothering to examine anything else along the way. My depression was enhanced by the chill of the room, the cold numbing my mood along with my bones.

I was amazed to see how much Cal had accomplished in such a short time, until a glance at my watch informed me that we had been here for well over two hours. Another twinge of guilt. All that work on one, measly peanut butter sandwich. But he looked cheerful enough as he emerged from behind a dilapidated chest of drawers, pointing out the peeling veneer to Bo, who nodded agreement.

"Right, then, I'll have it chopped up for firewood. Well, hello, gal," she said, spotting me. "Any luck? Say, if that face gets any longer you'll be sweeping the floor with your chin. What's the matter?"

"Nothing," I mumbled. "You've got some terrific stuff here, Bo. You're going to pull in big bucks at the sale."

She snorted. "Money's the least of my worries. Just time to get rid of all this. Past time. So what caught your fancy? Something Cal can help you carry?"

"Cal couldn't begin to lift it," I said. "Doesn't matter, though, because I couldn't afford it anyway. Cal, I guess you'd better be getting back to work, hadn't you? Sorry I stayed so long."

Bo raised a hand. "Hold your hosses, gal. What is it you think you can't afford? Maybe I can cut you a deal."

I swallowed painfully, unwilling to even talk about it. The sooner it was out of my mind, the better. But she kept after me until I finally told her.

Her face darkened. “That big desk? Way in the back?”

I nodded. “Mahogany. I’d advise you to contact a dealer about it, Bo. Don’t stick something like that in a yard sale.”

“You can have it,” she said, her words clipped. “Gratis. Cal, take a look and see how much help we’ll need to get it out of here.”

My head was spinning, a combination of disbelief, consternation and utter joy. Consternation took the forefront. “Bo, you don’t know what you’re saying. It’s worth hundreds of dollars, maybe even thousands. I couldn’t let you—”

“You could and you will. I don’t want it...don’t ever care to see it again, to tell the truth. Hope you’re plannin’ to put it out of sight somewhere, or I just might not even come visit you anymore.” Her voice was harsh. “I hate the damned thing.”

“But why?”

She squinted at me and seemed to snap back into focus, grinning like the old Bo. “Makes no difference why, does it? You got yourself a desk. For pity’s sake, child, you’re trembling. And no wonder. Them sweat suits are right comfy, but a coat on top would help. Don’t tell me you’ve lived here since May and still haven’t bought yourself a decent coat.”

“Didn’t need one up ’til now,” I retorted. I looked around the room and noticed, for the first time, that a fireplace was lodged in the western wall. Cal’s labors had cleared away the junk that had hidden it before. “Well, for heaven’s sake, Bo. Weren’t you just saying you were planning to break up that old chest for firewood? I’ll make a deal with you.” I gestured at the fireplace. “If you’ll burn it now and get this house warmed up, I’ll stay here all afternoon and help you work. You can pick me up later, right, Cal?”

“Sure. I’ll even take an ax to the chest, Bo, and get the fire started for you before I—”

“No!” Bo planted her back against the chest as if willing to protect it with her life.

Cal looked as startled as I felt. “Sorry, Bo, did I misunderstand? I won’t bust it up if you don’t want me to.”

Her tense shoulders slumped and she let out a bark of laughter. “Didn’t mean to snarl at you. All I meant was, it wouldn’t be a good idea to use that fireplace. Hasn’t been cleaned in over thirty years and there’s no tellin’ what kind of critters mighta built nests in there. But Taylor did remind me to be a better hostess than I’ve been. Tell ya what, I’ll run up to the house and make us a thermos of hot chocolate. It’ll warm you up for the drive back to town, at least.”

"Think she's trying to get rid of us?" I asked Cal as she slammed the door behind her.

"I'd just as soon she was," he replied, flexing his back. "Didn't wake up this morning with this kind of activity in mind."

I felt myself blush, remembering the activity he *had* had in mind. "Want to see my desk?"

"Sure."

We maneuvered back through the piles and stood before it. Cal let out a low whistle.

"It'll take the whole Perdue football team to get this outta here. And somebody's pickup. A big pickup."

"But isn't it beautiful?" I asked dreamily.

"I refuse to agree with that until I make sure I'm not the one who's going to be wrestling with it. I think I've done enough lifting for one day. Hell, for a week."

"Well, I haven't. Cal, really, I'd like to stay and help for a while. A woman in her eighties can't be moving this heavy stuff around. You really wouldn't mind coming back for me this evening?"

He smiled. "Bribe me."

I did, but not for as long as I would have liked. We were interrupted when I gave a mighty sneeze, and not from the dust this time. "Crap, I think I'm catching a cold. Cal, we've got to get some heat in here. My fingers won't even bend anymore."

"Okay, let's see what I can do."

We traipsed back to the fireplace. Cal got down on his knees and craned his neck to peer up the chimney. "I'd say she's right. There's definitely something blocking the sunlight."

"Can't you get it out? Would this help?" I handed him a broom.

"We'll give it a try." He poked the broom handle up the opening and jiggled it. Something clattered to the hearth, but was swallowed up by the mound of dusty ashes before I could see what it was.

"I'd better clean this out," I said, and found a flat sheet of cardboard which I used to begin scooping away ashes, depositing them in a trash bag. While I was working, Cal decided he needed his flashlight and went out to the patrol car to fetch it.

Men, I thought, exasperated. *A man will mess around for hours and never get the damn fire started, and I'm freezing my butt off.* I picked up the broom and went to work on the chimney, muttering to myself. "Why on earth he thinks he has to see something...poke...in order to be able to get it loose...prod...is something I'll never...grunt...understand." The obstruction gave way, tumbling out onto the metal grating that my scooping had uncovered. I looked up to see Cal, accompanied by Bo, standing in the doorway.

Cal dropped his flashlight, Bo her thermos bottle.

"Holy shit," said Cal.

Bo said nothing. As if in slow motion, she slithered down to join her broken thermos on the dirty floor.

From amid the jumble of bones, a skull gazed up at us, its jaw agape as if in surprise.

Chapter Two

IF THE SKULL'S expression was indeed one of surprise, then the two of us had something in common. Make that the three of us. Cal hadn't moved from the doorway, not even to check on Bo.

"Holy shit," he repeated.

"Uh-huh," I agreed weakly. The thing's empty eye sockets stared back at me, and a gold incisor twinkled through the soot coating its teeth.

Bo groaned. The sound broke our horrified trance, and we both rushed to kneel beside her.

Cal lifted her wrist, checked her pulse. "Taylor, use the squad car's radio and call for an ambulance."

Bo clutched at my sleeve as I tried to rise. "Don't," she croaked. "I'm okay. Just help me sit up."

We complied, bearing her not insignificant weight between us. She glanced at the collection of bones littering the fireplace, shuddered, and squeezed her eyes shut. "I don't believe it," she said, so softly we had to lean closer to hear her. "It's just like him, though. After all these years, still causing me grief."

Cal's eyes narrowed. "You mean you know who it is?"

She glared at him. "Well, of course I do. It's my husband, Ralph. My late husband. Of course I was never sure until now that he was really dead."

Cal and I looked at each other.

"She's in shock," he murmured. "Doesn't know what she's saying."

Bo jerked her arm from his grasp and, using me as a brace, pushed herself to her feet.

"I know exactly what I'm saying, youngster, and I'll thank you not to talk over my head as if I'm deaf or dotty." She trembled, but remained standing, one hand still clutching my shoulder for balance.

"I'm sorry," Cal soothed. "Didn't mean to imply any such thing. But if you won't let me call for an ambulance, I'm at least going to insist you let us get you back to the house. It's too friggin' cold out here for any of us."

She gave in. "Bourbon," she said. "That's what we all need.

Nothin' like a swig of good whiskey to warm a body up."

But once we got her inside the big farmhouse, Cal had me brew a pot of tea instead, and forced her to drink two cups of it.

"*Gaaa*," she said, choking down the second dose. "Never did like sweet tea."

"The sugar offsets shock," Cal reminded her. "And it seems to have worked. Your color is coming back."

"Good." She got up from the kitchen table and rummaged in a cabinet. "Now I'll take an antidote for the cure." She poured us each a shot of whiskey, then drained her own and was pouring another before I had taken the first sip of mine.

I didn't care much for the taste of bourbon, but the effect was worth the initial bitterness. A shaft of heat followed the liquor down my throat, spreading to warm my fingers and toes and relaxing the tense muscles in my neck.

Cal pushed his glass aside, still full. "I need to ask you some questions," he told Bo.

"I 'spect you do at that." She leaned back in her chair and propped sneakered feet on the worn tabletop. "Thing is, I don't know what to tell you. I have no idea what he's doing there."

"Are you sure it's your husband?" I blurted.

"It's him all right. Didn't you see the gold tooth? Ralph's pride and joy that damned tooth, not that he'd ever admit to anything as sinful as pride."

Cal drummed his fingers on the table. "You said something about not being sure he was dead until now. What did you mean by that? I thought you'd been widowed for years."

"I have. Sort of. Oh, Lord, it's a long story. You've lived here most of your life, Cal, so it's hard to believe you haven't heard most of it before."

"Can't say I have."

Bo gave a short laugh. "Guess everyone's moved on to other gossip by now. It has been thirty-five years after all." She sobered. "Still feels like yesterday to me."

"What happened?" I asked gently.

She dug a filterless Camel from her shirt pocket and lit it, then offered one to me. I declined, opting for one of my own ultra-lights. Our smoke mingled above the table as she tilted her head back and closed her eyes.

"Thirty-five years ago today," she said, "Ralph Posey ran off." Her eyes popped open. "Well, that's what I thought at the time anyway.

That's what everybody thought. He took a bunch of cash from the church safe and left in the dead of night. No one ever heard from him again."

"He stole money from a church?" I'm not what you'd call a religious person, but the thought shocked me.

"His own church to boot." She grimaced. "He was a preacher. The theft didn't set too well with his congregation, but at least most of them were better off than he left me. I had to wait seven years before I could have him declared legally dead." She shook her head. "Never thought of looking up the chimney. Sure would've saved myself a tough seven years."

"It must've been very hard on you," I murmured, patting her hand.

She gazed at me for a moment, and then grinned broadly. "You're a sweet gal, but I think you're offering sympathy for all the wrong reasons. I didn't give a rat's ass that he was gone, wish he'd left sooner. I hated that bastard."

I gasped.

Cal's eyebrows shot up like startled geese.

"The hard part was that our bank account was in his name. Status quo for the 1950s, Taylor. Count your lucky stars you're living in a liberated age. I couldn't get my hands on a single penny for those seven long years it took to get myself officially widowed. And me with a seventeen-year-old daughter who wanted to go to college."

"What did you do? How did you live?"

"By the skin of my teeth. My Pop had given me some oil stock when I turned twenty-one, and I still had it tucked away. Ralph didn't know about it, though I can't imagine why I never told him during those early days of our marriage. I was so besotted with the son-of-a-bitch, I'm surprised I didn't lay the stupid stock certificate at his feet. Sure gave him everything else I owned, and then some." She mashed out her cigarette, lit another.

"That stock was worth about five thousand dollars. Doesn't sound like much, does it? But it didn't cost as much to live back then either. This house was paid for, which was a blessing, so all I had to come up with was tax money. My daughter, Faith, had a scholarship to Texas Tech, but I sent her some cash to pay for books and extras.

"The rest of the money I used to buy old Sammy Haskell's grocery store. Worked out for both of us. He was old and tired, wanted to retire and spend the rest of his days with a fishin' pole. I needed a way to make some money to see Faith and me through the lean years.

Wasn't easy, let me tell you. Sammy had let the store go to hell in a hand basket. I had to kill the rats before I could even restock." She sighed. "You can't imagine how frustrating it was to know that nearly fifty thousand dollars was just sitting in the bank and I couldn't get my hands on it."

Cal whistled. "Fifty grand was a lot of money back then."

"A fortune," she agreed. "Pop had given me a generous dowry. Ralph used what he needed to build the church, then tucked the rest into a bank account and left it there. We lived like paupers. Poor as church mice, you've heard that expression? Well, we lived like the fleas on those mice. Good thing he considered gardening the Lord's own work or we might have starved to death."

"I don't understand," I said.

She curled her lip. "Avoiding the sin of avarice, my dear."

Cal shook himself and got to his feet. "I've got to call Doc."

I looked at him. "Doc Neil? Why?"

"He's the county coroner, Taylor, and we've got a dead body out there. I've let procedure slide for too long as it is." He rubbed his forehead. "I'd better get in touch with the Lubbock County Sheriff's Office while I'm at it. Our crime scene kit consists of a few paper bags and a pair of tweezers."

"Crime scene?" I glanced at Bo, but she was staring off into the middle distance.

Cal sighed. "Yeah, Taylor, a crime scene. We can pretty much rule out suicide, in my humble opinion, unless you think Ralph Posey stuffed himself up the chimney and stayed there until he suffocated." He laid his hand atop Bo's and she flinched. "Got any ideas about who could've killed him, Bo? Any enemies that you know of?"

She broke into a hearty laugh. "Enemies? He had 'em, plenty of 'em. And I'll tell you something right now, Cal Arnette. I was number one on the list."

"I've already gathered that," he said, and left the kitchen.

I glanced heavenward. "That wasn't the brightest thing you've ever said, Bo."

"Somebody else would've told him if I hadn't. It was no secret that I detested Ralph Posey."

"I don't get it. If you hated him as much as you say, why didn't you just divorce him?"

She shook her head. "Spoken like a woman of modern times. There was no such thing back then as 'just a divorce.' Divorce was a dirty word." Her shoulders slumped. "Taylor, if you don't mind, I'm about talked out. Think I'll go stretch out on the bed for a while."

I felt terrible for not having suggested it myself. It was easy to forget how old Bo was. She had the energy and spunk of a much younger person. "Good idea, Bo. I'll go check on Cal." I stood up, hesitated, hardly knowing what to say. This was a long way from the normal condolence call. "If you need anything..."

"I'll let you know," she said wearily and looked away, summarily dismissing me.

I found Cal back at the little house, crouched by the fireplace. He gestured for me to join him. "Careful, we've already messed this up enough. Did you notice that before?" He directed his flashlight beam into the opening, and I caught a glint of dull metal.

I leaned a little closer, careful not to disturb the bones, and saw a small shovel propped against the rear bricks of the chimney. "No, I didn't. Where did it come from?"

He stood up, dusting off his hands. "I'm guessing it was up in the chimney along with the body. Don't know if it fell out when the skeleton did and we just didn't notice it until now, or if it fell out later while we were up at Bo's house."

"But why would a shovel be up the—oh."

"Yeah, it could be the murder weapon. We'll know more after Doc has had a look at the remains."

I followed him outside, where he bummed a cigarette from me and lit up, inhaling deeply. Cal only smoked when he was extremely upset.

"Cal, I know what you have to be thinking, but..."

He looked at me. "But what?"

"Don't. Just don't. She couldn't have. Bo talks tough, but you know she has a heart as soft as kid leather."

He opened his mouth to reply, but was interrupted by a squawk from the car radio. "Unit one," said a soft, female voice. Paula Forman, widow of a former deputy, had been office clerk and dispatcher for several months now. She was a petite brunette and drop-dead gorgeous, and I might have been jealous of her if I didn't know so much about her marital history. Paula didn't trust men, and with valid reasons.

Cal reached through the window and grabbed the mike. "Go ahead."

"Lubbock County is sending a team out. Should be there within an hour. Ollie says he'll handle anything that comes up in town, so you can stay put out there. Oh, and Doc should arrive any minute. Just saw his car go blasting past the S.O."

"Thanks." Cal's lips had tightened at the mention of Derrick County's newest deputy. I knew he didn't like Oliver Burke, but I didn't know why. Cal refused to discuss the man.

It seemed as good a time as any to try again. "What is it with you and Deputy Burke? If you don't like him, why did you hire him in the first place?"

He sighed. "I didn't hire him. I'm not the sheriff yet, Taylor, and until the election, Dave Underwood has pretty much taken over the administrative duties of the S.O."

"Oh, I didn't know that."

Dave Underwood was the other county commissioner, as well as the president of Perdue's only bank. A thoroughly pig-headed man, obsessed with his own power and prestige, he seemed to delight in keeping folks off balance.

"Burke retired from Dallas PD," Cal went on, watching the horizon where a cloud of red dust indicated someone tearing up the road toward Bo's house. "At least, that's what he told Underwood. My sources say it was more like a forced resignation."

"Really? Why?"

"Later. Here's Doc."

The battered, old Datsun slid into a wild spin before shuddering to a halt.

"He's gonna kill himself one of these days," Cal muttered as the old doctor stalked up to us.

"What the hell is going on here?" he demanded. "Paula was spouting the most ridiculous drivel on the phone, something about a skeleton and Bo fainting. Where is Bo? She okay? Why didn't you call an ambulance, Cal? Afternoon, Taylor. Maybe you can tell me what this is all about, since Deputy Arnette here seems to be tongue-tied."

"Just waitin' to get a word in edgewise, Doc," Cal drawled. "Which question you want answered first?"

Doc grunted and pushed past us. He came to a dead stop in the doorway, staring inside. "Well, I'll be hornswaggled," he said. "Paula wasn't kidding." We joined him inside the little house.

"She wasn't kidding," Cal agreed. "Take a look, but I'd appreciate it if you didn't touch anything just yet. I'm waiting on a team from the Lubbock S.O."

"Ralph Posey," Doc murmured.

Cal glanced at him sharply. "I didn't tell Paula that, so she couldn't have told you."

"No, she just said a skeleton. But I recognize the tooth."

"You knew him?"

Doc squatted close to the remains. "Not really, but I saw him around a lot. Couldn't miss that tooth, especially in bright sunlight. You could see the man coming a block away." He leaned forward, peering at the skull. "I can't just turn it over?"

"Not right now, Doc. I want the forensic people to see it just like this."

The old man grunted as he got to his feet. "So what am I doing here?"

"Well, you're the county coroner. Procedure."

Doc grinned wryly. "Wouldn't want to shirk my duties. I hereby pronounce him dead."

Cal's lips twitched. "Thanks. What can you tell me about him?"

"Don't know." Doc dug a cigar out of his jacket pocket and bit off the end, careful to spit it out the door. "I wasn't a member of his flock. Weird little feller, I'll say that." He found an old coffee can to use for an ashtray. "Travelin' preacher, evangelist type. Showed up in Perdue one day askin' where he could set up his tent for a revival. I remember, 'cause I was in Lucy's Café with old Doc Patterson when Ralph and his sidekick came struttin' in."

Cal looked interested. "Sidekick?"

Doc sat down in a wooden rocker and puffed his cigar. "Younger feller, name of, um, Neff, I believe. Harry—no, Harvey. He traveled with Ralph, made arrangements for lodging and food, collected the offerings, that sort of thing. He did most of the talkin' that day at Lucy's.

"Someone finally told 'em they could set up out near the festival grounds, and they left. That revival ended up attractin' a lot more folks that I would have bet on, but then that was back before we had the Rattlesnake Festival or the county fair, and hardly anybody owned a television set, so you took entertainment where you could find it.

"I went myself, long about the third night." He laughed. "Ralph put on a good show, I'll give him that. By the time he was through, everybody in that tent was dripping sweat and I, for one, went home almost convinced that my soul would burn in hell if I didn't forego my wicked ways and give all my money to Ralph Posey.

"Not that I had much to give. I was interning for Doc Patterson, and in those days doctors were as like as not to get a scrawny chicken or a sack of potatoes for payment. Cash money was hard to come by. I was stunned at how many greenbacks landed in Ralph's collection plate that night."

"He must've been some preacher," I said.

"Oh, he was at that. But the whole town was still shocked when Bonita Trent up and married him."

It was hard to think of Bo as Bonita—such a delicate name for a lady who seemed more a mighty oak than a daffodil. "Why did she, I wonder?"

"Don't know for sure, but my guess would be that she was tired of bein' a spinster. Bo was close to thirty years old then, and it didn't look like anyone was ever going to pop the question. Funny thing, when you consider that her daddy was the richest man in these parts. Doc Patterson cheered when he got called out here to treat a sore throat or a turned ankle. He knew he'd get his bill paid in cash." He shrugged. "On the other hand, Bo wasn't exactly what most men had in mind when it came to picking a wife. She was a tomboy through and through, and plain as mud."

I was still fuming over the 'spinster' remark. "So what's wrong with being unmarried at thirty?" I asked heatedly. I was pushing twenty-nine myself.

Doc looked startled. "Nothin' at all, not these days. But back then, well—"

"I know." I sighed. "Times were different. Still, she wouldn't have married him just because she wanted to be someone's wife, would she? I mean, that seems a little drastic."

"Oh, I doubt that was all there was to it. She probably fell for him, along with half the other ladies in Perdue."

I stared at him. "Fell for him? Come on, Doc, the man you're describing doesn't sound like centerfold material to me."

"Ugly as sin, if you want my opinion," Doc agreed. "But then I'm not a female. There was something about him, I don't know what. Maybe that boomin' voice or maybe those eyes. That man had deep set eyes, black as coal. When he looked at you, it was like being stripped bare to your soul." He shook his head. "Whatever it was, Doc Patterson and I ran a whole spate of pregnancy tests about two months after Ralph Posey showed up in Perdue."

That remark even brought a gasp from Cal.

"I'm not saying it was anything more than a coincidence," Doc went on, "but those women were worried, I'll tell you that. Most of 'em married, too, so no reason to fret about bein' in the family way unless..." He let it hang there.

"And Bo married him anyway?" I couldn't believe it.

Doc looked insulted. "Well, it's not like Doc Patterson and I spread it around, you know. And the women weren't likely to talk about it among themselves, but even if they did, Bo wouldn't have been included. She was a loner, that gal. Didn't mingle with the other ladies. Never quite fit in."

"How did Bo's parents take her marriage?" Cal asked.

"I have a feelin' her mother would've raised hell, had she still been alive. But Bo's daddy had been a widower for nigh onto twenty years and, as far as I could tell, he was all for it. See, Nelson Trent made his money in oil—a wildcatter, they called 'em back then. The man had itchy feet, didn't like to stay put. If it hadn't been for Lou Ann, Bo's mama, he probably never would have settled down at all. But Lou Ann snared him good.

"Once they were married, she nailed his wanderin' feet to the ground, made him buy up this land and build her a house. Once she was gone, I 'spect Nelson felt obligated to stay on with his daughter. He bent over backward when someone finally offered to take her off his hands. Bo had inherited her mother's hankering for permanent roots, so Nelson built Ralph a church right here in town." He gestured around us.

"Bo's the one who had this place remodeled. It used to be the foreman's cabin when this was a working ranch, but Nelson never raised anything except scrub mesquite so this little house had been empty for years. Bo had it done up as a honeymoon cottage."

He laughed. "A lot of wasted effort. Not six months after the wedding, Nelson high-tailed it outta here. Stayed gone, too, and I'll bet he never looked more than once at a pretty woman after that for fear of being trapped again. Anyway, after he left, Bo and Ralph moved up to the big house."

"Poor Bo," I said. "A father who wanted her off his hands and a husband who treated her like dirt. What a life."

"Speaking of Bo," Doc said, "she's the one you should be askin' about all this. It's mostly hearsay on my part, you know, made up of faded memories and town gossip."

"Oh, but Bo's a suspect," I put in, ignoring Cal's glare. "Deputy Arnette is going to need some unbiased testimony."

Doc choked on a puff of cigar smoke. "You're not serious. Bo Posey isn't a killer, Cal. Have you lost your mind?"

Before Cal could answer, we heard a car pull to a stop outside. Both men went out to meet the newcomers, but I stayed where I was, gazing at the skull.

"I wish you could talk," I told it. "Because I know Bo couldn't have done this, and you'd damn sure be able to tell us who did."

I stepped back as a fortyish woman and a much younger man followed Cal and the doctor into the house, crowding what space was available among the stacks of junk that surrounded us like extra walls. Cal pointed out the skeleton, but the woman ignored it for the moment, looking at me curiously.

Cal relented, performing the introduction. "Taylor, this is Sergeant Molly Sullivan with the Lubbock Sheriff's Department forensics unit. Sergeant, Taylor Madison, our local celebrity. She's a mystery novelist."

I grimaced as I shook the woman's hand. Not only did I dislike being described as a celebrity, but part of me resented that Cal couldn't come up with a better title for the woman who had shared her bed with him the night before. "Nice to meet you, Sergeant."

"Molly, please. I'm a big mystery fan, but I'm not sure...

"My pen name is Maddy Taylor," I told her, and she broke into a grin.

"*Last Call*," she said, naming my latest novel. "Excellent book. I enjoyed it." She cleared her throat, as if suddenly realizing this was not a social occasion. "This is my assistant, Deputy Chris Upton."

Deputy Upton nodded vaguely, his attention already focused on the skeleton. "Cool," he whispered. "Wow, Molly, come look at this."

Molly winced. "Don't touch it, Chris."

"I know, I know. Want me to take some pictures?"

"Good idea. The camera's in the trunk."

The kid bounded out of the house, his loose-fitting uniform flapping about him like the garb of a scarecrow. Molly sighed, watching him go.

"Rookie," she told Cal, who nodded sympathetically.

Her own uniform fit like a glove, showing off ample curves. She pushed a loose hairpin back into the thick wad of dark hair piled atop her head and moved to kneel beside the remains.

"Small bones for a man," she commented.

"Ralph Posey was just a speck of a feller," Doc said. "A strong wind would've blown him over. Hell of a voice, though. You could hear him preachin' damnation and brimstone to his congregation whether you attended his church or not. Church of the Rapture, it was called." He nudged Cal. "Old Sheriff Mason used to get complaint calls every Sunday. He was itchin' to arrest Ralph for disturbing the peace, but figured it wouldn't look good to hassle a man for spreadin' the word of God, even if he did do it at the top of his lungs."

Molly moved out of the way as Chris came skipping in with his camera. "Get shots from as many angles as you can," she said. "And for heaven's sake, don't step on the bones."

Chris nodded, holding a light meter over the hearth and making an adjustment to the camera's settings. "Awesome," he said as he began snapping pictures.

"At least he's enthusiastic," Molly said under her breath. "You say this body has been here for thirty-five years? That's fascinating. I've never worked a homicide this old. Got any suspects?"

I opened my mouth, but shut it again as Cal shot me a warning glance.

"Nothing written in stone yet," he said.

Molly shook her head. "It won't be easy. We'll do our best to give you some evidence to work with, but after all this time I can't guarantee we'll come up with much."

"I understand that."

Cal had managed to stifle my comments, but not so Doc's. "You're barking up the wrong tree if you're looking at Bo," he said gruffly.

Molly lifted a dark eyebrow. "Bo?"

"The victim's wife. Widow, rather," Cal explained.

"Well, the spouse is always a good place to start," Molly agreed.

Cal seemed impressed with her, and I felt a flare of jealousy. It didn't mean anything really. I had been jealous of brunettes all my life. Too many dumb blonde jokes over the years had put a serious dent in my self-esteem. Maybe I should take Pearl Miller, the owner and operator of Hair Today, up on her offer to dye my pale hair to a rich shade of chestnut. But who wants white-blonde roots?

I shook my head and snapped back to the conversation. Cal was telling Molly what we had learned from Bo.

"Sounds like a motive to me," the sergeant agreed, and that did it. I couldn't stand it any longer.

"Bo Posey," I said through gritted teeth, "is not a murderer. She is a decent, warm-hearted woman who—"

"Oh, c'mon, Taylor, let's not get carried away," Doc broke in. "I like Bo just fine, but warm-hearted is not a term I'd use to describe her."

"Whose side are you on?" I asked him angrily.

"No one's takin' sides," Cal said in the reasonable voice that always made me want to kick him. "We have to start somewhere."

"Well, start with someone besides Bo," I retorted.

"Why don't we try to piece together what happened?" Molly broke in calmly. "We don't yet know how the man was killed, and I don't intend to hazard a guess until we've gotten those bones back to Lubbock for analysis." She stopped, shooting a look at Doc. "Er, if that's all right with you. You're the coroner and this is your jurisdiction."

"Can't say I've ever performed an autopsy on a heap of bones before," Doc said. "Besides, your lab has fancy equipment I've only dreamed of. You're welcome to them, if it's okay with Cal."

"I'd appreciate it," Cal said.

Molly couldn't hide the gleam in her eyes. "Good."

"As to the method," Cal went on, "did you notice the spade that's leaning against the back of the chimney?"

"I got at least a dozen shots of it," Chris called out gleefully and Molly groaned.

"You're thinking that might've been the murder weapon? Just a second." She shooed Chris out of the way and bent to turn the skull over. We all inched closer. Sure enough, the back of the skull bore a four-inch crack.

"You could be right," she said. "We'll know more when we do some comparisons with the blade of that shovel. Then again, he could have fallen against something, or, for that matter, this could've happened when the skull struck the hearth a couple of hours ago." She tilted her head and peered up the chimney. "Interesting. Got a flashlight, Deputy?"

Cal moved to crouch beside her, directing the beam of his flashlight up into the dark shaft.

"See the marks?" Molly asked. "Apparently whoever hid the body stuffed it up the chimney and then wedged the spade diagonally across the opening to hold the body in place. Now, Doctor Neil says the victim was skinny, but even so it would've been a relatively tight fit. I imagine the body would've stayed put for several days. Only when the flesh was decimated, due to decomposition or insects, would the corpse have fallen from its hiding place. But the shovel kept it up there." She turned her ice blue eyes on me. "Deputy Arnette told me you had to poke it loose with a broom handle."

"Right."

Molly gave a final glance up the chimney. "Thirty-five years," she marveled. "Clearly, no one used this fireplace in all that time. Odd. Of course, the killer would've prevented that if at all possible."

"Bo didn't want us to build a fire," Cal reminded me in a low voice. He didn't look at all smug; he looked sad.

And that scared me.

Chapter Three

DOC CONSULTED HIS pocket watch and said that, if he was no longer needed, he ought to be getting back to his office. Cal asked if he would drop me off in town.

The elderly man gave me a little bow. "I'd be honored," he said.

"Thanks anyway, Doc," I said. "But I'll just wait and ride back with Cal."

It was a good try, but it didn't work, and Molly shot me a sympathetic glance as Cal propelled me to the door. He watched to make sure I climbed into the passenger seat of Doc's old Datsun, then gave a brief wave and went back inside.

"Damn," I said under my breath.

"It *is* a crime scene, Taylor," Doc said as he steered down the gravel road. "Not really a place for spectators."

"I used to be a deputy," I reminded him.

"A temporary position. And as I recall, you couldn't wait to leave the first murder scene you came across."

"That was different." I shivered a little, remembering the late Sheriff Crawford slumped in the recliner in his living room—now my living room—fang marks in his neck and his skin as cold as a refrigerated roast. "I didn't know this victim. Besides, a heap of bones is a far cry from an actual dead body."

Doc dug one of his foul-smelling cigars from his shirt pocket and plugged in the car's lighter. "I can't get over it," he mumbled. "Ralph Posey dead for all these years, and no one the wiser."

I studied his sagging profile. "You don't believe that Bo could have done it, do you?"

He snorted. "'Course not. Bonita is a clever woman." He lit his stogie and took a couple of puffs, squinting at the road ahead. "Now, I'm not sayin' she wouldn't have killed the old bastard, given the proper motivation and circumstances—"

"Doc!"

He waved his cigar. "Let me finish, will ya? I've lived a long time, Taylor, and I've come to the conclusion that no one is incapable of murder. Different people have different breaking points, that's all. Sure, Bo could've done it, but would she have been stupid enough to leave the body in that chimney for all these years?" He gestured at the land that stretched around us, empty but for the clumps of mesquite scrub that seemed to spring up overnight in this part of Texas.

"Think about it, gal. She might have stuffed him up there temporarily, sure—not a bad hiding place. But if I know Bo, she'd have grabbed the first opportunity to get him out of there and into the ground. She's got around four hundred acres out here, and this land hasn't been worked for half a century. A million potential gravesites where he'd never be found."

"Good point," I had to concede. "Why hasn't Cal thought of it?"

"He will. Give him time. Cal thinks of most things, sooner or later."

Doc turned the car onto smooth highway, and I relaxed a little. "Then it's going to be okay."

"I didn't say that." He chewed on his cigar. "Depends on what kind of evidence they uncover. 'Course, after more than thirty years, there probably won't be much left."

"Whatever they come up with, it won't point to Bo," I said stubbornly.

He lifted a bushy, white eyebrow, but remained silent for the rest of the drive to Perdue.

Paula was on the phone when I walked into the sheriff's department. I gave her a little wave, and continued into the small office that had once been occupied by Miles Crawford. The threadbare carpet still held the scent of his favorite pipe tobacco, as did the upholstery and curtains of the little house that now belonged to me. I had never actually seen his ghost, but I smelled it all the time.

Tucked between the filing cabinets was a tiny refrigerator where the employees kept their lunches, creamer for their coffee, and, sometimes, perishable evidence. One never knew what surprises lurked within. Fortunately, all I discovered this time was the quart of milk and the frozen dinners I had stored earlier before Cal and I made the drive to Bo's house.

Paula looked up from her typing as I walked back into the front room. "Is it true?" she asked. "Did a skeleton really fall out of a chimney? Who is it, do you know? How long has it been there? What did the folks from Lubbock say? How—"

"Good afternoon, Paula," I interrupted. "Yes, I'm fine, thanks for asking, and you?"

She laughed. "Sorry. This is just so weird, you know? Nothing like this ever happens around here. The most excitement we have is when Puffy gets stuck up a tree." Puffy was a mean-spirited cat who, I firmly believed, purposefully got himself into trouble periodically just to keep his human on her toes. "Considering that Puffy is pushing thirty pounds, I'd say there aren't many trees left in town that'll support him."

"So he'll come up with another method of tormenting Mrs. Matladge."

The phone rang and she reached to pick up the receiver. I watched her as I poured coffee for both of us. Hard to believe this was the same woman I had rescued from an attic where her abusive husband had chained her after breaking a few of her bones and loosening her teeth. It had only been about seven months since her release from that hideous marriage, but her physical and mental recovery had been amazingly swift.

I was glad Cal had thought to offer her the position of dispatcher/clerk/secretary when Billy Jackson, the former dispatcher, took a leave of absence to attend the police academy in Lubbock. The job gave her confidence and purpose, two things she had been in short supply of—she was even contemplating enrolling in the academy herself as soon as Billy returned.

I perched on the edge of her desk as she hung up the phone. "To answer your question, yes, it's true about the skeleton."

"Really?" Eyes the color of violets sparkled above the rim of her coffee mug. "Well, for heaven's sake, Taylor, spill it. Details, gossip and speculation, please."

I smiled, but hesitated at her demand for information. "I'm not sure how much Cal wants revealed right now."

She scowled at me. "Hell, Taylor, I'm not a reporter. I work here, remember? I'm sure Cal will fill me in when he gets back, but I'd rather hear it from you. Women know how to tell a story—men just list the basic facts and grunt a lot."

I snickered. "Okay, you twisted my arm."

When I finished, she gazed at the star-shaped paperweight on her desk, her lips pursed thoughtfully. "Bo didn't do it," she said at last.

It was a relief to hear those words spoken aloud by someone besides me, and I told her so.

"Cal doesn't believe it either," she assured me. "He's just being official right now. He takes this job very seriously, you know."

"I know." *Especially with the sheriff's election coming up*, I thought but didn't say aloud. Surely Cal wouldn't throw Bo to the wolves simply to earn some free publicity? I shook my head. How could I even think such a thing? I knew Cal better than that. "I've got to get home before my frozen dinners thaw," I told Paula. "Come over for coffee some evening, why don't you? We don't get to talk very often."

She said she would, and I had my hand on the doorknob when it turned of its own accord and a man in a Derrick County deputy's uniform entered the office. I took a step backwards as he stared at me, peeling off mirrored sunglasses to reveal eyes the color of blue steel.

"How you doin', Ms. Madison?"

"Fine. You?" I had to force the words through gritted teeth. This was only my third time to come face to face with Oliver Burke, and there was no reason for the hairs at the back of my neck to prickle as they did whenever I saw him.

He certainly wasn't unpleasant to look at. He couldn't have measured more than an inch above my own height of five-ten, but he stood with a ramrod straight, almost military, bearing that made him seem much taller. He wore his light brown hair slicked back in a style that made me think of James Dean, and he must have shaved three times a day in order to achieve that utterly smooth, almost polished, complexion.

At the moment, his lips were parted in a smile that revealed perfect whiter-than-white teeth, but the smile didn't reach those cold eyes and I wasn't fooled for a minute. My stomach rolled as if I had taken a swig of sour milk, and the image made me realize I had a perfect excuse for not pausing to chat. Throwing out a hasty explanation about my melting groceries, I squeezed by him and out the door. A backward glance at Paula revealed she was no more impressed with Deputy Burke than I was. But then, Paula was no longer a fan of the male sex in general. I wondered if she would ever recover from the experience of being Lester Forman's wife.

As I pulled my Volkswagen into my driveway, Dorothy Stenson waved at me from her yard across the street where she was busily raking leaves. "Little nip in the air today!" she shouted when I got out of the car. "Come on over for some hot cider."

"Sure," I yelled back. "Let me put this stuff away first."

I stashed my groceries, poured a bowl of cat kibble for Hazel and grabbed a sweater on my way out the front door. What people in Perdue considered a "nip" felt like a full-fledged bite to a girl from South Texas.

Dorothy settled me into a living room as cozy and overstuffed as the lady herself, and handed me a steaming mug. The fragrance of apples and spices filled my nose as I warmed my hands on the cup, and took a cautious sip. Heaven. As soon as she felt the first hint of winter chill, Dorothy put a gigantic pot on the stove and started the delectable concoction simmering. She called it Rattlesnake Cider because, she said, it bit into your taste buds and wouldn't let go. I'd begged her for the recipe, but she guarded it like a family jewel. I took another sip, tasting cinnamon and nutmeg and a hint of orange, and waited for Dorothy to lecture me about Cal.

She opened her mouth, but what came out was, "Misty! No! Bad girl!"

I turned around and saw a tiny Cocker Spaniel puppy engaged in a joyful battle with the hem of Dorothy's drapes.

"How adorable!" I cried as Dorothy scooped the pup off the floor. "May I hold her?"

"Anything to keep her away from my curtains," Dorothy said, but she really didn't sound angry. "I found her doing that first thing this morning. Just look at this."

I tried not to smile as I examined the drapes, shredded by Misty's needle teeth.

"When did you get her?" I asked. Misty wriggled in my lap, alternately licking and nipping at my wrist.

"Yesterday. I thought a dog might make a good companion, but I'm about to change my mind. At this rate, she'll tear up everything in my house before she's finished teething." She took the puppy and her stern tone changed instantly. "Isn't that wight, puppems-wuppems. Won't her just tear up my whole house? Yes. Isn't her a cutie-wootie?"

I looked at her in combined amazement and amusement. All in all, I was delighted. First, despite her collection of friends, Dorothy spent more lonely hours than she liked to admit. Second, I was now pretty sure the curtain-twitching Cal had observed this morning had not been Dorothy spying on us, but Misty beginning her morning exercise.

"So they found old man Posey in a chimney, huh?" Dorothy said as calmly as a woman asking the time of day.

The abrupt change of subject almost made me drop my mug. "How on earth did you hear about that?"

Her painted lips curved into a smile that went yards beyond smug, and she took the time to carefully pat her shoe-polish colored hair into place before answering. "Rita told Sally Nelson, who told Frances Walters, who phoned me."

"Well, sure, why didn't I guess that?" I mumbled, taking another sip of cider.

"Come now, child, you've lived in Perdue for almost a year. Secrets don't stay that way for long around here."

"I know, but it's only been..." I glanced at my watch. "...a few hours."

"Time enough for those folks from Lubbock to stop off at the diner for a quick lunch on their way back." She winked. "They requested a private booth."

I groaned. "So they got the one back in the corner by the kitchen door." I was convinced that Rita, the waitress at Lucy's Café, could lip-read from a distance of thirty paces, but if she could manage to lure the unsuspecting into the corner booth, she didn't have to bother. A poster of John Travolta, gussied up in his western costume from the movie *Urban Cowboy*, was pasted discreetly over an opening that had once served as a food pick-up counter before the café's remodeling job some years back. The poster hid the hole nicely, and was cheaper than new sheetrock.

Now, any customers in the rear booth had better be sure they didn't discuss anything more scandalous than the upcoming church picnic because Rita could perch on the little stool just inside the kitchen, filing her nails and soaking up every word. Hometown folks were well aware of the trap, but strangers fell into it regularly.

Dorothy was still wearing that smirky little grin and I had to grin back.

"So, are you going to tell me the story?"

"Why should I? Thought you got it all from Sally Nelson."

"Frances Walters," she corrected. "Which is just my point. After a bit of news has made the rounds, you can't be sure it hasn't been altered a little in the process. I want the straight version, if you don't mind."

I didn't even hesitate this time. If Rita knew, then most of Perdue was clued in by now, and I might as well make sure the tale that circulated was the truth. I had no doubt Dorothy would make sure any twisted facts were properly straightened by nightfall. Her smile faded as I recounted the events of the afternoon.

"Oh, my," she said when I had finished. "Doesn't look good for poor Bo, does it?"

"Dorothy, you can't think—"

"Of course not. Well, probably not."

"Dorothy!"

She stroked Misty's silky ears, and spoke without meeting my eyes. "Has anyone notified Faith?"

"Who?"

"Her daughter."

"Oh." I remembered now—Bo had spoken of the daughter who she had managed to send to college using the money from the sale of the stock. "I have no idea."

Dorothy handed Misty back into my care and grunted as she pushed her stout body out of the chair. "Never mind. That was a dumb question. Bo wouldn't call her in a million years, and no one else would think to do it." She rummaged through a drawer and pulled out an address book. "Faith should be with her mother at a time like this."

"At a time like what?" I was getting angry. "Bo hasn't been arrested."

Dorothy finally looked at me, and I didn't like the expression in her eyes. "Not yet," she murmured.

I bit my lip to keep from saying something I knew I shouldn't and watched as she flipped through the little book, then picked up the phone and dialed. "Busy," she said. "I'll try again in a minute."

"Are you friends with Faith?" I asked, draining the last of my now cold cider and wishing it were a shot of something stronger. If Dorothy wasn't sure of Bo's innocence, how would the rest of the town react?

She refilled my mug from a thermal pitcher. "I don't know that you'd call us friends now. We send Christmas cards, and that's about the extent of it. But we were best friends in high school."

"Really?"

"Sure. She was pretty close to your aunt, too." Dorothy's tone implied she couldn't imagine why anyone would bother to be friends with someone like Tessa, and since I didn't want to discuss my aunt—who had recently been revealed as my birth mother—I ignored the reference.

"What was she like? Faith, I mean."

"Kept to herself a lot. Intelligent. Pretty, but always embarrassed about her clothes. She wasn't shy, though most folks took her to be just because she tried not to call attention to herself. Some of the nastier kids would make jokes about her, called her Raggedy Ann, things like that."

Bo had said that they lived like paupers. "I take it she wasn't the most popular girl in school."

"She wasn't on the cheerleading squad, if that's what you mean. But most of the kids liked her well enough. Especially after she started dating Lewis Tucker." Dorothy smiled a little, remembering. "You could've knocked the lot of us over with a feather when he asked her to the homecoming dance our junior year. They were inseparable after that."

"What was so special about dating Lewis Tucker?" I asked, and Dorothy looked at me as if I'd lost my mind before she connected the past with the present and realized that I hadn't known him.

"Lewis was what we used to call a big man on campus. Not only was his family the wealthiest in the county, but he was Perdue's star quarterback, junior and senior class president—"

"I get the picture." Kevin Gerard had been my high school's version of Lewis Tucker, but he had dated a vapid, little redhead who achieved the honor of senior class queen based on her chest measurement. I couldn't imagine Kevin dating someone who fit the description of Faith Posey. "Did they end up getting married?"

"No, and we were surprised. After graduation, Faith went on to college at Texas Tech, but Lewis stayed here. Just lived off the family money."

"Nice work if you can get it."

She frowned at me. "It wasn't his choice, Taylor. Lewis loved animals, and all he ever talked about was becoming a veterinarian. But after the accident..."

I leaned forward.

"It happened the night of our graduation dance." She closed her eyes and shivered. "He lost control of his car and went into a ditch. For a while, we weren't sure he'd even live, but he pulled through. Paralyzed, though, from the waist down."

"How awful!"

"He thought about going on to college, but vets around here don't deal with dogs and cats as much as they do horses and sheep, and he knew that. There's no way he could've handled that kind of work from a wheelchair."

"Poor kid. But what about Faith? She just abandoned him?"

"I really don't know. Nobody does. She shared an apartment in Lubbock with six or seven other girls. You know that Bo didn't have much money back then?"

I nodded.

"But Faith hardly ever came back to Perdue, not even for a visit. We never saw her and Lewis together after graduation night." She reached for the phone. "I'd better try her again."

This time, someone answered. I rubbed Misty's plump belly and listened as Dorothy filled her old friend in on the situation, and I had to admit she handled it well. She made no mention of Bo being under suspicion, just emphasized that the discovery of the body was a shock to an elderly woman and that she felt Bo should have some family support. Dorothy listened for a few minutes, her usually pleasant face drawing into grim lines.

When she spoke again, her voice had roughened. "I can't believe you'd say such a thing. You're the only family she has left, and you're coming if I have to fly to Boston and drag you here, understand? You know I'd do it, too."

Another silence, and Dorothy's expression softened a bit. "That's better. What? Well, yes, I suppose you can stay with me, but don't you think—? No, all right, fine. Tonight? Good...see you then."

Dorothy dropped the receiver into its cradle and stared at the phone as if it was a goldfish that had just jumped out of its bowl and lunged for her throat. "They used to be so close," she murmured.

"Bo and her daughter?"

"Yeah. More like best friends than parent and child. I was sort of jealous, to tell the truth. My mother and I have fought like cats in a sack since the day I was born."

"So what happened to them?"

"I don't know. But at least I convinced her to come. Taylor, Faith is flying in tonight. I hate to impose, but could you pick her up at the Lubbock airport?"

"I guess so, if she doesn't mind riding in a Volkswagen."

"I think it might be better if you borrowed my car. I'd go myself, but I don't see too well at night anymore."

I pretended to be insulted. "My VW isn't fancy enough, huh?"

"Just not big enough. Her daughter is coming with her."

"I didn't know Bo had a granddaughter! She never mentioned it."

Dorothy looked sad. "Hard to talk about someone you've never met."

BY SIX O'CLOCK I was back in my own house, waiting for a container of frozen lasagna to heat in the old gas stove's oven and wishing for a microwave. Every five minutes or so, I reached for the phone and dialed the sheriff's office. Paula had left for the day at five, and I kept hoping Cal would walk in and answer my call.

I lit a cigarette and sipped from a cup of hot tea as I thought about Bo and the granddaughter she had never laid eyes on. According to Dorothy, on the day Faith graduated from Texas Tech with a virtually worthless degree in liberal arts, she returned to her home in Perdue for just long enough to pack a suitcase and say goodbye to Dorothy and a few other friends. She had been aboard a Greyhound bus by midnight.

Dorothy had heard from her several months later—a brief note, simply explaining that she had settled in Boston and was working for a small art gallery during the day, waiting tables in the evening. Why Boston? Dorothy had no idea. Knowing Faith, she had thrown a dart at a map.

When I asked if Bo ever heard from her daughter, Dorothy replied that Faith kept in touch with her mother in a formal way, sending a Christmas card every year and a short letter when she married Alexander Weathered on her twenty-third birthday.

I had stopped her at that point. "The sculptor? *That* Alex Weathered?" His work was famous the world over, so even a relatively uncultured twit like me had read about him in *People* magazine and *Newsweek.*

Dorothy assured me that Faith's husband was indeed the man Newsweek referred to as "the Picasso of marble." Bo had received another letter upon the birth of Faith's daughter, three years later. But Bo had never been sent a picture of her only grandchild, much less met her.

"She sent one to me, though," Dorothy said, and showed me a photo that had been tucked into a Christmas card she'd received from Faith years ago.

I examined the picture of a ten or eleven-year-old girl with golden blonde curls and strangely piercing dark eyes. The notation on the back read, "Keron Weathered" and I asked Dorothy about the unusual spelling.

She shrugged. "Probably her daddy's idea. You know how those artist types are. It's pronounced Karen, so I don't see why they couldn't have just spelled it the same way. Yankees!"

I hid a smile.

"I took the picture with me the next time I went to Posey's," Dorothy went on. "Of course, I was expectin' Bo to drag out a whole album full of snapshots to show off. You know how grandmothers are. That's when I found out Bo had no idea what her own grandchild looked like." Dorothy's eyes misted. "Darn near broke my heart, the way she stared at this picture, like she was starving and I was waving a steak under her nose. I tried to make her keep it—seemed only fitting. But she wouldn't. Said it had been sent to me, not her. You know how stubborn she can be."

The oven timer buzzed and I got up to remove the cooked

lasagna, but my appetite was gone. Bo was one of my favorite people, and, at this point, I had no desire to provide a taxi service for the daughter who had treated her so shabbily. I had said as much to Dorothy, pointing out that Bo's state of mind at the moment was shaky enough without throwing in a reunion with a daughter who didn't even want to be here. And I was beginning to feel more and more certain Dorothy was using this entire mess as an excuse to bring mother and daughter together again.

"I'm not sure I want to be a part of this little scheme you've cooked up," I'd told her.

Dorothy simply gave me that smirk I had come to fear, and seemingly changed the subject. "By the way, dear, Cal's birthday is coming up next month, did you know? You might consider buying him a nice bathrobe. I'm not easily shocked, and personally I thought he looked sorta fetchin' in those white boxer shorts, but you have other neighbors who might think it unseemly for the future sheriff to appear on the front porch of a certain unmarried female in such attire. Of course, it's possible no one else noticed him this morning, and I certainly wouldn't dream of breathin' a word to anyone."

In most parts of America, people would certainly be outraged by such blatant blackmail. In small towns, it's simply a part of life. Scratch my back; I'll scratch yours. I've been here long enough to learn that.

Faith's flight wasn't due in until nine, but I was tired of fidgeting and picking at food I didn't want, so I set out for Lubbock. Accustomed to my Volkswagen, Dorothy's sturdy, box-shaped Ford sedan made me feel as if I was driving a tank. There was no way I would dare to sully the car's pristine interior with cigarette smoke, so I gritted my teeth and listened to the muzak station Dorothy had set on the radio, breathing the scents of talcum powder and Juicy Fruit gum. I was glad to arrive at the airport, find a parking space, then spend some time browsing the gift shop, drinking coffee and people watching.

It hadn't occurred to me to ask Dorothy what Faith looked like, so I was a little worried about recognizing her. But as the passengers began filing off the plane, I spotted Keron immediately. She hadn't changed that much from the photo Dorothy had shown me. Her hair was longer, darkened now from gold to deep honey, but her eyes were the same, huge in her small, heart-shaped face, and black as midnight. Tall and slender, she towered over the slight figure beside her.

Faith was so tiny that, at first glance, she looked like a little girl, but a second look revealed the faint lines around her eyes and mouth, and besides, no little girl I knew would have been dressed to kill in a designer suit. I wondered where on earth she shopped for Italian pumps in what had to have been a size three.

I approached them and introduced myself. Faith gave a ghost of a smile and ran a hand through her shoulder-length, silver hair.

"We appreciate the ride, Ms. Madison."

"Call me Taylor. Did you have a nice flight?"

"Fine, except for its destination. Where are you parked?"

Her speech was a study in contrast—a West Texas drawl, influenced by her childhood, overlaid with a thin veneer of Bostonian. She'd said "packed" instead of "parked."

"Close by. Let's go get your luggage first."

"No need, we just brought carry-ons." She must have noted my surprise. "We're not planning a long stay."

"I see," I said shortly, matching the tone she had established. "This way then."

Keron sat up front with me, Faith in the back seat. After the first few miles, I gave up on trying to make conversation. Faith's responses were clipped to the point of rudeness, and her daughter simply closed her eyes and pretended to be dozing. It was a relief to drop them off at Dorothy's, and I was even happier no one encouraged me to stick around once I had walked them to the door.

Drat Dorothy anyway for sticking her meddlesome nose into this. I couldn't shake the feeling that Bo would be better off if the two visitors turned around and went back home.

Chapter Four

WORRIED THOUGHTS ABOUT Bo invaded my dreams, so it wasn't surprising that I overslept the next morning.

At ten-thirty, I was seated at the kitchen table, still yawning over my second cup of coffee, when the doorbell rang. Hazel, who considers herself a watch-ferret, nipped my ankle to make sure I understood that I had a visitor, and I was standing on one foot when I opened the door.

Keron lifted an eyebrow at my pose, but otherwise made no comment.

"Sorry to bother you," she said. "Could I come in for a minute?"

"Um, sure." I moved aside, wishing I had at least thrown on a sweat suit. My ratty old robe and fuzzy slippers looked even shabbier than usual next to her designer jeans and Angora sweater.

"Coffee?" I offered, leading her into the kitchen.

"I'd kill for a cup," she said so solemnly that it sounded as if she really would. "Dorothy doesn't believe in the evils of caffeine. She served herbal tea for breakfast."

I poured her a cup and sat across from her, moving my chapter notes out of the way.

She eyed the stack of paper. "New novel? Dorothy told me you're a writer. I used to love mysteries, but for the past few years I haven't had much time for pleasure reading."

I made polite noises and waited for her to tell me what was really on her mind.

She took a sip of coffee, opened her mouth to speak, then closed it again, her eyes widening. A soft chattering clued me in to what was happening as Hazel climbed up a denim clad leg and settled herself in Keron's lap.

I got up, intending to snatch her away and apologize, but Keron had broken into a huge grin. It was the first time I had ever seen her smile, and it transformed her face from merely pretty to stunning. I was glad Cal wasn't here to see her.

I sat back down. "That's Hazel," I told her.

"What a darling! Hi, Hazel. Oh, you're a beautiful girl, yes you are." She launched into a stream of baby talk, then broke off, blushing a little. "Sorry, I'm a sucker for ferrets. An ex-boyfriend raised them."

"She likes you, too." That was an understatement. Hazel had died and gone to heaven. She twisted onto her back, offering her belly for Keron to scratch. Keron did.

"I'd like to ask you a favor," she said, placing Hazel on her shoulder.

I have come to regard those words as among the most frightening in the English language, but I'm pretty sure I successfully avoided wincing. "Ask away," I said. Notice I did not say, "Sure, anything."

"Would you drive me out to my grandmother's house?" Whatever I might have been expecting, that wasn't it. "I hate to ask," she went on. "I'd borrow Dorothy's car, but I really don't want Mother to know where I'm going." She sighed. "You've probably caught on by now that Mother doesn't want to be here in the first place. I'm not sure myself what the whole story is, but she and her mom obviously have some unresolved issues between them. I thought if I could meet my grandmother alone first, maybe I'd be in a position to play mediator."

She noticed the look on my face and laughed. "Oh, hell, forget all the mumbo-jumbo. I'm a psychologist, and psychobabble tends to leak from my pores when I'm not looking. What I'd really like to do is get to know my grandmother without my mother breathing down my neck and making it harder than it's already going to be. So, will you drive me out there? I'll pay for the gas."

I laughed, too, at that. "I think I can afford it," I said. "Just give me five minutes to put on some clothes."

Before setting out, I called the grocery to find out whether Bo was there or at home. Arnold informed me she was taking a few days off. He'd heard the news, of course, and tried to probe for details, but I cut him short.

I then suggested calling Bo's house to give her some warning, but Keron didn't want to. "Mother hasn't even let her know we're here yet," she said. "It might as well be a complete surprise, right?"

"Whatever you say."

Keron didn't wrinkle her nose at the sight of my fifteen-year-old Volkswagen. Another point in her favor.

We chugged up the street. Keron watched as I lit a cigarette and rolled down my window to keep the smoke out of her face.

"Times like this," she said, "I wish I smoked. Or drank. Or popped pills. Something. I'm afraid this meeting is going to be awkward."

"Hey, you can handle it. You're a shrink after all."

"Shrinks aren't immune to nerves," she responded, but seemed to relax a little.

Since I had managed to veer the subject away from her main concern, I kept going. “Where’s your practice?”

“Boston. Wanted to stick close by home so I could keep an eye on Mother—I sometimes pitch in and help her out at her art gallery on weekends.”

I wanted to pursue the “keep an eye on Mother” remark, but restrained myself. “She owns an art gallery?” I asked instead.

“Yes. Dad bought it for her years ago. As a substitute for his presence, I suspect.”

I couldn’t let that one pass. “Meaning what?”

She looked startled, as if she had been talking to herself and someone had overheard. “Dad lives in Europe. Mother hates Europe. So they compromised. Very sophisticated, don’t you think?” Her tone was dry.

“They’re divorced?”

“Oh, no, nothing so crass. Not even separated, not legally, anyway. Mother panics at the thought of losing him permanently, and Dad doesn’t care enough to press the issue, so they just rock along. He visits two or three times a year.”

She shifted in her seat to face me, and abruptly changed the subject. “Do you know, until last night, I didn’t know I had a grandmother? Mother has always implied she had no living relatives.”

I turned onto the dirt road that cut through Bo’s property. “From what Dorothy tells me, they haven’t spoken for years.”

“Do you know why? During the plane ride, Mother didn’t hesitate to talk about her father and what a bastard he was, but she’s being really tight-lipped about my grandmother.”

“Maybe Bo can tell you.”

She nodded and lapsed into silence, her hands clenched so hard on her lap that her knuckles were white.

I pulled to a stop in front of the big house, but left the motor running. “Why don’t you give me a call at home when you’re ready for a ride back? Bo has my number.”

Her dark eyes widened. “But I thought...aren’t you coming in with me?”

I looked at her in surprise. “You said you wanted to do this alone.”

“Wrong. I said I didn’t want Mother here. Moral support I can use.”

I supposed I could relate to that feeling. “Okay. C’mon.”

Keron stood behind me as I knocked, and remained there even after Bo opened the door. I was struck by how shrunken she looked, like a doll with part of its stuffing removed.

"Taylor!" she said, brightening. "The one person in Perdue I don't mind seeing today. Come in, gal. I'll put the coffee on."

"Um, I hope you don't mind two visitors, Bo." I stepped aside.

Bo's mouth dropped open. There was obviously no need to introduce the two women. Before I could say a word, Bo had Keron enfolded in her arms. I was happy to see that Keron returned the embrace, though somewhat shyly.

"Little Keron," Bo kept repeating as she led us into the living room. She pronounced the name "keer-own," but Keron didn't correct her. How, after all, was Bo supposed to know how to pronounce a name she had rarely even seen in print? I could tell Keron was thinking along the same lines, and that it made her sad.

"How on earth did you recognize me?" Keron asked.

"You have your grandfather's eyes," Bo said. From anyone else, the words might have been doting. Bo sounded almost fearful.

Keron picked up on that and laughed. "Don't worry. From what I've heard, it's my only similarity to him."

"Glad to hear it. Sit, both of you. I'll bring us something to munch on."

Keron settled onto a cherry-and-chintz sofa, while I took the matching armchair. She glanced around the room approvingly. "Nice. I think I was expecting a hovel. Mother harps on the fact that she grew up poor."

"That's a long story, and something you should get your grandmother to tell you. Bo's not poor anymore, not by a long shot."

"Really? I thought you said she ran a little grocery store."

Bo came back into the room in time to catch that. She slapped a heavy silver tray onto a low table, and started pouring coffee. "In the first place, Posey's is the only grocery store in Derrick County. It might be small, but I've got what you might call a captive audience." She cackled. "I don't need the income from it anymore, true enough, but I'm not the type to sit on my butt and knit shawls.

"Besides, it keeps me up on the local gossip. What is it that the politicians like to say? Keeps my finger on the pulse of the community."

"Bo is also a county commissioner," I put in.

"No kidding?" Keron looked impressed. "I'd like to see Posey's."

"Sure, we'll go by." Bo turned to me. "I'm letting Arnold run it for the next few days. He'll probably bankrupt me, but until this mess is cleared up, I think it's best if I stay away. I've never cared much what folks say about me, but I'll admit that right now I'm just not up to facing all the questions. Especially since I don't have any answers." She patted Keron's knee. "Enough about that. I can't tell you how good it is to see you, child. I was beginning to think I'd never get to meet you at all."

"You probably wouldn't have, if Mother had her way. But when Dorothy called—"

Bo shook her head. "Well, that clears up the mystery of who spilled the beans. I gotta tell you, though, that bein' able to finally hug my grandchild is worth bein' charged with murder."

Keron looked stunned. "What?"

I put a hand on Bo's arm. "You're not serious. Cal hasn't charged you, has he?"

"Well, not yet," Bo admitted. "But it's only a matter of time. When he took my fingerprints yesterday, I saw the writin' on the wall. Now, Taylor, don't glower like that. It'll give you wrinkles. The man's just tryin' to do his job, and even I can see that I'm a logical suspect." She gave a weary chuckle. "It's almost funny. I must've fantasized about killing that nasty man a thousand times."

"But you didn't do it," I asserted.

Bo smiled at me. "I noticed that wasn't a question. Thanks. But just to set the record straight for Keron here—no. I didn't do it. I probably should have, but I didn't."

"Cal really took your fingerprints? When did he do that?"

"Yesterday, before the folks from Lubbock left. 'Just procedure,' he told me."

"Well, that's probably true."

She snorted. "I wasn't born this mornin', Taylor."

Keron dived in. "Now, look here, if my grandmother is being accused of a crime, I think we'd better find her a lawyer. Taylor, is there a good one around here that you know of?"

"Hold your horses, gal. There's no need for that just yet."

"No, I think she's right, Bo. Do you have an attorney?"

"Yeah, I got one, for taxes and such, but he charges by the minute. Now, I'm not a miser, but I'll be damned if I start payin' through the nose for some yahoo to sit around making phone calls and billin' my account. Let's wait and see what's gonna happen first." She poured more coffee into her cup, her mouth set in a rigid line that told me there was no sense arguing.

"What I really want to do is get to know my little Keron. Not so little, though, are you? Tell me all about yourself, honey. We got a lot of years to talk over." I heard a tremor in Bo's voice. She was covering well, but the poor woman was obviously scared to death.

I stood up. "That's true, you do. And now that the ice has been broken, Keron, I really am going to leave you here for a while, if that's okay. I have an...er...errand to run and the two of you should have some time alone to get acquainted. How about if I pick you up in a couple of hours?"

Keron agreed, and I made a dash for my car. I was so furious with Cal that I nearly ran off the road twice before I had even gotten back to the main highway.

The slam of my car door sounded like a gunshot in the quiet parking lot of the sheriff's office, and I saw Paula's startled face at the window. She glanced over her shoulder and shook her head at me. Warning me not to come in? To hell with that idea.

I slammed the front door as well. "Where is he?" I demanded, glaring at poor Paula, whose gaze slid from me to someone behind me.

"Who're you lookin' for, Ms. Madison?"

I turned. Dave Underwood, the other county commissioner and president of Perdue's only bank, grinned at me. A stubby man with a gray crew cut, he always made me think of a partially smoked cigar.

I tried to answer in a normal tone, but my voice shook from the rage bottled up inside me. "I wanted to see Cal for a minute." The door to the back office was open a crack, and I heard a voice from within. "Is he in there?" I asked Paula.

"No, that's Burke. Cal's in Lubbock, Taylor. He probably won't be back for a couple of hours."

"Want some coffee, Ms. Madison? Paula, fetch our visitor a fresh cup, why don't you?"

Paula lifted an eyebrow at being treated like a servant, but rose to do as she was told. I gestured her back into her chair. "No, thanks, Paula. I can't stay."

"I've heard that you and Deputy Arnette have become quite an item," Underwood said with a sneer. "Guess he's filled you in on the case of Ralph Posey."

"I know about it," I said tightly, ignoring the first half of his comment.

A whoop from the back office interrupted the tense conversation. Burke burst into the room, his eyes shining like polished steel. "You were right, Mr. Underwood. I just talked to Neff on the phone."

"Good work," Underwood told him. "Paula, if Cal calls, tell him Burke and I have done part of his job for him." He put his hands on the edge of her desk and leaned into her face. "This new information, along with the Lubbock team's little revelation this morning, should make it easy to get an arrest warrant for Bo Posey. That old bitch is gonna fry this time."

The fury I had been holding back exploded before I knew what was happening. I grabbed his arm and swung him around to face me. "How dare you talk about Bo like that, you horrid little bastard?"

I was at least five inches taller than Underwood and had more muscle tone in my left hand than he had in his entire flabby body. There was a flicker of real fear in his eyes as he looked up at me. Burke made a move in our direction, but Paula came around the desk and beat him to it. Gently, she pried my fingers from the commissioner's arm and gave me a push toward the front door.

"Taylor and I are going across the street for a glass of iced tea. Burke, you'll answer the phone for a few minutes, right?" She didn't wait for an answer.

The weather was milder than it had been the day before, but I was shaking as if I were on the verge of frostbite. Paula wrapped an arm around my waist and led me across to Lucy's Café. "Stop grinding your teeth," she whispered. "If Rita thinks anything is wrong, she'll hover over our table the whole time we're there, and you need a cooling off period."

I nodded, and allowed her to lead me to a booth. Not, of course, the back booth near the Travolta poster.

Rita, the café's waitress, was in the running with Dorothy for the title of Perdue's Biggest Gossip Award, but we had arrived at the tail end of the lunch rush and she didn't seem inclined to bother with us. Her red hair disheveled, her expression harried, she took our order and scurried away.

Paula rested her elbows on the table and propped her chin in her hands. "I know how you feel—" she began, but I cut her off.

"Do you? That son-of-a-bitch."

She smiled a little. "Which one? Cal? Burke? Underwood? Men in general? You'll have to be more specific."

I had to laugh, and the tension in my shoulders eased a bit. "All of the above, at the moment," I said. Rita brought our tea, and I took a sip. "Jeez, I really made a fool of myself, didn't I? Wouldn't put it past Underwood to press charges for assault."

"And admit that a mere woman could hurt him? Forget it."

"I doubt I really hurt him, but did you see the look on his face? Stinking little coward."

"That's exactly what he is, Taylor, and it would probably be smart of you to remember that a cornered coward is a dangerous animal. Underwood can make things really rough for Cal, you know."

I felt the anger simmer again. "You picked a bad time to use that argument, Paula. If Cal had been there, he'd have been on the receiving end of my temper." I slammed my fist against the tabletop. "Damm it, why is everyone ganging up on a little old lady? I just found out that Cal took her fingerprints, for God's sake. She's scared out of her mind."

"Keep your voice down," Paula warned. "I'm sure Bo is scared, Taylor, but what do you expect Cal to do? It's a murder case."

"It's been thirty-five years!"

"Doesn't matter. There's no statute of limitations on murder, and you know that. Cal is just as responsible for investigating this case as he would be if it had happened yesterday. Why am I telling you this? You write mystery novels for a living. I'm sure you know the law as well as I do, if not better."

"But Bo didn't do it," I insisted for what felt like the fiftieth time.

"I agree with you. But she's the only suspect at the moment, isn't she? Others will crop up. Give it time."

I slumped in my seat. "Will they? If Underwood has his way, no one will look any further." I gripped my tea glass. "Am I missing something? What does Underwood have against Bo?"

Paula gave an exasperated sigh. "You really do live in your own little world. Don't you even read the county newspaper? Bo Posey and Dave Underwood are bitter enemies, politically speaking. See, Bo has this old-fashioned idea that her purpose as county commissioner is to serve the public. Keep the budget down, save the taxpayers some money. Underwood, on the other hand, tends to use the office for his own gain."

I tried to focus on what she was saying. "For instance?"

"I'll give you a good for instance. You've been out to Bo's house?"

"Just came from there."

"Is the road to her house paved?"

I shook my head. "Gravel."

"Take a run out to Underwood's place sometime. He's set as far back from the main highway as Bo is, but it's blacktop all the way to his front door. Same with his cronies. A lot of mutual hand washing goes on in that man's office, if you get my drift. Bo's been trying to get something on him for years. Something that'll stick, that is. The guy's as slimy as a day-old dead fish."

"So," I said thoughtfully, "it's a matter of him getting her before she gets him."

"That's about it."

"Paula, what was Underwood talking about? Did the Lubbock forensic team come up with something?"

"Apparently. Molly Sullivan called about fifteen minutes before you came in. That's why Cal went to see her. Before you ask, though, I don't know exactly what it was all about."

"But Underwood does. And if he's happy about it, you can be sure it's not good news for Bo. Neither, obviously, is whatever Burke found out from that phone call he made. I don't get it. Bo told me that Harvey Neff was a good friend to her, so what could he possibly say to hurt her?"

"Knowing you, you'll find out." Paula looked at her watch and slid out of the booth. "I've got to get back, Taylor." She hesitated. "Listen, I understand why you're upset. All of Bo's friends are upset right now. We all want to help her. But you've got to believe that Cal isn't ready to lock her up, okay?

"Burke, on the other hand, is in Underwood's back pocket, and the two of them make a nasty team. Try not to make things worse for Cal than they already are. We both know he's the good guy." She grinned. "As guys go."

After she left, I made myself stay put for long enough to finish a second glass of tea and calm down a little more. Rita found the time to stop by my table for a fishing expedition, but I managed not to tell her more than she already knew. Frustrated, she finally left me alone.

I was beginning to be glad Cal had not been at the office when I went storming in. Paula was right. He was only doing his job, however repugnant it might seem to me. I intended to keep a close eye on this investigation, and, personal relationships aside, the last thing I needed to do was alienate my best source of information.

By the time I drove back out to Bo's, I was feeling better.

Keron answered my knock, her pretty face glowing. "My grandmother is such a sweetheart."

I laughed. "Agreed. But only if you stay on her good side."

"I heard that, Taylor!" Bo peered at me from behind her much taller granddaughter.

"You can't deny it," I retorted. "Ready to go, Keron?"

"Not really. I could listen to her stories for a week. But I guess I'd better get back and check on Mother."

Bo laid a hand on her arm. "You're a lovely child," she said, then wiped furiously at her eyes. "Y'all git. Keron, I'll see you again before you head home, right?" The pleading in her voice broke my heart.

Keron wrapped her in a hug. "You bet you will," she said. "I'm not going anywhere until this whole mess is cleared up. Count on it...Grandma."

"I DON'T UNDERSTAND," SHE told me a few minutes later as I steered back down the gravel road. "Mother only said a few words about my grandmother last night, but managed to make her sound like some sort of ogress. What in the world could've happened?"

I shrugged. "You know as much as I do. All I've heard is that there were money problems when your mother was growing up. And apparently, Bo's husband was not a nice man."

"So I gathered. But in that case, why the animosity between Bo and my mother? You'd think the circumstances would've drawn them closer if anything."

"There's only one way to find out." I glanced at her as I flipped on the turn signal. "Ask your mother."

"Oh, I intend to," she said grimly. "And this time, damn it, she's going to answer me."

I dropped her off at Dorothy's, and then trudged into my own house, suddenly weary to the bone. Hazel came chattering into the living room and I scooped her up, nuzzling her against my cheek.

"Hazel, being human is the pits," I told her and she looked up at me as if to say, "You're just now figuring that out?"

I wasn't hungry, so I brewed a pot of tea and sat down at my computer, hoping to finish a chapter before it was time for bed. I might as well have just sat on the couch and stared at the wall. At least my eyes wouldn't have been aching two hours later from staring at a blank computer screen.

At eleven, I showered and put on my nightgown, and was walking around the house turning off lights when the doorbell rang. Cal stood on the front porch, the circles under his eyes making him look as if he hadn't slept for a week.

Any lingering inclination I might have had to yell at him dissolved when I took a good look at his expression. Tired, discouraged; verging on hopeless.

"Come in," I said instead. "I'll fix you a drink. Scotch okay?"

"I'd prefer arsenic," he said, settling on the couch with a groan and tossing a sheaf of papers onto the coffee table.

I put some ice in a glass and poured the liquor. "I'm afraid to ask, Cal, but I have to."

"It's not good, Taylor."

I sat beside him. "Tell me anyway."

He drained the contents of the glass, then leaned back and closed his eyes. "Fingerprints. The lab found Bo's fingerprints on the handle of that damn shovel."

I gasped. "How is that possible? Prints don't last that long, do they?"

"Depends on a lot of things. The surface of the object, whether or not it's been in a protected environment." He took another sip of scotch. "In this case, though, it's mostly a lucky break. For the lab, that is, not for Bo. These prints were left in the form of what they call plastic impressions."

I looked at him blankly. "I've read a lot about latent prints, but I can't say I remember that term."

"It happens when a finger is pressed into a soft surface that molds itself to the friction ridges. What we're talking about with the shovel handle is mud." He sat up and shuffled through the papers on the table. "See for yourself. They faxed me the report. Plain old mud might or might not have lasted this long, but in this part of the country, the soil is red clay. Her prints are almost as fresh as if she had touched that damn shovel this morning."

As I scanned the report, a yellowed newspaper clipping fluttered to the floor and I bent to retrieve it. A wizened, little man with eyes as black as fresh sin stared up at me from the front page. *Preacher Vanishes*, the headline blared.

My brain was spinning. "Cal, the prints alone don't mean anything, do they? So Bo was using the shovel...that doesn't necessarily make it the murder weapon."

He shook his head sadly. "But it was. The shovel blade conforms to the injury on the back of Ralph's skull, and Luminol even shows blood on the metal."

I had heard of Luminol, a chemical used to detect traces of blood not visible to the naked eye. Luminol is sprayed on the suspect surface, and then the room is darkened as much as possible, pitch dark being the preference. Any Luminol that has come into contact with blood will glow. I had even been told by a source at HPD that Luminol is especially valuable when working a case that has been re-opened after a substantial period of time because, for some reason, older blood samples will actually produce a brighter glow than will fresh ones.

I stood up and began pacing the room. "Well, then, there's another explanation."

"Maybe." He drained his glass and got up to refill it.

"That isn't what I want to hear you say, Cal."

His face contorted. "Well, I'm damned sorry, Taylor, if I'm not saying what you want to hear. What is it you want me to do? Ignore the evidence? I couldn't, even if I wanted to. Burke knows about it, and because of his big mouth, so does Underwood." He sat back down abruptly, rubbing a hand across his forehead. "Didn't mean to blow up."

"It's okay."

"No, it's really not. See, there's more. Underwood got a bee in his bonnet this morning and had Burke start making some phone calls, trying to track down Harvey Neff."

"I was at the S.O. during part of that."

He gave a tiny smile. "Yeah. I heard about a little altercation between you and old Dave."

"Sorry." I smiled, too. "Not that I did it, just that you found out about it. So what's up with Harvey Neff?"

"Well, Burke found him. Seems he lives right in Lubbock. He worked in real estate for years, and still dabbles in it, though he's mostly retired."

I poured a slug of Scotch into my teacup. "And what did he have to say that got Burke and Underwood all excited?"

Cal patted the couch next to him, and I sat.

"Underwood, with Burke's help, got his hands on my preliminary report. What caught his eye was the stuff Bo told us about the money, remember? How, when she couldn't access the funds in the joint bank account, she sold some stock her father had given her? Do you recall how much she said she got from that stock?"

"Five thousand dollars. Not much to start a new life on, even in the early '60s."

"Enough, though, as she proved."

"Cal, what does this have to do with the murder?"

He took my hand and examined it as though he'd never seen it before. I realized it was an excuse not to meet my eyes. "Underwood wanted to find out how much money went missing from the church safe when Ralph 'disappeared.' Harvey remembered. It was just over five thousand dollars." He released my hand. "We're talking motive,

Taylor. I only hope Bo can prove she sold that stock."

Chapter Five

BY SEVEN O'CLOCK the next morning, I had been wide awake for an hour, my mind racing in circles. Deep down, I agreed with Doc. No one was really incapable of murder, given the proper set of circumstances. And, by all accounts, Bo had put up with more than the average woman could bear, and had done so for seventeen years. But she had looked me straight in the eye and denied killing her husband, and I believed her.

Next to me in the bed, Cal rolled to his left and moaned into the pillow. Bad dreams? Well, who could blame him? He had stayed over at my insistence, not because of any romantic inclinations on my part, but simply as a matter of his own safety. During the course of hashing over Bo's predicament, he had consumed my scotch at a rate that made me determined not to let him drive. He'd been barely conscious when I tucked him into bed, and I felt sure he'd sleep until noon if I didn't wake him. Luckily, he wasn't due at work until the afternoon shift.

But I sure had work to do. I eased out of bed, pulled on jeans and a sweatshirt, then headed to the kitchen to make coffee. I had no doubt that the first thing on Cal's agenda—after he downed a half-dozen aspirin—would be to confront Bo, and I wanted to get to her before he did.

I had moved Cal's squad car into the garage the night before, secure from Dorothy's prying eyes, so it was a simple matter to slip my VW into neutral and push it out into the street before starting the noisy motor. Lucy's Café was open and packed with the breakfast crowd by the time I got there, and I asked Rita to put a dozen fresh doughnuts in a bag. I had already filled a thermos with coffee, so I just nabbed a couple of Styrofoam cups and beat a retreat before Rita could start questioning me.

Manners dictated a phone call to Bo's house before such an early morning visit, but I was halfway there before the thought occurred to me.

When she didn't answer my knock, I went around to the back door. She denied it, but Bo was getting a little hard of hearing, and if she was in the kitchen, she might not have heard me. I spotted her as I rounded the corner of the house. She was gathering dark leaves from her garden, perhaps turnip greens. I was struck again by how small and frail she looked, though frail was not a word I had ever before applied to Bo Posey. Her diminutive stature had led to one of the many arguments between Cal and myself the night before.

"Be rational for once," I'd told him heatedly, "and consider the fact that Bo is by no stretch of the imagination a large woman. Do you really believe she would've had the strength to stuff a full-grown man up a chimney? For God's sake, Cal, you're a big man, and I'm not sure you could've done it yourself. It would take a hell of a lot of upper body strength.

"And a chimney is a tight fit, you know. Whoever did this would not only have to balance the dead weight of a body, but would also have to supply considerable force to jam him up there."

"I'm not an imbecile, Taylor," he had replied, laying on his West Texas drawl so thickly I could have cut it with my fingernail. "Of course I thought of that. But if you'll remember, Doc told us that Ralph Posey had a very small build for a man. I needed to find out just how small, so I did a little checking this morning." He pulled a folded sheet of paper from his pocket and handed it to me. "I got this from the *Gazette's* morgue. It's a photocopy of the original picture, but you can see enough to answer your question."

I unfolded the paper. Bo and Ralph stared up at me from nearly half a century ago—she in a white, floor-length wedding gown, he in a dark suit. The reproduction was grainy and slightly blurred, but it seemed to me that she looked optimistic, while Ralph bore the expression of a man making a necessary sacrifice. It was easy to see what Cal was trying to tell me. Bo was a petite woman, yes, but Ralph was even shorter than she, and had the build of a praying mantis, barely more than skin and bone.

"According to the medical records Doc dug out for me, Ralph weighed around one hundred and ten pounds. Hell, Taylor, even you could probably have lifted him. As to the chimney, take a good look at it sometime. You have to remember it was built during an era when folks relied on a fireplace for heat, not just ambiance. The one in that house is twice the size of any you'd find in a modern home, and the chimney is quite a bit wider.

"No, the biggest problem facing the murderer would've been keeping him jammed up there, which is why the shovel was braced diagonally beneath him to act as a wedge."

So much for that theory. And if Cal could see Bo this morning, he would probably point out that a lifetime of gardening had built up the muscles in her shoulders and arms—something else I couldn't deny. The first time Bo had shaken hands with me, she had damn near broken my fingers. But I was wasting precious time.

"Good morning," I called out, and she straightened, smiling when she saw me.

"Didn't think city girls got up this early," she said. "Keron with you?"

I hated to disappoint her, but I shook my head. "Just me. Have you had breakfast yet?"

"Nope, needed to get this done first. Want some greens? Grab a basket and help yourself."

"Maybe later, Bo." I moved closer so we could stop shouting. "I'd appreciate it if you'd come for a little drive with me."

She started for the house. "What you got in mind? If it's breakfast at Lucy's, I think I'll pass. I don't feel up to facing that crowd just yet."

I took the basket of greens from her hand and set it in the shade of the back porch. "I do want to take you to breakfast, but not at the café. How does a picnic sound?"

Her mouth quirked. "Can't say I've ever been on a picnic this early in the day. Sure, okay. What can I bring?"

"Nothing, as long as you can put up with doughnuts and coffee. C'mon."

Bo has a sharp mind, and I hadn't driven ten feet from her house before she started asking questions. I fended them off, wanting a little time to relax her before I did what had to be done.

At the tiny city park on the edge of town, I pulled my Volkswagen behind a clump of trees where it would be hidden from the road. Bo and I tramped through the still damp grass to a small clearing where the morning sun gathered like a warm blanket. I seated her on a low stump and poured her a cup of coffee.

"Nice," she said approvingly. "Much cozier than a witness stand. Ready for the interrogation when you are, Taylor."

I told you she was sharp.

"Spill it," she said, so I did.

I shared everything I knew with her, as gently as I possibly could. Cal was going to be livid, but at this point I was much more concerned with Bo's reaction.

When I had finished, she was quiet for a time, sipping her coffee and nibbling a doughnut. At last she looked down at me, where I was sitting cross-legged on the ground.

"Wouldn't blame him if he did lock me up," she said. "Sounds pretty cut and dried, don't it?"

I put a hand on her knee. "No one is going to lock you up, Bo, not if I can help it. We've just got to find some answers, that's all."

"Doesn't appear we'll have the chance. If Underwood's pushin' for my arrest, you can bet it'll happen. The man's a scumbag, but he's got clout."

I smiled for the first time in an hour. "Well, that's something I didn't tell you. Mr. Underwood had a little knot tied in his scheme yesterday."

Bo's glum face brightened. "Yeah?"

I nodded. "According to Cal, Underwood was all set to take their findings to the justice of the peace and ask for an arrest warrant."

"Judge Prescott," Bo said sourly. "Well, that's it then. I'm done for. Sam Prescott and Dave Underwood have been wipin' each other's butts for the past twenty years."

I laughed. "Well, not for another week, they won't. Seems Judge Prescott is on a fishing trip in East Texas, and won't be back until next Tuesday. Cal said Underwood looked like he'd been socked in the gut when he found out."

Bo looked hopeful for a split second, and then shook her head. "So what? If our judge is unavailable, all Dave has to do is take their case before a judge in Lubbock County."

"Which is exactly what Deputy Burke suggested, but Underwood said no, he'd wait for Prescott to come back."

"I don't get it."

"Burke didn't either, but Cal thinks he understands. See, just like you said, Prescott and Underwood are pals, so there's little doubt he'd get his warrant just by asking. But if he takes the evidence to a big city judge—a total stranger—there are too many things that could go wrong. After all, the evidence is pretty circumstantial at this point, and it's entirely possible an impartial judge might be reluctant to lock up an eighty-two-year-old woman for a murder that occurred three decades ago."

"Good to know that old age comes in handy now and then," Bo said dryly. "Usually, it's just a pain in the ass. Cal's probably right, though, 'cause that sounds like the slimy way Underwood's mind works."

"So, we've got a reprieve."

She squinted at me. "Reprieve, huh? Delaying the inevitable, if you ask me."

"Come on, Bo, don't talk like that. Now, you told me you were innocent, and I believe you. Let's start figuring out how to prove it, okay?"

"What happened to innocent until proven guilty? Forget it...stupid question. Where do you want to start?"

"With the shovel." I poured more coffee for both of us, and settled my back against the stump. "That's a real problem, since your fingerprints were on the handle."

She grimaced. "Hardly surprisin', since it was my shovel. You think that good for nothin' Ralph Posey ever did a lick of gardening in his miserable life? 'Woman's work,' he called it, just like every other chore that meant liftin' a finger."

I sighed, and tried another direction. "Suppose you tell me everything you remember about the night before he came up missing?"

She rested her chin on a gnarled fist, her forehead crinkled in thought. "Well, I remember Ralph and me had a fight. We argued a lot, but this was a real humdinger. Harvey and Gertrude came runnin' into the church office to see what was going on."

My heart sank. "There were witnesses?"

Bo chuckled. "Don't look so gloomy, Taylor. If I'm gonna be convicted for yellin' at my husband, we might as well hang it up right now."

"What was the fight about?"

"Faith. She was goin' to graduate high school in a couple of weeks, and she wanted so bad to go on to college. Ralph didn't cotton to the idea. Said she'd just get her head filled with all sorts of evil thoughts. Besides, I'd known for a while that he had other plans for her."

"Such as?"

Bo fired up a Camel and spat a bit of tobacco from her tongue. "Wanted to turn her into a female evangelist and take her on the road."

"Eek!"

"Yeah. But she was doin' so well with the radio show—"

"Back up...what radio show?"

"Oh, hell, you don't think Ralph was satisfied preachin' to the measly thirty or so in his congregation, do you? The man thought he was destined for greatness. He and Harvey set up a call-in prayer line on a little Lubbock AM station." She grimaced. "Just another way to scam money out of folks who couldn't afford it."

"I get it—one of those pay-to-pray gimmicks."

"Yep. At least Harvey made sure the money actually funded a few worthy causes, and one of those causes was Faith."

"Huh?"

Her pinched mouth softened a little. "He felt sorry for Faith, wearin' rags to school and never even having pocket change to go get a soda with her friends. He cooked up the scheme to get her a job on the radio show." She shook her head. "Nicest thing anyone had ever done for my daughter, and I told him so.

"Since he was the bookkeeper, he was able to slip her some of the cash that came in. Ralph didn't know, of course. Harvey convinced him that Faith was donating her time to show support for her father, which was exactly the right thing to say."

"Ralph didn't care that Harvey donated most of the cash?"

"Naw, I told you, Ralph took his vow of poverty to heart. That's why I was so surprised when he ended up missing and the money from the church safe gone with him. Only thing I could figure at the time was that he'd decided to move on and start up a bigger and better church somewhere else."

"You were telling me about Faith's job," I prodded.

"Right. Well, Faith started out just screenin' calls, fetchin' coffee, things like that, but the station manager liked her voice so much he insisted they put her on the air now and then. So she read the opening and closing prayers, and joined in when Ralph and Harvey prayed together.

"Ralph decided she had the callin' to become an evangelist. The idea horrified her. I knew she would've been miserable, and I just couldn't let that happen." She laughed a little. "This has sure enough been a long, roundabout way to tell you what Ralph and I were fighting about, but now you know."

I thought for a minute. "So you and Ralph were shouting, and two people came in to break it up. Harvey and Gertrude. Now, who's Gertrude?"

"Gertrude Mason. She was the sheriff's sister."

"The sheriff's *sister?* What was she doing there?"

"Oh, Gert was a leadin' member of Ralph's congregation," Bo said, her lips twisting. "She thought Ralph was the cat's meow and I was the litter box. Anyway, Gertie just poured fuel on the fire. When the little hussy started lecturing me on decorum, I was fit to be tied. I stormed outta there and went on home before I could give in to the temptation to knock the bitch down and stomp her guts out."

"What time was this?"

She considered. "Early evening. Sun just starting to sink. I remember, 'cause it was in my eyes all the way to the house."

"What did you do when you got home?"

She grinned. "I attacked the garden. I'd found it the best way to deal with my temper, you see. Gardening is good, hard labor, and takes the edge right off a hissy fit. And I needed to calm down if I was going to think of a way to get my daughter where she wanted to go."

Underwood would say that she thought of a way, all right. I lit a cigarette of my own, my hands trembling a little.

Bo shifted. "I've figured out that you brought me here so Cal can't find me yet, but do you s'pose we could go sit in your car for a while? My rear end is goin' to sleep on this stump."

"Sorry, sure." What was I thinking? I still tended to forget how old she was.

We moved to the VW and rolled down the windows to take advantage of an Indian summer breeze.

Bo sighed, snuggling into the upholstery. "Where was I?"

"Gardening."

"Yeah, that's right. I was diggin' potatoes, and cursin' Ralph under my breath when it started drizzling. It was this time of year, you know, and storms would drop without a minute's warning. The wind whipped around to where it was all of a sudden coming from the north, and it didn't take long before I was shivering. The potato patch is down close to the little house, so I headed in there to warm up a bit."

I'd had my eyes closed, picturing this as she told it. Now I turned to look at her. "You were using the shovel?"

"It's hard to dig taters with your bare hands."

"What did you do with it when you went inside?"

Her brow furrowed. "Can't rightly say I remember. Probably just carted it with me."

"You wouldn't have left it in the garden?"

She shook her head in disgust. "Spoken like a city gal! Tools rust when you leave 'em out in the weather, child. I wouldn't have done such a thing."

"Okay, keep talking."

"Well, I had a notion to light a fire and warm my hands, but Ralph never cared much for the smell of wood smoke, and there was no kindling in the wood box. Would have been too much work anyhow. I'd have had to clean out the fireplace before I could've used it. I'd be willing to bet that the ashes in there were left over from the fire I built on our weddin' night." She snorted. "That's the last time I remember tryin' to be romantic with the bastard."

Her words made me realize that the ashes I had scooped from the fireplace the day Cal and I had discovered the skeleton were most likely the same ashes Bo had contemplated cleaning out on that fateful night. The thought made me shiver.

Bo peered at me. “You all right, hon? You look like a goose walked over your grave.”

That particular old country adage didn’t make me feel any better, but I nodded. “I’m fine. Go on.”

“Anyway, I turned on the gas furnace and fixed myself a cup of hot tea. I hung around for thirty minutes or so, thinkin’ the drizzle would let up and I could finish my digging, but it started raining harder, and the wind was really howling by then, so I just took a raincoat off the coat rack and ran back to the big house.”

“Leaving your shovel in the little house?” My voice rose in excitement. “Bo, don’t you see? If you left the shovel there, anyone could’ve come along later and used it to kill Ralph. Think about it. You were digging potatoes in the rain, probably got mud all over the handle. Your fingerprints would be in the mud. Then you leave it in a heated house, so what happens? The mud dries and your prints are still there like they’re cast in cement.

She frowned. “But if you’re right, whoever killed him would’ve left their own prints on it.”

“Not on a layer of dried clay, they wouldn’t.” I tried to contain my enthusiasm, but it wasn’t easy. “Let’s go on. What did you do when you got home?”

She shrugged. “I was chilled to the bone by that time, so I ran myself a hot bath and dug out a bottle of my Pa’s brandy that I kept hidden from Ralph.”

“Didn’t Ralph come home eventually?”

“Yeah, about an hour later I heard his old rattletrap pick-up comin’ up the drive.” She smiled a little. “I had fallen asleep in the tub, and all I could think was, ‘Oh, shit, he’s gonna see the brandy bottle in the bedroom and pour the last of my booze down the sink.’ But he didn’t stop at the big house, just continued on down the road.” She glanced at me. “Before you ask, that wasn’t unusual. Ralph slept out there more times than not. We weren’t what Oprah would call compatible sex partners.”

“Oh.” Something else occurred to me. “Where was Faith during all this?”

“She had gone to her senior prom. She left early and got dressed over at Dorothy Stenson’s, and spent the night there afterwards. I felt like I might be catching a cold, so I went on to bed and slept ’til morning. When Ralph turned up missing, I was as surprised as anyone."

"All right." I chewed my bottom lip and considered her story. "We've explained the fingerprints, so that's good. Now about the stock, Bo? Can you prove you sold it?"

"Never thought I'd have to, but maybe I can. I sold it to a friend."

I sat up straighter. "Someone here in Perdue? That will help. Who?"

She shook her head. "Don't count on it helping. He's dead. Passed away about ten years ago."

"Who?" I asked again.

"Henry Tucker."

"Tucker. I know that name."

"His son was dating Faith. Lewis Tucker. Maybe she mentioned him."

"No, but Dorothy did."

Bo cackled. "I should've known."

"Does Lewis still live here?"

"If you can call it living," she said, rather mysteriously.

"Good grief, Bo, stop playing word games. This is serious. Is he still in Perdue or not?"

"Yep."

I started the car. "Let's pay Mr. Tucker a visit, shall we?"

"He won't like it, but why not?"

She refused to elaborate further, but I soon found out for myself what she meant. As directed, I drove into town and parked beside Perdue Pharmacy. Instead of going inside, Bo led me around to the back of the red brick building, where a rickety looking metal staircase ascended to a door on the second story.

"The birdman," she muttered, and gave me a little shove to start me up the steps.

There was barely enough room on the tiny landing for both of us, and we were huddled together so closely we must have looked like a two-headed mutant to the man who opened the door.

I had forgotten Lewis Tucker was confined to a wheelchair. His legs, though concealed by a blanket, were obviously wasted and his face seemed too narrow for his size. His shoulders, however, bulged beneath his shirt, pumped by the effort it took to maneuver a non-electric wheelchair day after day. Though he bore little resemblance to the football hero Dorothy had described, I could see lingering traces of what a handsome teenager he must have been. His hair, more silver now than brown, was still thick and full, and his eyes were a clear, beautiful gray.

Those eyes glanced up at me, then widened as they focused on Bo. “Mrs. Posey?”

“Call me Bo, for heaven’s sake. Want to make me feel like an old lady? Yeah, it’s me, Lewis. Can we come in for a spell?”

“Uh, sure, sure.” He backed his chair out of the doorway and we followed him in.

The upper floor seemed to consist of a single, good-sized room, with a kitchenette lining the rear wall. Plants hung everywhere, their lush greenery disguising the drab walls, and birdcages stood or hung in every spare nook where there wasn’t a plant. Most of the cages were filled with colorful finches that went into flurries of activity when touched by the breeze from the open door. I closed it behind me, and the little birds settled down.

There wasn’t much furniture, but Lewis gestured at a daybed strewn with pillows, and Bo and I took a seat.

She glanced around the apartment. “I’d heard you withdrew from the human race, Lewis, but I can think of worse places to hide out. You’ve really fixed this place up nice since last time I saw it.”

“Thanks.” He still seemed nervous, his thin hands plucking at the chair’s rubber-coated wheels. “Um, I’m a little out of practice, but I guess I should offer you something to drink?”

“Guess you should at that,” Bo said. “But what I really need is a place to get rid of some coffee. You do have a bathroom, don’t you?”

“Of course I do.” He seemed sincerely insulted at the question. “Right back there.”

Bo got to her feet and disappeared behind a gigantic banana plant, leaving two very uncomfortable people staring at each other.

“I have you at a disadvantage,” I said at last. “I know who you are, but you don’t know me. My name is Taylor Madison.”

His face contorted into a smile, but the process seemed painful, as if he had forgotten how. “Maddy Taylor,” he said. “The local author. I’ve read your novels.”

“You have?” Bo emerged from behind the plant. “I’m surprised. Thought you never went anywhere.”

I gave her a curious glance, but she didn’t explain.

“Miss Klune brings me a stack of books every couple of weeks when she delivers my groceries.”

Sadie Klune was Derrick County’s librarian. It didn’t surprise me that she did favors for Lewis; she volunteered for everything from the

Saturday children's reading circle to the Methodist Church's annual white elephant sale.

"She told me a lot about you," Lewis said to me. "I really enjoyed reading your mysteries."

"Thank you."

"If Sadie keeps you up on the local gossip, then you know what's happening with me," Bo cut in.

"Can't say I do."

"That's odd. I've been the main subject of conversation for the past two days."

"Then that explains it," Lewis said. "I haven't seen Miss Klune for over a week. Looks like you'll have to catch me up."

"Well, it all started when my husband's skeleton fell out of a chimney," Bo began.

I would have sworn on a stack of Bibles that Lewis Tucker's pale face was incapable of losing any more color, but it did. I thought for a moment that he was going to topple out of his chair, and I rose to catch him, just in case.

"Maybe you'd better let me explain, Bo," I said. She had a habit of being painfully blunt, and I wasn't sure this poor man could take it.

She shrugged. "Go ahead."

I filled him in on the barest of basics, leaving out all gory details, and he watched me carefully the entire time as if trying to decide whether he could trust me or not.

"You're being charged with his murder?" he asked Bo when I had finished the story.

"I haven't been yet, but it's danglin' over my head," she told him. "Which brings me to why we're here."

His hands moved to the wheels of his chair, and he backed away as far as the room would allow, which wasn't all that far. His breathing grew loud and ragged, and I finally caught on to what was happening.

"He's hyperventilating, Bo! Help me find a paper sack."

The two of us rushed into the minuscule kitchen and rummaged frantically through the cabinets. I located a small grocery bag and carried it to Lewis, pressing it over his nose and mouth.

"Take slow, even breaths," I instructed him. "Easy now, you're okay. We didn't mean to upset you."

A little color returned to his face and he pushed the bag away, still gasping a bit. "I'm fine, thank you. Sorry."

"I'm the one who's sorry," Bo said, leaning over him worriedly. "Taylor, maybe we'd better come back another time."

"No!" I almost shouted it, and Lewis looked startled. "No," I repeated, in a more normal tone. "Mr. Tucker, this is important. We just need to ask you if you can locate your father's business records."

Lewis's gray eyes fluttered, then locked with mine. "My... father's—"

"I sold some stock to him soon after Ralph disappeared," Bo explained. "Seems the sheriff's office needs proof that I did. Has to do with motive."

Lewis shook his head, clearly bewildered. "I see. I think." He pondered for a moment. "Dad passed away about ten years ago, and you probably heard I sold the house soon after. Mom is in Restful Haven in Lubbock."

"I know," Bo said gently. "I meant to ask after her."

"She's well, as well as she can be, considering. But as to what you're asking, I really can't tell you. I stored a few things, and Dad left some papers in his safety deposit box, but I honestly don't know what all I have. I hired an auction firm to sell off the contents of the house, and afterwards gave them permission to dispose of what was left. I'll look through what I held onto and get back to you. Would that be all right?"

"But as soon as possible," I urged him. "Please, you must understand how badly we need this information."

Bo nodded. "We've only got until next Tuesday, Lewis. That's when the hanging judge gets back."

Lewis stared at her as if she had begun speaking Greek, and she waved a hand. "Never mind. Listen, I've been thinking back to when I approached your father about selling him the stock. My timing was awful. I realize that now. You were still in the hospital, hadn't been out of the coma for more than a few hours. Your mother and father were home for the first time since your accident, probably trying to get a little rest, and here I came barging in.

"Point is, I recall your mother being present for part of the conversation, though I'm not sure she was still in the room when the actual sale took place. But the thing is, if she remembers what I came to talk to him about, it might convince the authorities I sold the stock to him, even if we can't come up with any paperwork to prove it."

Lewis had started shaking his head even before she was through speaking. "I thought you understood why my mother is in the rest home."

Bo raised her eyebrows. "Nerves, I supposed. Dinah was always such a skittish little thing. I figured your father's death hit her pretty hard."

"This started before Dad died," Lewis said. "I really thought everyone knew. Mom has Alzheimer's."

Bo, for once, was stunned into complete silence for almost a full minute, and then she began stammering apologies.

Lewis interrupted. "Please, Mrs. Posey...Bo, it's okay. Look, let me get us all something to drink. Cola? Spring water? Something hot? Name it."

We both opted for water, and he rolled into the kitchen to fetch it. That's when I spotted something crouched on the wide windowsill. Black fur, a stub where a tail ought to be.

"A Manx!" I cried, delightedly. "Look, Bo."

"A who?" she asked.

I got up and crept over to the creature, my hand extended. The black lump uncoiled, a pink tongue reached to touch my finger, wide ears pricked with interest. Not at all shy or indifferent, it leaped bodily into my arms and began purring.

"Oh, you little sweetie," I cooed, as if I were holding a week-old kitten instead of nearly twenty pounds of feline. "Lewis, this is absolutely the most beautiful—"

He had glanced over his shoulder, and his eyes grew huge. "Wait!" he cried. "Don't—"

"—cat," I finished.

A soul-shaking shaking scream split the air, the sound of a woman in mortal terror.

Chapter Six

BO, WITH AMAZING agility, made a dive behind the daybed. The cat clawed his way out of my grasp and bolted for a potted fichus tree, which groaned under his weight as he attempted to climb it. Lewis hadn't moved. He sat near the kitchen counter, a glass of ice water in each hand, his eyes squeezed tightly shut.

Nursing my scratches, I hurried across the room and knelt by the bed. "Bo? My God, are you all right? Why did you scream?"

Her head bobbed up from behind the pillows. "Me? What are you talking about? You're the one who screamed!"

"I did not!"

We both looked at Lewis who seemed frozen in place, his lips quivering. Certain he was going to hyperventilate again, I grabbed the bag and started toward him. Before I was halfway there, he leaned his head back, opened his mouth and...howled with laughter.

It sounded rusty, as if he didn't do it often, but he was obviously enjoying himself. Bo came and stood beside me, hands on hips, scowling down at him. He opened his eyes, saw her face and laughed even harder.

"Sorry, sorry," he gasped after a moment and pulled off a sheet of paper towel to blot up the water he'd spilled all over his lap. "It's just...the two of you...your expressions...oh, Lord."

"Who the hell screamed?" I demanded.

"Cecilia did," he managed to choke out.

"Cecilia who?" Bo asked. "Damn it, Lewis..."

Lewis launched into another gale of hilarity, but he pointed.

We turned. Tucked behind a five-foot bamboo plant, visible only from the perspective of the kitchen, stood an enormous brass cage with ivory trim. Inside, a white cockatoo the size of a toaster danced from one side of her wooden perch to the other, her feathers poofed out in a fuzzy halo. Her head was tucked under one wing and she was trembling violently.

I approached the cage and tapped gently on a brass bar. "Cecilia?"

The ruffled head emerged, and one black button eye studied me warily. "Cat," she croaked.

"Cecilia is terrified of C-A-T-S," Lewis said, finally in control enough to speak. "I never say the word aloud. Same thing applies to K-I-T-T-Y, P-U-S-S, F-E-L-I-N-E, or any other variation I've been able to come up with. She has quite a vocabulary."

"So what do you call the—"

Lewis shook his head warningly.

"—the black, fuzzy thing over there?" I finished weakly.

"Watch this." Lewis whistled. The cat trotted across the room and leaped into his lap. "Good dog," he said, stroking the velvety fur.

Bo and I stared at each other, then burst out laughing.

"That's the most absurd thing I ever saw!" I said at last. "That poor ca—um, creature doesn't even know what he is! You do realize that eventually you're going to have to shell out some big bucks to an animal therapist."

"Hey, it keeps the peace. Nigel doesn't seem to mind."

"Well, hell, I'd mind," Bo said. "Especially if you added insult to injury by naming me Nigel. Jehosaphat, Lewis, when are the men in white coats coming to take you away?"

"Why do you think I've hidden away like a hermit for the past ten years? They haven't found me yet."

The man in the wheelchair was still grinning, and suddenly my heart went out to him. I didn't know the real story behind his decision to alienate himself the way he had, but it was obvious that, no matter what he said otherwise, our visit was providing him with more fun than he'd experienced in a very long time.

I'd never match Bo's talent for bluntness, but it was on the tip of my tongue to simply ask him why he'd withdrawn from the world. Fortunately, I came to my senses in time and picked up my glass of water instead.

Cecilia was beginning to recover. She cocked her head at us, made a gurgling noise in her throat, then proclaimed, "Nasty cat!" Whereupon she turned her back and began attacking her food dish.

"How about if you pry open a window so I can have a cigarette?" Bo said to Lewis. "My nerves are fried to a crisp."

Lewis obeyed, and as I watched her light one of her ever-present Camels, a thought occurred to me.

"What would you do if, God forbid, a fire broke out up here?" I asked him. "You couldn't get down those metal steps in a wheelchair."

Lewis rolled back into the kitchen and fetched a saucer for Bo to use as an ashtray. "I've got an electric lift rigged to the inside staircase that leads down to the pharmacy's storeroom. And another wheelchair waiting at the bottom."

"Well, that's fancy plannin' for a man who never goes anywhere," Bo said, ignoring the saucer and tapping ashes into an African violet that blossomed on the windowsill.

Lewis smiled tightly. "I know that's what most people think, but it's not true. For one thing, I visit my mother at least twice a month."

"In Lubbock? How do you get there? Don't tell me you've learned to operate a car?"

I shot her a look, confused by the sudden venom in her voice.

Lewis tensed in his chair. "A friend drives me. Any more questions?"

It was clear we were beginning to wear out our welcome. I carried my glass to the kitchen and put it in the sink. "We'd better be going," I told Bo. "Mr. Tucker, thank you for seeing us. Please don't forget to look through those papers."

"I'll call you," he promised, his stiff posture relaxing a little. "Maybe next time we can talk about mystery novels. I'm a real fan."

Was that an invitation? Poor guy was probably lonelier than he'd admit.

"Sure. How about if I cook you dinner sometime?"

His thin face lit up. "Really? That'd be great. I'm not much of a cook, and there's only so much frozen food a person can eat."

"Try heating it first," Bo suggested sarcastically.

What in hell had gotten into her? I took her arm and propelled her toward the door.

As soon as we had negotiated the creaking steps to the ground, I turned to her. "You were pretty hard on him there at the end. What's the matter?"

She grimaced. "I know it was rude, but it galls me to see a man shut himself away like that. Lewis has a good brain, and he had the most potential of anyone in his graduating class. How could he just give up?"

I remembered what Dorothy had told me about Lewis's plans to become a veterinarian and Lewis's reasons for putting that ambition aside.

Bo harrumphed when I passed the story along to her. "He didn't have to be a farm and ranch vet, you know. Could've moved to a city and opened a dog and cat practice." She got into the car with a grunt.

I slid into the driver's side and started the engine. "Well, but he was just a kid when all this happened, Bo. Sometimes it doesn't occur to the young that their dreams can be modified," I said as I pulled out onto the street.

"So he could've at least gone on to college and found somethin' else he liked."

"Maybe he couldn't afford to. I'm sure his medical bills were horrendous, and—"

"Stop the car," Bo said.

"Huh?"

"Stop!"

I did as I was told, coming to an abrupt halt at the corner of the courthouse square and thinking how lucky it was that Main Street's traffic was pretty much limited to three cars per hour.

"Look to your right. See that house with the tower and all the gables?"

"Yeah, I've always wondered about that place." The house rose four stories into the air and I'd often wondered if Edgar Allen Poe had left a few bodies bricked up in the walls of its cellar or a tell-tale heart under the floorboards.

"That's the Tucker mansion. Ol' Henry just kept addin' on. I 'spect that place has thirty rooms or so. He and Dinah were hopin' for a passel of kids, but Lewis turned out to be an only child. I know for a fact that his trust fund kicked in when he turned eighteen, and it was enough to pay for two or three college degrees. When I think of livin' on red beans and rice while I was putting Faith through college—and with her workin' on the side to help out, at that—I could just strangle Lewis for turnin' his back on his good fortune.

"Now, you tell me why on earth a man with money oozin' outta his pores would hole up in a dinky apartment over a drugstore unless it's to cut himself off from civilization and sulk?" Her shoulders suddenly slumped. "Oh, heck, ignore me. I'm just disappointed. I was really hopin' he'd be able to help with the stock thing. I don't know what to do now."

"It's not a lost cause, Bo. He promised to try and dig up the record."

"If there's one to dig up. Suppose Henry turned around and sold that stock to someone else a couple of years down the line. I doubt he'd hang onto any of the paperwork involved. Suppose—"

"Suppose we stop supposing and go on from here."

"Where? Seems to me all we can do is wait and see if Lewis comes up with anything."

"Good thing you're not a detective," I told her. "Or even a mystery writer, for that matter. Waiting is not something I do well. Just ask Cal."

"Got a plan in mind?"

"You bet." I rested my hands on the worn steering wheel. "First of all, how well did you know Mrs. Tucker?"

"Well enough to call her Dinah, not well enough to flirt with her husband. Why?"

"I think we should go visit her."

Bo gaped at me. "What for? You heard Lewis. She has—"

"Alzheimer's disease. Yes, I heard him. Bo, have you ever known anyone with Alzheimer's?"

"Can't say I have." She shuddered. "Horrible thing. I believe I'd rather be paralyzed from the neck down than have my mind go like that."

"Yeah, it's bad. My college roommate's grandmother had it. Jean and I used to visit her in the nursing home." I tapped the steering wheel thoughtfully. "It's a weird disease. Sometimes, Granny Newman thought Jean was her sister, sometimes a nurse. But other times, she knew perfectly well that she was looking at her granddaughter. There were days when she couldn't remember how to tie her shoes, but she could tell you what she'd had for breakfast on the day Japan attacked Pearl Harbor. She could tell stories about her honeymoon, but had no idea what toothpaste is used for."

Bo grinned. "I'm catching on. Just because Dinah might not know the time of day, she could very well remember my discussion with her husband, is that it?"

"Bingo."

Her face fell. "But Taylor, even if she does, what good will it do? She wouldn't exactly make a prime witness, now would she? Can't you just hear the prosecutor if my lawyer tried to put a woman with a diagnosed mental disorder on the stand?"

"Yeah, but I don't care about that right now. Point is, it would convince Cal and, more than anything, I want him squarely on our side."

"Can't think of anyone I'd rather have in my corner," she agreed. She looked at me, and her gaze softened. "Except maybe you. And you're already there, aren't you?"

"I am indeed." I started the engine. "Okay, how do I get to—what was it? Restful Haven?"

"Easy. You just..." She broke off, slumping forward in her seat.

"Bo?" I peered into her face, which had gone almost as white as Lewis's. "Are you all right?"

She tried to wave me away. "All...right. Just got a little...dizzy there for a minute."

"I'm taking you to the clinic." Gunning the motor, I forced the VW around the corner with a squeal of its balding tires. Bo fumed and protested and grumbled, but I ignored her.

"Good thing you brought her in," Doc told me thirty minutes later. "Her blood pressure is through the roof. Poor old soul, I guess this mess is weighing on her more heavily than she'll admit, and ten to one she's been neglecting her medication."

"Then this has happened before?"

"Not recently. We've had pretty good luck keeping it under control, but if she doesn't take her pills, they can't help her." He glanced over his shoulder into the cubicle where Bo was stretched out on an examining table, making sure she wasn't within earshot. "She's really in bad shape—babbling about Lewis Tucker of all people."

I had to smile. "She's not hallucinating, Doc. We just went to pay him a visit."

"Oh! Well, that's a relief. How's the boy doing?"

Only a man of Doc's years could refer to a fifty-plus man as a boy. "Seems okay to me. A little reclusive."

Doc poured muddy coffee into a Styrofoam cup and offered some to me. I declined.

"Poor kid," he said, sipping. "Wish I could do more for him. He's lucky, I suppose, to have full upper-body function. If the injury to his spine had been even a little higher, he'd be paralyzed from the neck down, and would probably be on a respirator."

I shivered. "Things could always be worse, I guess."

"Yeah." Doc added sugar to his muddy brew. "Lucky is probably too strong a word, though. Lewis had so much ahead of him." He sighed. "The night of the accident should've been one of the happiest of his life. He was graduating with honors, going on to Texas A&M to study veterinary medicine. Took the prettiest gal in town to the senior prom, where he was named MVP of Perdue's football team. Then—wham! It all changed in an instant."

"Do you know what caused the wreck?"

"A sheep had gotten loose and wandered out onto the road. Lewis was on his way back to Perdue after taking Faith home, and you know how dark it is outside the town limits. By the time he saw the sheep in his headlights, he had to swerve hard to miss it. Hit a fence post at sixty miles per hour."

"When am I gettin' out of this place?" Bo bellowed from the

cubicle.

"Hold your horses!" Doc bellowed back at her, then lowered his voice. "Taylor, I'm not sure what to do. I'd like to admit her to the clinic for a couple of days, just to monitor her medication and get her back on track, but I have no doubt she'd pitch a fit at the very idea."

"I could take her home with me, or...Wait! I've got it, Doc, the perfect solution. It's safe for her to be at home as long as she's being looked after, isn't it?"

"Sure, I just don't want her to be alone for a while. What you got up your sleeve?"

"I'll need to check before I can say for sure, but don't worry. If this plan falls through, I'll stay with her myself. Thanks, Doc."

Bo was sheepish as I helped her out to the car. "Dang fool thing to do," she muttered. "I know better than to skip my medicine like that. Just had a lot on my mind."

"I can't imagine why," I said dryly. "Let's get you home. I've got a phone call to make."

"What about Restful Haven?" she fretted, easing into the car seat.

"I'll go by myself. Well, why not, Bo? Not to sound unfeeling, but I probably won't seem any more a stranger to her than you would. Relax. I'll handle it. Trust me."

"I do," she said. "More than you know. Taylor, there's no way I can ever thank you enough—"

"Before you get sappy on me, I should tell you that Doc said no booze for the next few days."

That succeeded in switching her gears. She bitched and moaned and groused all the way home.

I settled her in bed, ordered her to take a nap, then descended to the den where I picked up the phone. As I had expected, my plan went off without a hitch—all it took was a flying trip back to Perdue.

By the time Bo, wrapped in her bathrobe, came looking for coffee an hour later, her surprise was seated at the kitchen table.

"Keron!"

"Hi, Grandma. How'd you like a houseguest for the next week or so?"

Even Bo couldn't manage a gruff reply. Wordlessly, she put her arms around her granddaughter.

"Thank you," I mouthed to Keron, and she nodded, shooing me away with her free hand.

The clock on my dashboard told me it was only just past noon, though I felt as if I had been awake for at least thirty-two hours. I wanted to stop by the house and look through the Lubbock phone directory—Bo hadn't had one—for Restful Haven, but I had no desire to take a chance on running into Cal. I knew I'd have to face him sooner or later, but hey, I'm a procrastinator from way back.

Turns out it wasn't my decision to make. As I pulled off the highway and onto the main street of Perdue, flashing red lights in my rearview mirror informed me that the mountain had come to Mohammed.

He was wearing a pair of mirrored sunglasses, whether in an attempt to look like a movie cop, or whether to relieve his hangover I wasn't sure. I didn't ask. He leaned through my open window, breathing mint mouthwash into my face.

"Missed you at breakfast," he remarked mildly, and the tension in my neck eased a bit.

"Sorry, errands to run. You know how it is. Besides, I'm surprised you were able to keep any breakfast down."

"Didn't try," he admitted. "So, what have you been up to?" His tone was still pleasant, conversational, so I tried to control a guilty flinch and returned the smile.

"Oh, this and that. You know."

"Yeah, I know. I ran into Doc."

I gulped. "You did?"

"Bo's feeling fine, by the way. I called to check on her just now."

"You did?"

"Of course, I s'pose you know better than I do how she's feeling, since you've been with her all morning." His voice cracked a little on the last two words. "Taylor, what the hell have you done?"

My mouth opened and closed a few times, but nothing came out. Finally, I gave up trying to think of a plausible fib. "We're blocking traffic and the good citizens of Perdue are gawking at us. I'll meet you at Lucy's, okay?"

"I'll give you a police escort," he said grimly, and climbed back into his squad car.

We avoided the John Travolta booth and sat as far away from the counter as possible, but still we leaned across the table and spoke in whispers.

Cal had plenty to say, and it was like listening to the hiss of a furious snake.

"I thought I could trust you," he said. His eyes were still hidden behind the tear-shaped mirrors, but I could hear as much hurt in his voice as anger.

"I'm sorry," I said. "Not that I'm trying to help Bo, but that you feel I've let you down."

Rita brought our iced tea and lingered at the next booth, apparently trying to polish a hole in the tabletop. Cal glared at her and she reluctantly retreated.

"I don't know what you think you've accomplished," he continued, "but you have royally screwed this investigation."

"By being the one to tell Bo that she's a suspect? What difference does it make that I told her instead of you? I just wanted it broken to her gently."

I could hear his teeth grinding. "But along with being the bearer of that particular news, you also spilled your guts about our evidence. The first thing she told me was that the two of you had come up with an explanation for her prints being all over the murder weapon."

"Well, we did. A logical explanation, too. You can't deny that."

"I can't?" He forgot to whisper, and eighty percent of the café's occupants turned to look at us. He dropped his voice again. "Taylor, for God's sake, what did you expect her to say? You take her out to a quiet spot, tell her about the damning evidence against her, give her plenty of time to think it through, and presto! She comes up with a story that makes perfect sense all the way around."

"I suppose you'd have preferred grilling her under hot lights and beating a confession out of her with a length of rubber hose?"

He removed his sunglasses and stared at me. "What have you been reading lately? Mickey Spillane? I just wanted an element of surprise when I talked to her. I can tell a lot by the way a suspect reacts to a question."

"Okay, then I'll tell you how she reacted. She was scared."

"Most murderers are when they're caught."

I couldn't believe my ears. "You think she's guilty, don't you?"

"That's not what I said."

"That's what it sounded like to me." I studied his bloodshot eyes. "Or maybe the political pressure is getting a little too hot for you, is that it?"

"What a rotten thing to say."

We scowled at each other for a few seconds, then I stood up.

"She didn't do it," I said. "And I'm going to prove it."

"Well, you sure as hell won't get any more help from me," he retorted.

"Glad to hear it. Help like yours I don't need." I turned on my heel and stalked away. I thought I heard him say my name, but it was probably just the blood pounding in my ears.

I burned rubber as I reversed out of the parking space, silently daring Cal to come after me with siren blaring.

He didn't.

I made it home and spent a good thirty minutes tearing my house apart in search of the Lubbock phone book, Hazel watching me nervously from beneath the couch. I finally gave up on finding the stupid thing and stomped across the street to borrow Dorothy's.

She gave me such a warm smile when she answered the door that I did my best to smile in return.

"Sure, I've got one," she said in answer to my question. "Come on in."

She'd no doubt ask all about what I was looking up and why. "Uh, I'm sort of in a hurry, Dorothy. Could I just take it with me and bring it back later?"

She nodded and went to fetch it, but I should have known I couldn't get off that easily.

"Why don't you come to dinner tonight?" she suggested when she returned with the book. "I'd like for you and Faith to get to know each other."

Or I could brush my teeth with a razor blade for the same amount of fun, I thought. But if I was going to help Bo, I needed to find out what had happened the night Ralph Posey disappeared, and Faith was a valuable source.

Agreeing on seven o'clock, I carried the phone book home and scribbled down the address for Restful Haven. I even took the time to comb my wild hair, so as not to frighten any elderly residents.

The address alone didn't do me much good, but a quick stop at a Lubbock gas station earned me decent directions. Restful Haven wasn't at all what I'd been expecting. Instead of a sprawling pink brick institution, I found myself wending up a curving driveway to an old Colonial manor house.

The ambiance inside was that of an exclusive and expensive health spa; the nurses padding past in their silent, rubber-soled shoes were dressed in tailored, gleaming white uniforms. A fragrance not unlike Chanel No. 5 replaced the usual antiseptic odor most nursing facilities exuded. Looking around, I told myself that Bo was dead wrong about Lewis being able to pay for a place like this out of petty cash.

When I asked for Mrs. Tucker, a nurse had me sign in and then escorted me to a cheerful sunroom. Walls of curved, slightly tinted glass showed a vista beyond of a sweeping lawn, still green despite the recent cold spell. I suspected most of the maintenance fund went toward keeping that grass alive, since Lubbock's typical landscape is dry, brown, and often dotted with tumbleweeds.

Dinah Tucker, seated in a well-padded easy chair, was gazing off into the distance. The nurse had to repeat her name twice before she glanced up.

"Mrs. Tucker, this is Taylor Madison."

"Hello," I said. "Would it be all right if I visit with you for a few minutes?"

She smiled. Dinah Tucker was a beautiful woman whose looks had not been ravaged by time, though she had to be in her seventies. Carefully arranged silver curls framed a porcelain complexion, unmarred by wrinkles.

"Are you with the Gallup Poll, dear?" she asked brightly. "I'll admit that I'm hoping to see young Kennedy elected president." She lowered her voice. "Don't tell my husband I said so. Henry is campaigning for Nixon."

I rummaged through my feeble knowledge of history, and determined that Dinah was currently living in 1960. So much for questioning her about the stock certificate.

She was a pleasant woman and, despite my disappointment, we chatted for a while about the possible consequences of a Catholic president. Then a pretty, young nurse approached and told Dinah it was time for her afternoon nap.

"Thank you, Liza," Dinah said. She began gathering crochet yarn, half-spectacles, and various other items into a tote bag.

"She's a sweetheart," I whispered to the nurse. "Take good care of her—Liza, was it?"

The nurse grinned. "My name's Marie. From what I can gather, Liza was the name of Mrs. Tucker's maid, but that was a long time ago. It's less traumatic for her if we don't attempt to yank her back into the here and now." She glanced fondly at Dinah. "If she was happier back then, why shouldn't she live there? At least in her own mind."

"Wow, I hope all the nurses here are like you."

She blushed. "Thanks. Listen, do you know Mrs. Tucker's son, Lewis?"

"Yes, why?"

"She seemed to enjoy your visit very much. She does get lonely sometimes. I understand Lewis can only visit when his friend is able to drive him here, but—"

"Maybe I can drive him once in a while, myself," I said.

"Oh, that would be great! The, um, rather portly gentleman who brings him never seems very happy about it."

Dinah waved a cheery goodbye as I took my leave, promising to pay her another visit soon. I intended to keep that promise, too, whether Lewis came along or not.

So many thoughts were rushing through my head during the drive back to Perdue that it's surprising I was able to keep the little car on the road. When the transmission groaned, reminding me to downshift for a sudden incline, I was snapped back into the here and now and found myself amazed all over again at the abrupt change in terrain. The countryside surrounding Lubbock can only be described as flat, but Perdue is an anomaly, enclosed on all sides by craggy hills that seem to erupt from the ground like deformed, prehistoric beasts.

Sometimes I wondered if being hemmed in by these abnormal hills added to the townsfolk's illusion of isolation from the modern world and, like the citizens of Brigadoon, their reluctance to join it.

The bright afternoon sun was swallowed by shadow as I drove through a narrow pass cut through the outermost bluff, keeping a wary eye out for snakes. My passenger window refused to roll up all the way, and I harbored an absurd fear a rattlesnake would launch itself from the rocks and make its slithery way into my car. Cal kept reassuring me that they hibernated when the weather turned cold, but I still saw one crossing the road now and then. I breathed a sigh of relief when my VW and I emerged into open spaces again.

Instead of turning towards home, I headed out to check on Bo. She was napping, but Keron asked me in for coffee.

Settled in Bo's warm kitchen, we wrapped our hands around the thick mugs and tried to chat about inconsequential subjects, but that didn't last long.

"I'm worried about her, Taylor."

"So am I."

She got up and rummaged through the cabinets. "I need chocolate."

I watched her pull out a package of Oreos and dump them onto a plate. "Keron, have you questioned your mother about what happened between her and Bo?"

She sat back down and crammed an entire cookie into her mouth, gesturing for me to wait until she had chewed enough to speak around it.

"Sorry," she mumbled. "Freud would have a field day with my

penchant for eating when I'm upset." She swallowed. "To answer your question, no. Mother refuses to discuss it. I'll tell you something, though. She's been having nightmares ever since we arrived in Perdue."

"Oh? What about?"

"She won't tell me that either. But they're dillies. We're sharing that big bed in Dorothy's guest room, and Mother has been pummeling me in her sleep, screeching at the top of her lungs." She pushed up one sleeve of her powder blue sweater and showed me a bruise the size of an apple.

"Damn." I barely breathed the word. "No wonder you didn't hesitate when I asked if you'd move in with Bo for a while."

Keron smiled a little. "Self-preservation aside, I'm glad you came up with the idea. Not only because Bo needs someone here, and I'm happy for the opportunity to get to know my grandmother, but...well, I've been working on this puzzle from the other end."

"And?"

She shrugged, reaching for another Oreo. "Bo seems genuinely baffled by Mother's attitude."

I took a cookie myself, dunking it into my coffee. "Dorothy said Bo and Faith were close at one time."

"Yes, Grandma said so, too."

"So, when did that change?"

Keron frowned. "You know, I asked her the same question. She said she really didn't remember, but..."

"But?"

"For some reason, I got the feeling it was just something she didn't want to talk about."

"Hmm. Well, your mom obviously hated her father from the beginning."

"And with valid reason, from what I've come to understand about Ralph Posey. But Bo—at least according to what she's told me—was squarely in Mother's corner. I guess I'll try again to make Mother talk to me. It'd sure be easier if her only problem was this issue with Grandma, but she's got enough hang-ups to fill a psych text."

"Has she ever seen a shrink? Sorry, forgot who I was talking to. A psychologist? A therapist?"

"No. She's a very private person and not the type to seek out that kind of help."

"What about the psychologist in her own family?"

Keron hesitated. "It would be totally against my professional ethics, of course, to treat a family member."

"Of course," I agreed solemnly.

She grinned. "That doesn't mean I haven't made some observations."

"Anything that would explain her attitude toward Bo?"

"Only if Grandma was secretly a man. Mother has an aversion to physical contact with men." She took a sip of cold coffee and grimaced, then got up to warm her mug and mine in the microwave. "She owns an art gallery, as I've said, and that's a huggy-kissy type of crowd, but Mother winces if a man puts an arm around her, and she's perfected the technique of air-kiss-and-run."

"What is your father like? How did they get together?" I asked.

She rested her chin in one palm. "Daddy's rather a free sprit, in true artist tradition, and he actually sat me down when I was about thirteen so he could explain it all to me. It was his version of giving me the facts of life lecture, I suppose." She nibbled another Oreo.

"He met Mother at a gallery where she was working as a secretary, and was, in his words, 'entranced by her willowy beauty.' You'd never know it, since his work is impressionistic, but he used her as a model for several pieces of sculpture.

"According to him, they got married for convenience. Both wanted to take themselves out of the marriage market, so to speak—Mother because she just doesn't like men, and Daddy because he was tired of being eligible bachelor material and being pursued by countless women."

"You're kidding."

"Nope. He said it interfered with his work time. He's no more interested in sex than Mother is."

"Then how—I mean, you—"

She laughed. "They both wanted a child, for different reasons. Mother, I suspect, was seeking a cure for loneliness, while Daddy was obsessed with the immortality factor. Once I was conceived, though, the sex stopped and neither seems to mind."

"Weird," I said.

"I'll agree with that assessment. Daddy's just eccentric, but I think Mother's reasons go a bit deeper." She shrugged. "It's possible that growing up in the shadow of a crazy father simply made Mother forever wary around men. I can't say I blame her from what little Grandma has told me."

I glanced at my watch and stood up. "I've got to go. Listen, Dorothy has invited me to supper tonight. Maybe I can do a little digging of my own."

"Good luck," Keron told me, but she didn't sound any more hopeful than I felt.

Chapter Seven

ON MY WAY home, I passed Cal's patrol car driving in the opposite direction. He pretended not to see me, and I pretended it didn't hurt that he pretended not to see me.

"A whole lot of pretending going on here," I told Hazel a few minutes later as I poured food into her dish. "I'm glad you still love me."

She chittered, hopefully in agreement, before crunching the first bite of her kibble.

I was hungry myself, but knew I'd hurt Dorothy's feelings if I didn't tuck into her meal like a starving truck driver, so decided to appease my stomach with a cup of tea while I changed clothes.

The phone rang as I was rummaging through the closet.

"What the hell is going on?" Paula demanded without preamble.

"Hello, Paula," I responded politely, casting aside a purple blouse I hadn't worn for eight years. "Something on your mind?"

"I heard," she went on, ignoring my feeble attempt at humor, "that you and Cal had a fight at Lucy's Café."

"Small town rumor."

"Really? Then why is Cal stomping around and growling like a mountain cat with a burr under its tail? C'mon, Taylor, 'fess up."

I sighed and sat down on the edge of my clothes-strewn bed. "Okay."

After I'd filled her in on the argument, she was silent for a moment.

"You were pretty hard on him, weren't you?" she asked finally.

"He's being pretty hard on Bo," I retorted, deciding on jeans and a thick cotton sweater and stuffing everything else back into the closet. "Doesn't sound to me as if he's even trying to prove her innocence."

"That isn't his job, Taylor," Paula said mildly. "He's not an attorney."

"Okay, but it *is* his job to conduct a thorough investigation."

"Looks to me like he is. He's spent the past few hours combing through old Sheriff Mason's reports from back when Ralph Posey disappeared."

I'd been holding the receiver between shoulder and chin while I poked one leg into the jeans. Now I sat down on the bed again. "Do you know what he found?"

"Well..."

"Hey, don't go ethical on me now, Paula."

"All I really know is that he's shaking his head over the lack of information. From what I can gather, he seems to think Mason was pretty haphazard about the investigation. There's not all that much in the case file, and what *is* there is sketchy."

I thought it over. "Maybe Mason was just one of those good ol' boy sheriffs like Hollywood loves to poke fun at. The laid-back, lazy type."

"No, that's what's got Cal bothered. Mason had a reputation for being tough, careful, and dedicated, with an eagle eye for detail. Cal actually pulled out some of his old cases for Billy to study before he left for the police academy."

"Paula..." I stopped. I'd been on the verge of asking her if she could find a way to make me a copy of Mason's case file, but that wouldn't be fair. She'd already told me more than she should have, and I knew it. I didn't want to put her job in jeopardy. "Um, thanks for calling. Stop worrying about me and Cal. I'm sure we'll work things out."

I hung up and finished pulling on my jeans, hoping I hadn't just told her one whopper of a lie.

Dorothy was laughing as she greeted me at her front door, and Misty tumbled out across our feet, her whole body wagging with puppy glee. I picked her up and cuddled her against my cheek as I stepped inside.

"Hope you're hungry," Dorothy said, taking the shawl I'd thrown on to combat the chill on my way across the street. Bo was right...I was going to have to break down and buy a real coat, and soon.

"I'm very hungry," I assured her.

Faith came bursting through the swinging kitchen door, still chuckling about something. When she saw me, her lips froze into a fake smile. "Ms. Madison."

"Please," I said again. "Call me Taylor."

"And you call her Faith," Dorothy put in since Faith didn't seem inclined to make the offer. "Would you like a glass of wine, Taylor?"

I tried really hard to hide my astonishment. "Sounds great." Dorothy drinking wine? Her church frowned upon anything stronger than milk.

"Faith brought it with her," Dorothy explained as she filled a juice glass for me.

The burgundy's bouquet invaded my nose and I sipped slowly, trying to remember the last time I'd tasted wine not purchased at the local 7-11.

"Thank you, Faith," I said with feeling.

Her posture relaxed a little and her smile became a bit more genuine. "I remembered Derrick County was dry when I grew up here, so I packed a little precaution in case things hadn't changed."

Dorothy filled another glass for herself and downed it like lemonade. No wonder she was giggly. I didn't envy the way her head would feel the next morning. When she excused herself and popped into the kitchen to check on supper, I sat down on the sofa and stared at Faith.

"How on earth did you persuade her to take a drink?"

"We just fell back into our old patterns," she said. "I was always the corrupting influence."

"Typical preacher's kid," I teased. "An angel on Sunday morning, a hell-raiser at night."

As usual, Dorothy had prepared enough food to last a family of four through a nuclear holocaust. I wasn't shy about shoveling roast beef and mashed potatoes into my mouth, and Dorothy beamed at me. I knew she suffered from an unrequited maternal instinct, and I was happy to help out whenever I could.

"How's your mother?" Faith asked me. What should have been a simple question threw me for a loop.

"Which one?" I asked idiotically.

Faith flushed. "Dorothy told me about Tessa being your...I mean..."

"Tessa and Wood took a cruise, and I think they plan on spending the winter in Italy." I didn't add, *Thank God*, but I thought it. Tessa and I had so many unresolved issues it would take us a full year to set them straight, and I wasn't looking forward to the process.

I couldn't resist giving Faith a return shot, though. "Speaking of mothers, how's yours?"

Her lips tightened. Before we could turn it into a hair-pulling contest, Dorothy stepped into the fray.

"I'm surprised Taylor decided to stay on in Perdue," she told Faith. "Big city gals aren't apt to take to small town life. I've never asked you straight out, Taylor, but why *did* you decide to stay here?"

"I don't know really. Feels like home, I guess."

Dorothy gave an angelic smile. "A certain Cal Arnette couldn't have anything to do with it, right?"

I mumbled something.

"Cal and Taylor fell for each other right off," Dorothy confided to Faith in a whisper as if I wasn't sitting right there. "We all sorta expected them to tie the knot, but you know young folks these days. No rush to do the proper thing."

She turned to me. "Cal's birthday's coming up in a couple of weeks, Taylor. Picked out a present yet?"

I shook my head, wondering if the local gift shop carried a bundle of switches. That's all I felt he deserved at the moment.

"How about a nice bathrobe?" Dorothy suggested.

I looked at her sharply.

"Just an idea," Dorothy said innocently. "It's one of those things men never think to buy for themselves."

I relaxed a little.

"Like pajamas," she went on. "Men would rather just sleep in their underwear."

Dang it, Dorothy!

"Or so I hear," she added. "Being a spinster, I couldn't know these things for certain."

I sighed.

"I hear you met Lewis Tucker," Dorothy prattled on, the wine apparently loosening her tongue. "How's he doin'? It's a shame the way he hermits himself away in that little apartment."

Faith had gone utterly motionless and her skin glowed like pale satin in the flickering light of the dinner candles.

"Lewis? He still lives in Perdue?"

"Well, sure he does. You didn't know? Whatever happened between the two of you anyway?"

"I think this is getting a little too personal for everyone concerned," Faith said firmly.

"I second that motion," I piped up, shooting Faith a look that said I was willing to call a truce if she was. I didn't want the conversation drifting back to Cal any more than she wanted to talk about Lewis. Faith nodded at me in silent agreement and popped open a second bottle of wine.

"Let's drink to that."

"You only brought carry-on bags," I said. "How did you find room for all these bottles?"

"I skimped on wardrobe," she replied, tipping me a wink. "Priorities, you know."

"I knew the two of you would like each other!" Dorothy announced, her words a bit slurred.

Faith avoided answering that. "What this party needs is some music," she said, and crossed the room to rummage through Dorothy's stereo cabinet. "Albums? For heaven's sake, Dot, the world has really passed you by, hasn't it?"

"I have a few 8-tracks," Dorothy grumbled.

"Ever heard of tapes? CDs? Well, doesn't matter, nothing to play them on anyway. I didn't even know they made turntables anymore." She slipped an LP from its cover. "This'll do." The Beatles filled the room with "Hard Day's Night," and Faith jacked the volume up to "wall vibrate."

"My neighbors will call the police!" Dorothy protested.

"Oh, loosen up. Kick off your shoes and come on. You, too, Taylor, though I suspect you're too young to remember the Twist."

"I've seen it done in movies," I informed her, and moved out into the middle of the room to show that I was a good mimic.

Misty ran between our sock-clad feet in barking ecstasy as we went from the Twist to the Frug and threw in a little Funky Chicken for good measure. Did I mention we were sipping wine between songs?

"No more!" I finally groaned, sinking into an overstuffed easy chair.

The music changed from pounding rock 'n' roll to a soft ballad. I watched Dorothy and Faith move unselfconsciously into each other's arms for a slow dance, wondering why my generation had taken it upon themselves to thoroughly screw up such easy friendships between women, cracking lurid jokes at the merest hint of affection. I applauded them when the tune ended. "You two should set up a dance studio."

They collapsed on the couch, Dorothy fanning her cheeks with a magazine. "That was nothing. We're rusty after all these years. You should have seen us back when."

"Dot was queen of the hop," Faith agreed.

"But you were the beauty," Dorothy told her.

"Me? Hardly. My school clothes looked like bleached potato sacks, remember?"

"Didn't matter...you were lovely. Still are."

Faith actually blushed. "Thanks, Dot."

Dorothy grew dreamy-eyed. "You should've seen her the night of our senior prom, Taylor. A vision, that's what she was—a vision in pink silk."

"Nonsense." Faith took a gulp of wine.

"S'not either nonsense. All those stupid kids who'd made fun of you couldn't pry their eyes away. You looked like a movie star."

Faith giggled. "Like Lassie, maybe. Arf."

Misty arfed in response and we all laughed.

Dorothy sat up straight and gazed at her friend. "How did you hang on to that figure anyway? Middle-aged folk like us are supposed to be well-padded." She pushed to her feet. "I'll bet you anything you could still fit into that pink dress."

"I doubt it," Faith said, still giggling.

"Only one way to find out—c'mon gals."

We managed to climb the ladder into her attic without breaking our necks along the way, even though the storage space was not wired for electricity and Dorothy had to precede us balancing a kerosene lantern.

"I can't believe you held onto my dress," Faith marveled, as her friend opened a huge wooden chest and we all gagged at the odor of mothballs. My wine-fogged brain wondered for a moment why Dorothy had Faith's prom dress in the first place, then remembered Bo had told me her daughter had gotten ready for the prom at Dorothy's house.

"Heck fire," Dorothy was saying. "I never throw anything away. I still have *mine*."

With a flourish, she produced both dresses—one dark pink, the other sky blue.

"Me first!" She stepped into the puff of blue chiffon. It fit—her left thigh.

Exploding into laughter, she tossed the dress to me. "You keep it, kid, in case you ever feel like wearing something besides denim. Now, Faith, here ya go."

Faith stepped out of her slacks and blouse and into the shimmering pink.

I drew in a breath. By the soft glow of the lantern's light, three decades vanished. Faith could have been seventeen again, and she was way beyond pretty—she was stunning. I no longer had to wonder how she'd managed to sweep a famous sculptor like Alex Weathered off his feet.

The dress was lovely, if a bit odd. What had begun as a simple sheath with a princess neckline had been transformed by the rather unusual placement of a swath of paler pink netting about the hips, making Faith look as if she'd just emerged from a fog bank. Maybe that was the idea the designer was going for—an ethereal quality.

Dorothy swiveled an old, full-length oval mirror on its stand so Faith could see herself. "Just look at you! I swan, I'm gonna have to go on a diet."

Faith chuckled. "It's not worth the effort, Dot. Staying thin didn't help me hang onto my husband."

"Sounds to me like you're better off without him," Dorothy said, and I wished I'd been around to hear *that* story. Oh, well, I could always pump Dorothy for information later.

"Your hair was pulled up on top of your head, I remember," Dorothy said, sweeping Faith's silver tresses into a topknot and holding it in place."

"Not quite like *that*," Faith protested.

"Close enough. And I loaned you a gold locket, didn't I? It really set off that princess neckline."

"It was beautiful," Faith said dreamily. "I'd never worn jewelry before. Ralph wouldn't permit it."

Ralph, huh? Not "Father" or "Daddy." Interesting.

"Oh, I'd forgotten all about this!" Dorothy fingered a rip in one shoulder seam of the pink dress. "You were so upset. I intended to sew it up for you, but I just never got around to it."

Dorothy was still giggling, but Faith had abruptly stopped.

"Did you ever tell me how this happened?" the plump woman asked.

"No." Faith reached behind her and unzipped the pink dress with apparent savagery. "I'm sorry, but I suddenly don't feel at all well...must be the wine. If you'll both excuse me, I think I'll go to bed."

She was climbing back down the ladder before either of us had time to react.

"What in the world?" Dorothy stared after her.

"Beats me." I picked up the pink dress from the floor and noticed from the label that it was, indeed, real silk. High quality silk.

"Dorothy, how could people as poor as the Poseys afford an expensive dress like this?"

"Hmm?" she asked, still distracted by her friend's odd behavior. "Oh, I don't know. I remember wondering the same thing at the time. Bo got it for her somewhere. Maybe from one of the charity bins Ralph's church set up."

"Right. I'm sure people donate silk dresses to Goodwill all the time." It suddenly hit me that a friend of mine in Houston had once bought a genuine cashmere sweater from a Goodwill store. "Well, maybe it does happen these days," I amended, "but I'll bet it didn't in the sixties."

"Does it matter where she got it?"

"I guess not," I said.

THE NEXT MORNING dawned bright and cold. I discovered Hazel curled up on my extra pillow, and realized, with a sharp pang, how accustomed I had grown to Cal's head being on that pillow.

A combination of warm blankets and too much wine had knocked me directly into deep slumber the night before, but now thoughts of Cal drew my mind back to the matters at hand.

"So here's the question of the day," I told Hazel. She yawned, but seemed to be paying attention. "According to Paula, Sheriff Mason was famous for writing detailed police reports, right? And considering Perdue isn't exactly a hotbed of crime, we're probably talking about cases dealing with petty theft, minor vandalism, and jaywalking.

"So why—are you listening, Hazel?—why would such a stickler for detail drop the ball when a major case comes along? Sounds to me like Ralph Posey's...disappearance barely rated a scribble on a Post-It note. Cal is puzzled, and I don't blame him." Hazel was snoring again. No help at all. I rolled over on my back and squinted up at the ceiling, thinking. Then I jumped out of bed and pulled on my warmest sweat suit.

Bo and Keron were having coffee when I arrived—decaf, much to Bo's irritation.

"I can't drink booze," she mumbled. "Can't eat fried foods. Can't even have real coffee." She lit a Camel.

"You can't have those either," Keron reminded her.

"Little gal, I loved you from the moment I laid eyes on you, but just try and take it away from me."

Keron shrugged and went back to her bowl of Special K. Not being the health-food type myself, I accepted a day-old doughnut from Bo and dunked it vigorously into my fake coffee.

"What can you tell me about Sheriff Mason's investigation at the time Ralph disappeared?" I asked Bo.

"Whattaya want to know?"

"Did he question you?"

She puffed on her cigarette, thinking back. "Well, yeah, he talked to me. I told him just about what I told you."

"He didn't seem suspicious of you, though?"

"No."

"If I needed to talk to someone about Sheriff Duke Mason," I said to Bo, "someone who knew him well, who would that be?"

"Easy," she said. "His sister, Gertrude."

"Oh, yeah. You told me she was an...um...upstanding member of your husband's church," I recalled. "She still lives in Perdue?"

"She's *back* in Perdue," Bo corrected. "Gertrude moved in with Duke right after his wife died—to keep house for him, she said. More likely to sponge off him. She drove him nuts, I know that. Dang, but that woman was loopy."

"How so?"

"I told you she had a huge crush on Ralph. 'Nuf said. Anyway, she moved away again not too long after Ralph...left. Probably, I thought at the time, to sponge off a different relative for a while, since Duke was obviously on the verge of strangling her. From what I hear, she got married, had a kid. She's widowed now and moved back into Duke's house after he passed away a few years ago. He willed it to her, so I guess she figured a free and clear mortgage was worth comin' back to. Her married name's...Snell, that's it. What do you want to talk to her about?"

"Just...things."

"Uh-huh." Bo looked at me sternly. "Listen here. It's *my* life on the line, Taylor Madison. Just because I can't run all over creation right now doesn't mean I don't want to help myself outta this jam."

"If I turn up anything important, you'll be the first to know," I assured her. "But I'm probably going to sniff down more than one blind alley along the way."

Bo snorted. "Some writer you are. That was a mixed metaphor if I ever heard one."

"Taylor's right, though, Grandma," Keron put in. "What you need right now is to stop worrying. A high stress level is worse for your blood pressure than booze would be."

"If you'd let me have booze," Bo grumbled, "my stress level would be non-existent." But her face had softened when Keron called her "Grandma," and she reached to pat my hand. "I know you're tryin' your best to help, hon. Okay, go for it, as long as you keep me up on what you find out."

As I drove back to Perdue, I considered how best to go about questioning Gertrude without raising her suspicions. My answer came in the form of a vision—well, a sign, anyway. The sign read: *The Derrick County Gazette, Est. 1955.*

Tucked into a tiny corner building catty-corner from the

courthouse square, the *Gazette* office appeared deserted when I stepped through the entrance. I glanced around the wood-paneled room, its walls studded with photographs. While the newsrooms of the *New York Times* were likely hung with pictures of Churchill and the first lunar landing, here in Perdue, the photos were all from Rattlesnake Festivals past: two men holding either end of the largest snake ever caught, its long body drooping like a thick cable between them; the current Miss Snakeskin, her crown skewed to one side; a fellow in the process of milking a snake for venom, his brow furrowed in concentration.

I was wondering where Jesse was when curses from the back room made me grin in comprehension.

"*¡Estúpido, repugnante pieza de mierda!*"

Jesse was confronting his nemesis—a printing press that might have been new when Moses was a kid in knee pants.

"Anybody home?" I sang out, not keen on entering the lair of the beast.

Something clattered, something else groaned, and I heard a thud that sounded like a well-aimed boot making contact with a solid object.

"Ow! *Estúpido...*"

"Jesse!" I yelled louder.

Jesse Alvarado, publisher/editor/star reporter, emerged, limping on one foot and sucking a fingertip. His once white T-shirt resembled the hide of a Holstein cow.

"*Buenos días*, Taylor. Come to help me out? Sit, sit." He gestured at a sagging swivel chair, then resumed scrubbing his stained fingers with an already black rag.

"Don't have time."

"Got another article for me? The piece you did on the bell tower was a hit. I've gotten at least ten letters about it."

High praise, considering his circulation was only about three hundred. "Thanks, I enjoyed writing it."

"I'd enjoy writing more myself if I didn't have to actually print it. That *estúpido*—"

"Jesse, when are you going to break down and get a computer?"

"What do I need with a computer?"

I sighed. It was a running argument.

"If you had a computer," I reminded him for the umpteenth time, "you could have a nice, big laser printer. Fancy fonts, snazzy graphics, and, best of all, no busted toes."

He grimaced, examining the dent in the tip of his boot. "They'd run me out of town on a rail."

"They" being the populace of Perdue, Texas, he was probably right. Since Jesse had taken over as publisher, he'd contributed a lot towards dragging the citizens of Perdue—kicking, screaming, and clawing at the red dirt—into the bright, new century, but he succeeded precisely because he knew when it was time to back off a little. We both knew his readers would feel cheated if their fingers weren't ink-stained when they finished reading their weekly newspaper, even if we didn't fully understand why.

"Maybe someday," he said to appease me. "Now, what can I do for you?"

"Lie. Just a little white one, though, and I'll make it up to you."

Jesse gave me a slow grin. "*¿Sí*? How?" He was well aware of how good-looking he was with his curly, black hair and dark-honey eyes. He also knew I was involved elsewhere.

"I'll buy you lunch at Lucy's."

"Gag. But okay. What's the lie?"

It was so nice to have at least one agreeable man in my life.

SHERIFF MASON'S FORMER residence was a tiny gray house with matching gray trim and a brownish-gray lawn. It huddled on its small lot as if ashamed to be seen in public.

Gertrude matched her residence—clothes, hair and eyes. "Who are you?" she asked upon opening the front door to my knock.

"Mrs. Snell, my name is Taylor Madison. I'm a part-time reporter for the *Derrick County Gazette*, and I'd like to interview you."

The door opened a little wider. "Me? Why me?" But she sounded flattered, and I knew I was in.

Once she'd seated me on a rather shabby sofa, she bustled into the kitchen to fetch a pot of tea. I heard her dialing the phone, speaking in a low mumble. Jesse, true to his word, must have confirmed my cover story because she appeared a few minutes later with a refreshment-laden tray.

"I'm doing research for an article about important figures in Derrick County history," I told her. "Your late brother is high on my list."

Her colorless eyes lost some of their sparkle.

"Naturally, your perspective is crucial," I added hastily. "You're the woman behind the man. Where would any of them be without us?"

"Don't I know it," she agreed, flattered once more.

After that, I sipped weak tea and let her ramble for a while, building trust.

"I don't get many visitors, you know. My son, he's in insurance, and the job keeps him busy. He hasn't come to see me since I moved back to Perdue because...well, but I go spend a day or so with him when I can. He—"

I interrupted gently, changing the subject to Duke. Then I listened some more to numerous stories about her brother at age twelve, when he'd made her life miserable as only a big brother can: lizards in her shoes, snakes (not rattlesnakes, though, just the green garden variety) in her bed. Teasing, hair-pulling, theft of candy, decapitation of dolls.

Concentrating on maintaining eye contact, I nodded now and then to show interest, wishing she'd hurry up and move the former sheriff into adulthood.

"Would you like a photograph to go with your story?" she asked suddenly.

I leapt at the offer, hoping a picture of an older Duke would jog her into the not-quite-so-distant past. I should have known it wouldn't be that easy.

Gertrude went to a bookcase and pulled out a dozen photo albums, each a good seven inches thick, some bristling with prints at the edges—either pictures not yet organized or (heaven forbid) pictures the pages had no more room for.

The latter proved true. I sneaked a peek at my watch as she opened the first album and began pointing out faces. Jesse would kill me if I stood him up for lunch at Lucy's. Worse, he might be pissed enough to give Gertrude a call and blast my little cover story to smithereens.

I looked at photos of Duke and Gertrude as infants, as children, as adolescents. I saw Duke proudly display the first fish he'd ever caught (the poor thing no bigger than an overfed minnow) and saw Gertrude brushing the hair of a splendid new doll (said doll later decapitated by her brother, she informed me). I held onto my sanity for a good twenty minutes, but when she opened the second album and started on "Duke and Gertrude: The High School Years," I couldn't take any more.

"Mrs. Snell," I said as gently as possible, "this is fascinating. In fact, you've given me a terrific idea for a future article, one on sibling relations. But right now, I really need to get the information I came for."

Her face fell and I felt a surge of pity. She may have been a rude, obnoxious know-it-all back when she and Bo were younger, but now she was just a lonely old woman.

"I *will* come back," I promised, realizing I'd made the same promise to Dinah Tucker and to her son, Lewis. I believed in keeping promises, too, but right now the one I'd made to Bo took precedence.

Gertrude had reached for yet another album and this one, I was glad to see, held more recent photographs.

"Here's Duke the day he got his first uniform," she said. "You ever seen anything so handsome?"

Based on the gilt-framed picture I'd seen hanging on a wall in the sheriff's office, Duke Mason had filled out into a husky guy in later life, but he'd begun his career as a Barney Fife look-alike.

"Here's Duke standing beside his patrol car his second day on the job," she went on.

I didn't have time to sit through "Duke: The Early Law Enforcement Years."

"You know, my story will actually deal with your brother after he was elected sheriff. Could we skip ahead in the photos a bit?" Of course, I didn't need to see any more photographs, but looking through the albums seemed to trigger verbal memories. Those I *did* need.

Gertrude complied, turning pages.

"Here we are," she said at last. "His swearing-in ceremony."

In the photograph, a slightly heftier Duke stood on the same bandstand that still graced Perdue Park. His left hand rested on a Bible as some unknown man in a shiny suit solemnly pinned a gold star to the newly elected sheriff's uniform shirt.

I dug a notepad and pen from my pocket, a subtle reminder that this was an interview and not just a gab session. "I'm curious to know why Duke decided to run for sheriff. Prestige?"

She snorted. "Duke didn't give a hoot about prestige. He just wanted things done right. Said it was time for the good ol' boy system to be done away with."

"What did he mean by that?"

"Oh, c'mon, you know how it is. Rich folk can get away with anything, as long as there's poor folk around to go to jail. My brother believed in justice for all, just like Ben Franklin said."

We were finally getting somewhere, so I didn't bother to correct her historical reference. "Everyone says he was a fair man with a passion for detail."

She nodded firmly. "That he was. Nitpicky, some called him. He took that as a compliment."

Gertrude was clearly incapable of simultaneous page-flipping and speech. This was getting me nowhere.

Feigning interest in a photo of Duke on horseback, I pointed and said, “Oh, that’s a great one. May I?” Without waiting for her response, I shifted the heavy book into my own lap and pretended to examine the picture more carefully.

“How old was Duke when he learned to ride?” I asked, and as she launched into a complicated story (as I’d known she would), I took the opportunity to turn the pages more rapidly.

Near the middle of the album, a group shot caught my eye. The same wizened, little man I’d seen in Cal’s old newspaper clipping stared up at me, his dark eyes somehow accusing. *Ralph Posey,* I thought, *would’ve delivered one hell of a frightening sermon.* To his left stood a much younger version of Bo, looking stiff and uncomfortable in a high-necked dress. Its frayed hem and too-short sleeves screamed flea market. Beside her was Paul Newman.

I blinked, looked again.

No, not Newman, but close. Blonde, tanned, and with a blazing smile that even a black-and-white photo couldn’t dim, the man rested one hand on Bo’s shoulder. Was it my imagination, or did she seem to lean into his touch?

I had no idea who he was, but the woman on Ralph’s right was easily recognizable as my hostess. She sported the exact same hairstyle—a tightly permed cap of curls—and the same prim lip line. Presently, those lips were still moving ninety miles a minute, supplying me with even more fascinating anecdotes pertaining to her late brother’s equestrian skills.

As soon as she paused for breath, I turned her attention to the picture. “This is amazing, Gertrude. You haven’t changed a bit.”

Her pale cheeks pinkened and she patted her hair. “Why, thank you, dear.” She squinted at the picture. “My goodness, that was taken nearly forty years ago.”

I finally had reason to be grateful for her garrulous nature—I didn’t have to prod her into telling me more.

“We were posing on the front steps of the Church of the Rapture,” she went on. “I wish I had more photographs of that lovely little church. It’s gone now. A twister damaged the roof in ’68, and the county finally tore it down in ’72.” She sighed. “I attend the Methodist church now, but it’s just not the same.”

“Probably not,” I was quick to agree. “I’ve heard Ralph Posey was...one of a kind.”

“That he was.” Her eyes misted as she reached to trace Ralph’s homely face with one fingertip. “We all miss him.” Her finger accidentally brushed Bo’s image, and she jerked her hand away as if stung by a wasp. "How he ever ended up with that—that woman is beyond me."

"Oh?" I bit back the urge to jump to Bo's defense.

"She never understood how fortunate she was," Gertrude murmured. "To share his name, to bear his child."

Oh, good grief, I thought, but didn't say aloud. An eavesdropper would think she was talking about Jesus Christ instead of Ralph Posey. But at least we had jumped ahead into the time period that interested me. I started trying to frame a question that would draw her brother into the conversation while she continued her rambling tirade against Bo.

"Do you know she often took the Lord's name in vain? Right there in God's own house! Harvey did his best to keep her in line, but it was a losin' battle." She touched the picture again, this time indicating the Paul Newman clone. So that was Harvey Neff.

Gertrude's phone rang. She bustled into the kitchen to answer and returned five minutes later, very flustered.

"Sorry, dear, I've gotta run. That was Sally at the beauty shop and I'm late for my perm appointment. Forgot all about it."

My protests fell on deaf ears as she practically pushed me out the door.

"I've got to hurry or she won't be able to fit me in this week, and I can't go to church on Sunday with stringy hair. Maybe we can talk some other time." At the last minute, she shoved the picture album into my arms. "Find a good one of Duke they can put in the paper with your story. Nice to know folks'll be able to read about him again after all these years. Be careful with the album now. I want my son to have it someday."

The door slammed shut behind me.

I lugged the bulky album to my car, where I kicked a tire in frustration.

Chapter Eight

JESSE FROWNED AT me as I slammed through the door at Lucy's Café. He glared at the clock above the counter and rubbed his stomach.

"Man cannot live on iced tea alone," he said as I slid into the booth opposite him.

"I warned you it'd be a late lunch."

"Yeah, but I was beginning to wonder if you meant lunch *mañana*."

I grabbed the ashtray and lit a cigarette. "At the rate things were going, you're lucky it wasn't lunch sometime next week."

He watched me inhale calming smoke. "Thought you were quitting."

"A vicious rumor, though what else should I expect from a tabloid publisher such as yourself? To set the record straight, I have cut down and may yet cut down even more, but quit? Nope. Have you ordered?"

"Hey, I was promised a free meal. If I'd ordered and you hadn't shown up, I'd have had to pay. How'd the fib work out for you?"

"The fib part worked great, thanks. But my mission, in the end, was not accomplished."

He leaned forward. "Are you going to fill me in on the details of said mission?"

Before I could answer, Rita appeared, pad in hand. Her gaze flitted from me to Jesse to the window (which framed a lovely view of the Sheriff's Office across the street) then back to me. One corner of her painted mouth twisted into a sly grin.

"Cheeseburger and onion rings," I told her. "Coke."

"Make that two," Jesse said.

We both watched her sashay to the order window.

Jesse stretched and grinned. "It'll be all over town by suppertime, you know."

"I know. Lunch with a friend is number sixty-seven on Perdue's list of unacceptable behavior."

"Lunch with a friend of the opposite sex," Jesse corrected. "Compounded by the fact that one of the parties in question is romantically involved elsewhere. How is Cal, by the way?"

"Stubborn, pig-headed, and maddening."

"Same as usual, in other words." Teasingly, he reached for my hand. "He's *loco*, too. If you were my girl, I wouldn't let you out of my sight for a minute, much less let you wine and dine a handsome newspaper publisher."

Cal, naturally, chose that moment to walk in.

My beau, as Dorothy calls him, has a temper, which he usually keeps under careful control. I saw him glance at Jesse's hand on mine, saw a muscle in his jaw tighten. Manners dictated that he acknowledge two friends, and he did so with a brief nod. Then he strode to the counter where Rita handed him a greasy paper sack, presumably containing lunch-to-go, threw money in her direction, and was out the door before I could clear my throat to speak.

"Oops," Jesse said.

I managed a shrug. "Don't worry about it."

One thing I like about Jesse is that he knows when to leave things alone.

"So back to my earlier subject," he said. "Gertrude Snell."

"It's complicated, Jess. I'm not sure if I should talk about it right now."

"Sure you should. I'll help. What does the esteemed Mrs. Snell have to do with Bo Posey's problem? Oh, don't look so surprised, Taylor. It's my job as local newspaper snoop to sift through tidbits of gossip."

"Guess I'm still getting used to that." A thought struck me as Rita served our cheeseburger platters. "Funny that Gertrude didn't pump me for information, isn't it?"

Jesse made an inquiring noise around a mouthful of meat and cheese.

"Heck, she was one of Ralph Posey's biggest fans. From the way she talked, I assumed he'd walked on water at least twice a day. So wouldn't you think the subject of his...reappearance would have been foremost in her mind? She never even mentioned it."

Jesse swallowed and grinned. "Well, let's look at it logically. Since the *Gazette* is a weekly, Ralph's story won't see print until tomorrow."

"What about the phone-a-friend grapevine?"

"Far as I know, Gertrude Snell doesn't have any friends. Most folks think she's more than slightly off her rocker. Pearl cringes when she makes a hair appointment. Says she lectures all the ladies on the evils of gossip, but only after she's listened for a while to catch up."

"Which she is doing at this very moment," I said, and explained why Gertrude had hustled me out the door before I could get the answers I needed.

"Just what answers were you looking for?"

I hesitated. "Off the record?"

He looked wounded. "I'm asking as a friend, Taylor, not as a reporter."

"Right. Okay, Jess, let's start with a question for you. Do you believe Bo Posey murdered her husband?"

His answer was immediate and vehement. "Of course not!"

"Good for you! Neither do I. But if the story's running in tomorrow's paper, I'm sure you're aware of how bad things look for her."

He snorted. "Circumstantial evidence."

I had to smile. "Thought you were supposed to be an impartial newsman. What happened to journalistic objectivity? Giving equal consideration to both sides of an issue?"

"I'll be bound by that, of course, in print. But this is a conversation between friends, remember? And *about* a friend. By the way, do I get dessert with this free lunch?"

I nodded, studying him as he signaled Rita for a slice of carrot cake. He did this by pointing at the pastry bin, waggling his hands beside his ears and making buckteeth. She rolled her eyes, but his pantomime worked because she fetched the correct dessert.

"I didn't realize you and Bo were such pals," I said as soon as our nosy waitress departed.

"How would you feel about someone who rescued you from the poor house?" He chuckled. "All right, so that sounded a little dramatic. I'm not even sure poor houses exist anymore, but the concept was terrifying to me at the time."

"What happened?" I asked the question gently because, despite his bantering tone, I detected a still-painful memory.

"*Padre* died when I was fourteen," he said. "And being a man entrenched in the old Hispanic culture, he'd never allowed my mother to work outside the home. So there we were—no life insurance, very little money in the bank, no income, no job related skills. *Madre* was in a state of combined grief and panic."

Having lived most of my life teetering on that narrow line between making ends meet and actual poverty, I understood. "Must've been rough."

Jesse pushed his cake away, half-eaten. "I quit school and took on whatever odd jobs I could find. To this day, *Madre* insists that an angel led me to Bo."

"She hired you to work at the store?"

"Yes, but that was only the beginning. Bo made me go back to school, and set my work hours so they wouldn't interfere with homework." He grinned. "She even made sure I had time for basketball practice. And when Bo found out my mother really did want a job of her own, she arranged that, too. While I was studying at night, Bo sat at the kitchen table and taught *Madre* bookkeeping."

I gave an involuntary shudder. "I'd rather shovel sludge than learn bookkeeping. It's all I can do to balance my checkbook."

"I'm with you. But *Madre* took to it like a duck to water. She eventually went to work at the county tax office, and started taking night classes."

"Hey, isn't your mom—"

He nodded proudly. "Yeah, she's a CPA in Lubbock. Came a long way in a hurry, didn't she? So, now you get it, Taylor. Because of Bo, I went from being a high school dropout with no future to a college graduate with my own newspaper. Bo Posey might be steel on the outside, but inside she's pure mush, and you know it."

"I'm not the one arguing that," I protested.

"How could anyone think she'd be capable of cold-blooded murder? I'm not the only person in this town she's helped through tough times."

"Cal might say she was trying to atone for past sins."

"Then Cal's *loco*." This time there was no humor in the word.

Jesse left to resume his battle of wills with the beast he called a printer. I lingered over a cup of coffee, watching the parking lot of the sheriff's department. Cal's car was gone, and I made a deal with myself: if he returned before I'd finished my coffee, I'd walk over and try to clear the air between us.

Fifteen minutes later, Rita came by with her carafe. "Refill?" she asked.

"No, thanks."

She squinted at the scant teaspoonful of cold coffee remaining in the bottom of my cup.

"I'm fine," I assured her. A second cup would be hedging the deal. Another ten minutes passed. I had given up and was digging in my pocket for cash to pay the tab when Oliver Burke dropped uninvited into the seat across from me, his spicy aftershave stinging my nose.

"Cal won't be back for an hour or so," he informed me.

"Is that so?" I hoped my tone displayed polite disinterest.

"That's why you're starin' a hole through the window glass, isn't it?" He picked up my empty cup and waved it at Rita. "Waiting for your boyfriend to come back?"

"Actually, I was just leaving." I dropped bills on the table and was sliding out of the booth when he put a hand on my arm.

"Hold on a second, sugar."

"Don't call me that." I didn't have to wonder anymore why Cal didn't like him. Everything about the man was oily, as if he bathed each morning in Crisco and gargled with it, too.

"Didn't mean to offend." He drew his hand back, but continued pinning me with his eyes. "Just wondered if you'd like to take in a movie sometime."

"With you?" I squeaked, torn between horror and laughter.

"Why not? Rumor has it you and Cal are on the skids."

"That's really none of your business."

He leaned across the table until our faces were almost touching. The high-backed seat gave me no room to withdraw. "In a small town, sugar, everybody's business is everybody else's. Personally, I think you're makin' a smart move. Your boyfriend's on pretty thin ice right now."

My hand itched to slap him. "Get out of my face," I muttered through gritted teeth, "before I plant my left heel where it'll hurt."

Burke backed away, but probably only because Rita was delivering his coffee. He took a sip, regarding me over the rim of the cup. "You're quite the little spitfire, aren't ya? I thought old Underwood was gonna pop a vessel the other day when you lit into him."

I tilted my head. "Aw, shucks, did I hurt your buddy's feelings?"

"I wouldn't call me and Underwood buddies exactly."

"Really? Then you're licking his boots just because you like the taste?"

He flushed. "Hey, he hired me to do a job, and I'm doin' it."

I smiled. "Might be wise to remember that, after the election, you'll be working for Cal."

"Maybe."

"No maybe about it, slick. He's the one and only candidate for sheriff."

Burke scowled. "You don't get it, sugar. If Arnette's fudging the Posey investigation to protect his pal, Bo, he's gonna be in a world of hurt. He can forget about being the next sheriff of Derrick County—hell, he can forget being a cop. Anywhere."

The threat gripped my heart like an icy glove. If someone had asked me five minutes before what I wanted Cal to do, I would have said, "Save Bo from jail, no matter what it takes." I really hadn't stopped to consider Cal's predicament.

I don't know whether Burke read something in my expression or simply realized that he'd said too much.

"I'll call you about that movie," he said, sliding out of the booth.

I sat like a statue, watching through the window as his patrol car pulled away. When I finally stood, I discovered my knees were shaking.

Dashing across the street, I burst in on Paula.

"What do you know about Oliver Burke's background?"

"Taylor, how many times do I have to remind you that hello is the standard greeting?" She got a good look at my face and dropped the joking tone. "What's wrong?"

Sinking into the first available chair, I repeated my question.

"I don't know much of anything except Underwood hired him and Cal wasn't happy about it. Why?"

"I think he and Underwood are teaming up to get rid of Cal." I told her what Burke had said.

Paula's lips thinned. "I'll find out what I can." She picked up the phone and started punching in numbers.

I was beginning to feel pretty rotten about how unfair I'd been to Cal. Talk about being caught between a rock and a hard place. He'd been catching heat from all sides, even from the one person who should have been squarely in his corner from the beginning. If I'd relied on logic instead of emotion, I'd have realized he didn't want Bo arrested any more than I did, but he had to do his job. I definitely owed him an apology. Even more than that, I owed him help out of the trap Underwood and Burke were setting for him.

Burke had talked about Cal "fudging" the investigation to get Bo off the hook, something I knew he'd never do. Question was, would Underwood manufacture evidence to make her seem guilty? It was clear the man hated her. And if he and Burke were teaming up to send Bo to prison, they were probably keeping information from Cal. If I could find out what it was...

An idea slowly took shape. I caught Paula's eye and mimed washing my hands. She nodded. The only way to the restroom is through the sheriff's back office, and after I ducked into the tiny bathroom to start water running for Paula's benefit, I turned my attention to Cal's desk.

As usual, its surface was compulsively neat with paperwork, stapler and day planner lined up so precisely that I suspected he'd used a ruler. Fortunately, I'm privy to many of Cal's secrets, and I'm aware his penchant for order applies only to objects within public view. Drawers, closets or boxes are a different story, and he'll put off taking out the trash until someone calls the health department. True to form, the wastebasket tucked beneath his desk was overflowing.

I'd been in the front office with Underwood the other day when Burke yelled out his success in locating Harvey Neff. Most people scribble notes while on the phone. With that in mind, I dumped wadded papers on the floor and sorted through them as quickly as I could. I wasn't really worried about Paula, although I didn't want to make her an accessory to my minor crime if I could help it. But if Cal or Burke walked in, I was in deep doo-doo.

Near the bottom of the pile, I found part of a yellow sheet from a legal pad. The writing wasn't Cal's, so I smoothed it out. Success!

Paula's voice floated from the front office. "Taylor, are you drowning or what?"

"Be right there!" I scooped trash back into the basket, dislodged a chunk of well-chewed gum from my finger and stuffed the yellow paper into a pocket.

"I've put out some feelers," she told me as I sauntered back into the front office, striving to look innocent. "My friend, Barbara, with Lubbock County dispatch, has a cousin who's a jailer with Dallas P.D. and he's dating the sister of a woman who—"

I had to laugh. "You've got to be kidding!"

"It's called networking," she said primly, then grinned. "I'll let you know what I find out."

"Thanks." I looked at my watch. Time enough to pay Mr. Neff a visit. "Gotta run."

"See you later. By the way," she added as I put my hand on the doorknob, "I hope you found what you were looking for in Cal's office."

"How did you—? I mean, what are you talking about?"

She pointed. "You have a crumpled Post-It note stuck to your butt."

"You should be a detective," I grumbled, removing the incriminating evidence. "Paula, I was only—"

She put her hands over her ears. "Stop! Don't tell me. I know nuh—think. Let's keep it that way."

"Yes'm," I said.

Sitting in my car, I studied the scrawl on my ill-gotten scrap of paper. Burke's handwriting was worse than my own, which is pretty awful. Neff's phone number had been obliterated by a grease stain, but the numbers of the address were relatively clear. I just had to figure out the street name. Dang it, the easiest way would be via the Internet and the wonderful maps, street lists, and driving directions available online. Unfortunately, my modem had died the week before, and I hadn't yet bought a replacement. Okay, then, I'd fall back on pre-tech research techniques.

I drove the two blocks to the library. Sadie Klune looked up and held a finger to her lips as I pushed through the door.

"Oh, it's you, Ms. Madison," she whispered. "Sorry. School will be letting out any minute, and I'm expecting a horde of noisy teenagers."

I've never heard Sadie speak above a whisper, not even outside the library. If she ever got married and had kids of her own, someone would have to give her screaming lessons.

"Do you have a Lubbock key map?" I asked, keeping my voice low, although hers and mine were the only breathing bodies in the library.

She nodded and pulled a bright orange book from a shelf behind her.

I took it to a nearby table and started decoding, feeling like a WWII spy. Neff's street name began with either an O or a D. The next letter could have been an R or an N. Methodically comparing the paper to the street index in the back of the key map, I achieved my goal in less than fifteen minutes.

"I heard you met my favorite patron," Sadie murmured as I handed the map back to her. "Lewis Tucker?"

"Yes, I did. Nice guy."

"He's so looking forward to having dinner with you," Sadie said.

I went blank. Dinner? Oh, yeah. I *had* said something about making him a home-cooked meal.

Sadie noticed my momentary confusion. "I do hope you hadn't forgotten. The poor man has so little company."

"No problem, as long as he likes spaghetti. It's the only thing I can cook from scratch that doesn't end up tasting like day-old oatmeal."

She brightened. "I'm sure he'll love it."

The expected throng of teens swarmed in, and I left Sadie hissing like a teakettle.

I had a vague plan to use my reporter cover again with Neff, but I wasn't happy about it. Some people don't like reporters, so I would be taking a chance.

I still hadn't come up with a good excuse for my visit by the time I reached his residence but, as it turned out, I didn't need it yet. The driveway of Neff's unassuming little tract house stood empty and no one answered my knock at the door. I decided to kill some time and check back later.

The golden arches of a McDonald's beckoned. I ordered a Cherry Coke at the drive-thru window, then headed for a small park I'd spotted earlier.

I sat on a wooden bench, shivering a little and wishing I'd ordered hot chocolate instead of a soft drink. A real winter coat moved to the very top of my shopping list. As long as I was in Lubbock, maybe I should swing by a department store—

"I don't want to!"

The little boy's voice cut into my thoughts. I glanced up.

"But why don't you want to play with the puppy, Joey?" a sweet-faced young woman asked. "Look, Missy wants you to throw the ball for her."

The wriggling brown puppy tried to lick Joey's cheek, but he turned away. I was close enough to see tears swimming in his eyes.

"She's not my dog. Rex was my dog."

His mother put an arm around him. "Honey, Daddy and I explained about Rex. He was old and very sick."

"I know he's dead," Joey said. "But he was *my* dog, and I don't want a new one."

The woman thought for a minute, then pointed to a towering sycamore. "Joey, see that tree? Most of its leaves are on the ground now, but next spring the branches will be covered with green buds. If those brown, dead leaves had refused to let go, there wouldn't be any room for the new green ones. It's called the circle of life, sweetheart. If you try to hold on to the past, you'll never get to see how beautiful the future can be."

As I silently applauded her explanation, Joey buried his nose in the puppy's warm fur and cried.

Life lessons are never easy to learn. We all make the mistake, now and again, of trying to live in the past.

Living in the past.

My thoughts tumbled over each other like agitated squirrels.

Living in the past, a maid named Liza...

I must have made some sound of triumph as I jumped to my feet because Missy yapped at me.

THE DESK NURSE at Restful Haven warned me that visiting hours were almost over, but agreed to let me have fifteen minutes with Dinah Tucker. Like a superstitious child, I crossed my fingers behind my back as I hurried to the sunroom.

Dinah looked up as I approached her favorite corner. Her china blue eyes showed no recognition, but her smile was immediate and welcoming.

My plan suddenly felt a little mean-spirited. Was it right to actually use the unfortunate woman's disease for my own purposes? No, scratch that, I had to go through with this. Bo's future might depend on it.

"Howdy, Dinah!" I grabbed her right hand and pumped it heartily. "Your boy doin' any better today?"

Dinah looked bewildered, her smile frozen in place. We were drawing stares from several other residents, so I plopped down in a chair across from her and leaned forward, lowering my voice a little.

"Guess it was sorta rude of me to just drop by unannounced, but then Bonita Posey's never been famous for her manners. My Daddy always said I acted like I'd been raised in the wild by coyotes."

I held my breath, watching her.

Slowly, the puzzled wrinkles in her forehead smoothed.

"Lovely to see you, Bonita." She glanced around her. "Where is my bell? I'll ring for Liza to serve tea."

My eyes closed briefly in relief.

"No need to bother your maid, Dinah, 'cause I can't stay long. Henry might've told you he bought some stock from me the other day. Just wanted to thank him, 'cause it looks like things are gonna work out for me now."

Please, I thought. *Please tell me that Henry confided in you.*

"Yes, he told me about that. I'm so happy he could help. Is there any news about Ralph?"

"Nope. Listen, Dinah, I sure hope partin' with five thousand cash didn't put a hardship on you, what with Lewis in the hospital and all."

"How kind of you to be concerned, Bonita, but please don't worry. Henry's business is thriving, and he does so love dabbling in the stock market. You did *him* the favor."

Next to the word "gracious" in the dictionary is—or should be—a picture of Dinah Tucker.

I stood up, offering my hand once more. "Lady," I said shakily, trying to maintain Bo's persona, "you're a peach. If there's ever anything I can do for you..."

"Quite seriously, there is, if it wouldn't be an imposition."

I hadn't been expecting that. "Sure, name it."

"Could you stop by the hospital and say a few words to Lewis? Despite the doctors insisting otherwise, I read somewhere that coma patients sometimes respond to voices. I sit with him as often as I can, but my health has been poor lately and Henry won't let me spend longer than two hours a day there."

Tears pricked my eyes. "You bet I'll go see him, Dinah. Be glad to."

"You're very sweet, Bonita. If it wasn't for Mr. Neff, I'd be worried to distraction about Lewis's lack of company."

I sat back down with a thump and stared at her. "Harvey Neff?"

"Yes, he's an angel. Do you know, he's been at Lewis's bedside almost constantly since the accident?"

"He has? Is he a friend of yours?"

"Oh, dear, no. We'd never even met the man until the night Lewis was injured."

"Then why—?"

A hand touched my shoulder. "I'm sorry, but you'll have to leave now," a soft-voiced nurse told me. "Mrs. Tucker's dinner is waiting."

Harvey Neff was becoming more interesting by the moment, and Dinah had unwittingly given me a cover story even better than my reporter ruse. This time, when I arrived at the little tract house, a white Toyota sedan was parked in the driveway.

Neff answered the door by opening it a scant inch, one pale eye peering cautiously out.

"I don't purchase goods from roving solicitors," he said. "Good day."

"Wait, Mr. Neff! I'm not selling anything. Dinah Tucker sent me."

The door eased open a hair more. "Did you say Dinah Tucker?"

"Yes."

The eye examined me from head to toe, then withdrew. I heard the rattle of a security chain, a sound that had become unfamiliar to me during my months in Perdue.

"Come in, Miss...er—?"

"Madison. Taylor Madison."

His entranceway was as narrow as he was fat, and I was forced to squeeze past him when he gestured me into the living room. I tried not to stare at him, but it wasn't easy. What had happened to the Paul Newman look-alike? Had he swallowed a whale, like Jonah in reverse?

"May I offer you refreshments?" he asked, a really lousy fake British accent spread like cheap veneer over a southern drawl. "I was preparing iced tea when you knocked."

"Fine," I murmured, not because I was thirsty, but because I wanted a few moments alone. The exterior of Neff's house concealed an incredible interior—it was like opening a plain, brown paper sack and finding it crammed with gaudy trinkets.

As soon as he waddled out of sight, I roamed the room, touching and gaping. To say Neff had an affinity for ballerinas would be a gross understatement. They were everywhere. Paintings ranged from a hideous oil-on-velvet rendition of a sad-eyed dancer in a pink net tutu to a small, rather appealing study of a willowy, young lady dressed in frothy white. Framed programs from various famous ballets dotted the walls anywhere they'd fit.

Dozens of ballet slippers were suspended from the low ceiling—my inadvertent collision with one cluster set them into motion like a weird mobile.

Every flat surface displayed ballerina figurines, and Neff returned to find me seated on the sofa, staring at a Buddha dressed in tights and toe shoes. This bizarre curio took pride of place at the center of his coffee table.

"Pretty," he said, setting a silver tray next to the Buddha.

"Um, yes, it is," I lied.

"What? Oh, the figure. Yes, an exquisite piece, but I was commenting on my visitor. Honey?"

"I beg your pardon?" The man had succeeded in flustering me.

"In your tea. Honey? Sugar?"

"Neither, thanks."

He settled next to me and offered a sweating glass. "Miss...Madison, is it? You say Mrs. Tucker sent you?"

"Who?" A ballerina doll perched on the mantel seemed to be giving me the evil eye. I tore my gaze away. "Oh! Yes, Dinah Tucker. You see, I'm a volunteer at Restful Haven." I felt no guilt at this untruth because I'd already decided to volunteer at the facility. Restful Haven was clean, posh, and—boring. I figured I could spend one afternoon a week reading to the residents, or even organizing a singalong. My piano playing was strictly by ear, but I'd worked up quite a repertoire of show tunes.

"And?"

"You might be aware Mrs. Tucker has Alzheimer's," I continued.

"I'd heard. Poor thing."

"Well, sometimes an Alzheimer's patient slips into the past. When this happens, memories more or less transform into current events."

"I'm afraid I don't see—"

"Mrs. Tucker regressed about thirty years today, and you seemed foremost in her mind."

"Me?"

"Yes, sir. All she could talk about was your kindness toward her son, Lewis. Do you remember?"

Neff set his glass down with a snap against the silver tray and struggled to his feet. He pulled a handkerchief from a hip pocket and began dusting the array of figurines on a nearby shelf.

"Lewis," he mused. "Yes, I remember. Tragic accident."

"According to Mrs. Tucker, you stayed by his hospital bedside for days, the entire time he was in a coma."

"It was the least I could do." He whisked the handkerchief around a ballerina music box.

"A very generous act, considering Mrs. Tucker says you weren't even a family friend."

"I was a church deacon. Our minister was...ah...indisposed, so I offered what comfort and prayers I could."

"Then the Tuckers belonged to your church?"

He became very interested in a speck of lint attached to the lower corner of the velvet painting and scratched at it with a fingernail. "No, the Tuckers were of a different faith. The boy's own minister never showed up. I felt sorry for him, lying there all alone."

My mind raced for a way to veer the conversation around to what I wanted to know. "You know, I just recently moved to Perdue, and I haven't found a good church yet."

He stopped dusting. "You live in Perdue?"

"Yes, for several months now. What's the name of your church? Maybe I'll check it out this Sunday."

"It was called Church of the Rapture, but it's not there anymore. The congregation drifted away after the minister...left."

I produced what I hoped was a look of dawning realization, one hand clapped to my cheek. "You're not talking about Ralph Posey?

Oh, my goodness. The news is all over town about his body being found in an old chimney."

Neff moved closer to me, his bulk trapping me in place so I would have had to leap over the back of the sofa in order to escape. "Madison," he muttered. "Taylor—why, you're a reporter, aren't you?"

"Me? No, I'm—"

"You most certainly are! I still subscribe to the *Derrick County Gazette*, and I remember an article you wrote about the bell tower."

Damn. "That was just for fun. I'm actually a mystery writer."

He glared down at me. "I also seem to remember reading that you were responsible for the death of a deputy some time back."

"Lester Forman was responsible for his own death."

His bulk was now pressing against my knees. "I don't appreciate trickery, young lady. The Derrick County Sheriff's Department has already contacted me to ask questions about Brother Ralph, and I was specifically instructed not to discuss this case with the media."

"But I'm not the media. I swear to you, Mr. Neff, I'm not here as a reporter."

Neff's eyes narrowed. "So maybe you're planning to write one of the grisly true crime books about poor Brother Ralph, is that it? Well, you're wasting your time. You won't get a shred of gossip from me. I'd appreciate it if you'd leave."

He stepped back just barely far enough for me to get to my feet, which I was only too happy to do. The ballerina doll that had been on the mantel was dangling from his huge hand like a recently strangled chicken and I sure didn't want those puffy fingers around my own neck.

Chapter Nine

AN ICY BREEZE snaked down my collar as I hurried to the car. I started the engine and turned the heater to high, remembering I'd planned to shop for a winter coat while in Lubbock. That would have to wait, though—it was getting late, and Hazel would be hungry. I stomped the accelerator and headed for Perdue.

The sun sets in a hurry once autumn arrives, and it was pitch dark by the time I got home. I was surprised to find Bo's rusty green pick-up parked in Dorothy's driveway. The ancient truck's windows were scarred from years of driving down gravel roads, and my headlights bounced off pitted glass, rendering it nearly opaque. I could just make out the shape of a human figure in the driver's seat. What on earth was she doing? I honked my horn to catch her attention as I pulled into my own driveway. It was Keron who climbed down from the cab, huddled into her jacket.

"Hi! What are you doing here?" I asked as she crossed the street.

"I came by to check on Mother, but she and Dorothy must've gone somewhere."

"Why didn't you go inside to wait?"

She looked at me oddly. "I can't just barge into someone's house when they're not home."

"You can in Perdue," I said. "Well, anywhere except my house, at least." I turned the key in my own lock. "I'm an anomaly, but as far as the rest of Perdue goes, you can forget them, thar, big city manners, gal. In these parts, folks wander in and out of each other's houses as if they all shared one big mortgage payment. Locking your door when you leave home makes everyone wonder what you're hiding."

"So what are you hiding, Taylor?" she teased.

"My remaining shreds of privacy. I'll admit that I sometimes leave the door unlocked while I'm home, but not when I go somewhere. Heck, though, give 'em time and they'll brainwash me eventually."

Hazel was attempting to climb up my pant leg, a good indication she was starving, so I gestured for Keron to follow me into the kitchen.

Keron accepted my offer of hot chocolate. She shook food into a bowl for Hazel while I got out the milk and cocoa.

"How's Bo doing?" I asked a little later as we settled on the couch with hot mugs. Logs blazed in my fireplace, so we were soon warm both inside and out.

"Better. She was getting cabin fever, so when I drove into town to pick up a refill of her blood pressure medicine, she insisted on coming along. She'd baked a batch of cookies and wanted to take a bag of them to Lewis Tucker—said something about an apology for being pissy to him."

"Good for her," I said, remembering with a stab of guilt that I still hadn't called Lewis to make arrangements for the dinner I'd promised to cook him. I wondered if seeing the daughter of his high school flame had made him melancholy. "Did Lewis ask about your mother?"

"I didn't meet him," she said. "I waited in the truck while Grandma went up. She told me he had a cat, and I'm allergic."

"Too bad. He's a nice guy. You'd like him."

"I'm sure I would. Anyway, we left there and went to the café to grab an early dinner. Doctor Neil showed up, and joined us for dessert. When I started making plans to stop by and see Mother, Grandma said she was tired and wanted to go home." She shook her head. "I doubt she was all that tired. I think she just didn't want to be around Mother, not that I can blame her. Doctor Neil offered to drive her back home and stay a while to play checkers. He promised he'd stick around until I got back."

"In case I haven't said so before now, Keron, I think it's really nice of you to stay with her during all this."

"I'm enjoying myself. I love listening to her stories." She grimaced. "Well, most of them anyway. Her life with Ralph would make *The Grapes of Wrath* read like a comic book."

"So she finally opened up about Ralph?"

"Oh, yeah. And once she started, it was as if I had unlocked a vault—all the stored up anger and frustration just tumbled out." Keron stroked Hazel, who had curled up on her lap. "Now, I wouldn't presume to diagnose anyone based solely on another person's description, but..."

"Hey, I won't report you to the shrink union. Spill it."

"I'm reminded of a case study we read in an Abnormal Psych class. The subject was suffering from Narcissistic Personality Disorder, and from what Bo has told me, the symptoms fit Ralph like a glove."

I moved to a chair near the window, raised the glass a couple of inches and lit a cigarette. My first in several hours.

"Explain, please," I said. "But try to make the explanation

resemble plain English."

She pondered for a moment. "In a nutshell, feelings of vast superiority."

"That's all? Heck, I've met more than one person who saw things that way."

"Probably, but not to this extreme. Someone with NPD has true delusions of grandiosity. In his mind, he's unique and far more special than anyone else. He, therefore, feels entitled to be treated better than anyone else. He may have above average social skills, and is capable of incredible charm, but this is used to gain admiration, if not downright awe, from others. Adulation is crucial to him, and any hint of criticism is likely to be met with rage.

"He expects automatic compliance with his wishes, no matter how unreasonable those wishes might be. And he has virtually no empathy for others because he simply doesn't relate to the fact that anyone besides himself has valid needs or emotions."

"Jeez," I said. "And you think Ralph...?"

"I think so, yes, but just from what Grandma has told me about him." She hesitated. "As long as I'm speculating, I might as well take it a step further. Assuming Ralph did have NPD—and I doubt that was his only mental aberration, since he might well have been manic-depressive, too—it was surely exacerbated by his chosen profession. Most NPD subjects are obsessed with their jobs because they consider their careers to be extensions of themselves and thus of great importance.

"And Ralph's "job" was religion. Consider that ministers wield a great deal of power, even the good ones. They even have a built-in book of rules, although an NPD subject would think himself entitled to rewrite those rules to his own liking."

I studied the glowing tip of my cigarette. "The Bible."

"Exactly. Believers and non-believers alike have always interpreted the Bible in multitudinous ways. Many people cling to what they want to believe, while discarding any passages which make them uncomfortable."

"Oh, sure. 'Thou shalt not covet thy neighbor's wife'—at least not out loud and not in front of your own wife."

"That's typical, yes, but in Ralph's case it was more like, 'Thou shalt not covet thy neighbor's wife'—but, then, she isn't really his wife in the eyes of God unless I say she is."

"Whoa!" I remembered something Doc had said and opened my mouth to ask Keron if Bo had known Ralph was a womanizer. Before the question found its way out, though, I decided I didn't need to hear an answer that might only supply Bo with an additional motive for Ralph's murder. I hoped Burke didn't get wind of it either.

I got up to throw a fresh log on the fire. "Bo's life must've been hell."

Keron nodded. "Living with a man who considered himself a supreme being? I can't even imagine it."

I couldn't either. "It was probably hard on your mother, too."

"I'm sure it was."

"Did you know Ralph was determined for Faith to follow in his footsteps? He wanted her to become an evangelist."

"That's almost laughable, except that, if Ralph had lived, he wouldn't have taken no for an answer. Remember what I said about NPDs thinking of their jobs as extensions of themselves? Well, that goes double for offspring and spouses. What he felt for them was certainly not love, as you and I know love, but ownership."

I didn't say so, but it struck me that Faith had never really escaped Ralph's clutches. She'd married a man at least twenty years her senior, probably still looking for the perfect father figure. On the other hand, when I considered what a strong, independent woman Bo had become, my admiration for her only deepened.

But, I reminded myself, *there were women in the world who would not only put up with a man like Ralph, they'd thrive on it.* Sad to contemplate, but true.

"Gertrude Snell," I said aloud.

"Pardon me?" Keron looked up from tickling Hazel's belly.

"I had a little talk with a lady this morning who apparently agreed with Ralph's assessment of himself." I went on to tell her about my encounter with Gertrude.

"Ralph would've eaten that up," Keron said. "Too bad you were interrupted before you got any answers about Sheriff Mason's peculiar attitude toward Ralph's disappearance."

"I'll try again. Hopefully, I'll figure out a way to get more information out of Harvey Neff, too."

"Who?"

I retrieved Gertrude's album and skimmed through it until I came to the picture taken on the church steps.

"That's Harvey," I told Keron. "Well, it was. These days, he more closely resembles an albino elephant."

She sighed. "Why do the gorgeous ones always go to seed?"

Moving Hazel to the arm of the sofa, she pulled the album into her lap and gazed at the picture.

"So that's what Ralph looked like. Needless to say, Grandma didn't keep any photos of him. Funny, I can't even think of him as Grandpa. I did inherit his eyes, though."

"Only the color," I assured her. "Yours are kind, not hard and cold like his."

Keron was still gazing at the picture. "Grandma looks so unhappy. My heart just aches for her."

"Mine, too. I wish I could travel back in time and warn her not to marry him. No, that wouldn't work, would it? Then you wouldn't be here." I patted her hand. "Don't worry, Keron. She doesn't deserve this mess she's in, and we're going to get her out of it."

Suddenly weary, I leaned my head back and closed my eyes, listening to Keron murmur comments as she turned the album's pages.

"Man, a shrink would have a field day with Ms. Snell. The lady was totally obsessed with her brother, wasn't she? Here he is, working at his desk. Sitting in his car. Napping in a hammock. Building a—what's that? Oh, a birdhouse.

"Hey, here's another picture of Ralph. Looks like she sneaked it one Sunday, because he's behind a pulpit. I have a feeling Ralph didn't like to be photographed from the way he was glaring at the camera in that other shot. Okay, back to Duke. Washing his car. Hanging Christmas lights. Oh, my God."

"What?" I mumbled, having been lulled into a near doze by her litany.

"Can you believe this? She has pictures of the poor man's funeral."

I sat up. "You're kidding."

"I know some people do that, I've just never understood it. I mean, if you believe in the religious version of an afterlife, then all you're photographing is an empty husk because the deceased's soul has already passed on. And, on the other hand, if you *don't* believe, why on earth would you want a picture of a corpse? No, I don't get it."

I peered at the album. Sure enough, there was Duke in his open casket, surrounded by flowers. Dozens of similar photographs followed, Gertrude's camera capturing each mourner who approached to say a final farewell. When Keron came to a group shot of the gravediggers, posing with their shovels, I closed my eyes again in self-defense.

"There's his tombstone," Keron went on. "Here's one of Harvey, putting flowers on the grave. Whoops, looks like she gave up on organization after that. There's just a jumble of photos stuffed in the back of the album." She shuffled through them. "Lots of people I don't recognize, pictures of kids, too. Ha! Here's another one of Ralph, looking a little less dreary in a red polo shirt, but still seeming irritated that she's pointing a camera at him.

'No, I take that back. This is obviously a studio portrait. Well, then, he's irritated with the photographer at—" She squinted at the picture. "—Discount King." Thumping the book closed, she stretched, then got up and went over to the window to peer out. "Looks like Dorothy and my mother finally made it back. Guess I'll go say hello before I head home to Grandma's."

"Catch Bo up on what I've been doing, okay? I'll keep y'all posted."

When I opened the door to let her out, I found a surprise package on my front porch. It weighed about one hundred and eighty pounds, and it was dressed in a brown uniform.

"Hi," Cal said.

Keron hid a grin, ducked past my new visitor and sprinted across the street. Clearly, Bo had filled her in on my stubborn deputy and our recently strained relationship.

"Hi," I said.

We were in each other's arms before Keron could knock on Dorothy's door.

I pulled him into the house. It had only been a few days since I'd last kissed Cal, but it felt more like a year and I couldn't get enough.

I have no idea how we got from the front door to the couch, but I didn't come up for air until Cal said, "Ouch!"

Hazel crouched atop a pillow behind our heads, chattering nonstop, and Cal rubbed his left earlobe where she'd nipped him.

"She's jealous," I said.

"Are you?" he asked her.

She replied by crawling onto his shoulder and nuzzling his neck.

"I missed you, too," he told her, then reached to stroke my cheek. "And you."

"Me, too, you." Rather than look directly at him, I pretended a sudden interest in the crackling logs. "I owe you an apology, Cal."

"For bein' loyal to a friend? I don't think so."

"No, for putting your career in jeopardy."

He lifted an eyebrow. "Who says you did?"

"Burke." I recounted my conversation with the surly deputy.

"Heck, don't worry about it, Taylor. Underwood's not goin' to get rid of me that easy."

"Of course not. Especially with me helping you."

Cal buried his face in his hands and moaned. "Taylor..."

"We'll discuss it later," I interrupted hastily. "Right now, there's something I need to show you."

"What?" he asked with a sigh.

"It's in my bedroom."

"Oh. Oh? Oh!"

NOTHING BUT EMBERS remained in the fireplace by the time hunger forced us to emerge from my bed. I padded into the kitchen and cracked a few eggs to scramble while Cal rejuvenated the fire.

Sitting on the floor with him, with our plates on the coffee table and Hazel begging bites, it hit me that I was happier than I'd ever been in my entire life. Even Bo's predicament couldn't detract from the overpowering joy of watching the firelight play across Cal's chiseled features and knowing he really did feel for me what I felt for him.

I'd been reluctant to use the "L" word and Cal, sensing my hesitation, had not pressed the issue. Love wasn't something with which I had experience.

The "mother" who'd raised me certainly hadn't heaped it upon me, and whatever emotions I evoked in my newly discovered biological mother, love didn't seem to be among them. A few men had held me, some had bedded me, but none had shown me what it's like to actually need another person.

Until now.

"A woman needs a man like a fish needs a bicycle." I used to chuckle in agreement at that particular feminist adage, but not anymore. Cal made me feel complete. His absence from my life, however brief, had been like losing an important body part.

"Okay, Ms. Madison." Cal spoke up after draining his glass of orange juice. "What kind of meddling have you done, and how much trouble is it going to cause me?"

The "L" word, apparently, would have to wait.

"First of all, Bo didn't take that money from the church safe." I went on to tell him about my visit with Dinah Tucker. He looked a bit startled when I outlined my ruse—pretending to be Bo—but allowed me to continue without interruption.

"Sneaky," he said when I had finished. "Good job, though. Only one problem."

"Her testimony would never stand up in court."

"No way."

"I realize that, Cal, but what's important is now *you* know the truth."

He gave a tired sigh. "I don't know one-tenth of the truth about this case."

"Well, if Bo didn't take the money—"

"Then who did? Have you stopped to consider that?"

"Yes, I have. And I'm beginning to think whoever robbed that safe wasn't really after the money at all."

"Meaning what?"

"Meaning it was just part of an elaborate scheme to make everyone in town think Ralph Posey had left of his own free will. The open safe, the missing money, his pickup left in the church parking lot." I ticked the items off on my fingers.

"That had occurred to me," Cal admitted. "But I don't see that it gets us any closer to figuring out *who* did it."

"Not yet. I'm still working on it, though, don't worry."

Ignoring his exasperated snort, I leaned my head on his shoulder, sharing space with Hazel. Maybe now was a good time for the "L" word. "Cal?"

"Yep?"

"Cal, I...I think I—"

Something beeped.

I lifted my head and stared at Hazel. I'd heard her chatter, burp, squeak and snore, but I'd never heard her beep.

Cal got up and retrieved his uniform jacket. He dug in a pocket and pulled out a little black device.

"A pager?" I was amazed. "Since when has the Derrick County Sheriff's Department gone high tech?"

"Had to happen sometime, Taylor." He pushed a button and peered at the box. "Crap, it's Lubbock County."

When Paula goes off duty, she transfers the S.O.'s incoming calls to Lubbock County's twenty-four-hour dispatch center.

Cal had already dialed my phone. "Who?" he demanded. "Are they sure? Okay. I'll be there ASAP." He disconnected, dialed another number. "Burke? I need you to get out to FM 24-40, about midway between the Culver farm and Bo Posey's place. 10-50 major. Work the scene. Victim's en route to Doc's clinic, and I'm on my way there."

"Damn," I said as he hung up. "How bad is it?" I knew a 10-50 was a car wreck, and "major" meant injuries, though not necessarily major injuries, as the term seemed to imply. I was already gathering his clothes from where he'd discarded them along the hallway that led to my bedroom.

To my surprise, he took the pile of clothing from me, set it aside, and held my hands.

"Taylor," he said gently. "The victim is Keron Weathered."

My knees went suddenly weak, and I sank down on the couch, narrowly missing Hazel. "Is she okay?"

"She was conscious when the ambulance transported her, that's all I know. I'll call you when I get to Doc's clinic and find out more."

I was already pulling on my clothes. "Don't bother. I'm coming with you."

He didn't even try to argue.

I KEPT URGING CAL to switch on his patrol car's lights and siren, but he refused.

"For God's sake, Taylor, we're in Perdue, not Houston. This time of night, we probably won't even pass another car on the road, so there's no sense wakin' up the entire population."

I crouched in my seat, shaking with cold and with fear. "If they took her to Doc's clinic instead of to a Lubbock hospital, she can't be hurt too badly, right?"

He didn't reply, just turned a corner and kept driving.

Reality sprang forth like an ugly weed. "Oh," I said. "Maybe she was in such bad shape they had to settle for the closest facility. Is that what you're saying?"

"I didn't say anything at all," he reminded me. "Stop speculating, Taylor. We'll be there in two minutes."

I flung open my car door and hit the pavement at a dead run before he'd even eased to a stop.

One of Perdue's volunteer paramedics, a plump, pimply-faced, young guy who looked scared to death, was hovering just inside the emergency room doors. A splotch of blood was drying on his white shirt, and the sight made me suck in a sharp breath.

"Where is she?" I demanded, but didn't wait for his stammered reply. Doc's voice drifted from a curtained exam room mingled with—not surprisingly—Bo's gruff tones.

I shoved the curtain aside without a second thought, startling Bo and Doc. They stopped talking.

In the bed, Keron opened her eyes and offered me a feeble smile.

Cal, by that time, had caught up with me, and I saw my relief mirrored in his face. I felt another surge of the "L" word, impressed by the depth of his compassion for someone he'd never even met. Some cops, confronted every day by the horrors people inflict upon each other, develop such a hard shell to protect their emotions that they eventually lose access to any emotion at all.

"How's the patient, Doc?" he drawled as I fumbled for his hand and held it tightly.

"Not bad, considering she demolished a section of fence. Can't say the same for Bo's truck, though."

"Hang my truck." Bo sneaked a wipe at a tear dripping from the corner of her eye. "High time that ol' heap was laid to rest in a scrap pile. I'm gonna break down and buy me one of them new SUBs.

"SUV, Bo," Cal corrected with a grin. "Unless you're planning an underwater vacation."

"Taylor, you're white as a ghost," Keron said. She patted the mattress. "Come sit down before you faint."

I sat down gingerly, not wanting to jar any sore places. "I was scared to death when I saw blood on that paramedic's uniform," I told her.

She touched a bandage on her head. "Scalp wound. They bleed a lot, so I'm told. Other than that, I got by with a few bumps and bruises, and maybe a cracked rib. Doctor Neil is waiting for the x-ray."

"I'm real glad you're okay," Cal put in. "Obviously, you're not in any trouble as long as you're willin' to pay for repairing the fence. If I'm straight on where this took place, it's Old Man Culver's fence, and he's meaner than a rabid badger."

"No problem. Grandma doesn't know it yet, but I'm springing for her new truck, too."

"Like hell, you are!" Bo said.

"We'll fight it out later. Listen, would you and Doc go get some coffee or something? You're both watching me so hard, I feel like a germ under a microscope." They complied, but grumbled all the way out.

"Guess we'd better go, too, and let you get some rest," I said, smoothing her bangs away from the stained bandage.

"No, stay. Both of you." She peered around the curtain to make sure Bo and Doc were out of sight, but lowered her voice anyway. "Grandma would have a fit if she heard this, but I thought you ought to know. This was no accident. Someone ran me off the road."

I gasped. "What?"

Cal pulled a wooden chair into place beside her bed and straddled it, his arms propped against its back. "Tell me what happened."

She reached for my hand and held on to it. “After I left Taylor’s, I spent about an hour talking to Mother and Dorothy, then started out to Grandma’s.” She glanced at Cal. “That farm-to-market road is bloody dark at night!”

“Dark as the inside of a cow’s stomach,” he agreed.

“I’m used to lighted highways, so it made me nervous as hell. One of the headlights on Grandma’s truck droops a little, which made it even harder to see.”

Cal frowned. “Damn it, I’ve been after her for years to get that fixed. She says it makes the pickup look like it’s winkin’ at folks when she drives at night, and she thinks that’s funny as all get-out. How she finagles it through inspections, I don’t know.”

“You don’t?” Keron and I chorused.

Cal gave a grudging chuckle. “Okay, dumb comment. Please go on, Ms. Weathered—Keron.”

“Well, I was creeping along and praying I wouldn’t miss the turn-off to her house.” Her hand squeezed mine. “I don’t know where that car came from. One minute I was alone on the road, and the next minute a set of bright headlights appeared out of nowhere. That stretch of road is straight as a stick, so the car couldn’t have emerged from a curve.”

“The driver might’ve been sitting there with his lights off,” I suggested.

She looked surprised. “I hadn’t thought of that, but it makes sense. Anyway, before I could blink, he was coming right at me. You know how scarred up that old windshield is, and when his high beams bounced off it, I might as well have been blind. I guess instinct made me jerk the steering wheel to one side, but the other car still grazed the truck. Next thing I knew, I was climbing out into a ditch.”

“Can you tell me anything at all about the other car?”

She shook her head. “Sorry, no. The last I saw of it was a set of headlights disappearing into the distance.”

“How’d you get help?” I asked.

“I called Grandma on my cell phone.”

I almost laughed at how alien the term cell phone sounded to me after several months of living in the Retro Land known as Perdue.

“I told her I didn’t need an ambulance,” Keron grumbled, “but she called one anyway.”

Cal was staring fixedly at a ceiling tile.

“Hello?” I said to him. “What’s churning around in that brain of yours?”

"Huh?" His gaze shifted to me. "Oh. Nothing, really. Keron, I'm right sorry this happened to you, and I'm sure happy you're not hurt any worse than you are. Taylor, how 'bout we let her get some rest now?"

"Good idea." I brushed a kiss against the patient's cheek and stood up. "When are you getting sprung from this joint?"

She wrinkled her nose. "Doctor Neil says I have to spend the night so he can watch me for signs of a concussion."

"Believe me, I know from experience that staying in this clinic isn't a barrel of laughs," I said. "But you must admit, it's a reasonable precaution."

"I suppose so, but I'm worried about Grandma. I don't like the idea of her being on her own just yet."

"Relax. I'll take her home with me." I ignored Cal's sigh of regret. We'd both planned for him to stay over so we could make up—for lost time, that is.

Convincing Bo wasn't an easy matter, but after checking with Doc to make sure it was okay, I bribed her with the promise of an illicit shot of whiskey before bed.

She finally agreed, and went to tell her granddaughter goodnight.

I had been planning to ask Cal something, but whatever it was went right out of my head when he pulled me into an empty cubicle and gave me a kiss I felt all the way down to my toes.

"Thought I'd better take care of that before I drive you two ladies home," he murmured. "Don't want to shock Bo."

Chapter Ten

BO SAT IN A chair by my fireplace, sipping scotch and complaining loudly that it wasn't bourbon. I could hear her clearly all the way back in the spare room where I had pushed junk up against the wall and was putting fresh sheets on the foldaway bed.

Bo's grumbling is a constant, like the ever-present howling wind of West Texas, and I paid no attention until her voice came to an abrupt stop, mid-syllable. Afraid she had passed out, or worse, I dropped a pillowcase and rushed to the living room.

I found her thumbing through Gertrude's photo album. She looked up as I skidded to a halt, her normally ruddy cheeks pale.

"Where did you get this?" she asked in the tone of a woman asking where that seething mass of maggots had come from.

"You knew I was going to visit Gertrude Snell."

"Oh. Sure, I did. Guess I forgot." She tapped a picture. "Been a long time since I saw Ralph's face. Would've been okay with me if I never did again."

"I can understand why."

She glanced at me sharply. "Keron been talkin' to you about Ralph?"

I hesitated. "Yes. She wasn't gossiping, Bo, and I'm sure she didn't intend to break a confidence."

"Naw, that's all right. I know you're doin' everything you can to help me outta this mess, so the more information you have, the better. I shoulda told you myself. It's just...hard to talk about, even after all these years."

"I'll bet it is." I sat on the hearth next to Hazel, who was curled up on the little pillow I keep there for her.

"How'd you get Gertie to talk to you? She's not exactly what you'd call sociable."

I explained the ruse I'd used.

"Ha! That's a good one."

"She loaned me the album so I could choose a picture of Duke to publish in the paper alongside his article," I said. "I suppose I'll have to end up writing something about him for the *Gazette* eventually. It wouldn't be fair to her if I didn't."

"Fair." Bo sneered and tossed back the last drop of scotch. "Like Gertrude knows the meanin' of the word."

I stopped my futile poking at the almost dead fire and studied her expression, surprised at the amount of anger in her voice.

She flushed. "Don't pay me any mind. You already know that me and Gertie weren't exactly chums. Considerin' you had to listen to her yak all that time, I hope you at least got some answers outta her about old Sheriff Mason."

"Not yet, but I'll try again. Returning the album will give me a good excuse to pay her another visit."

Bo traced the edge of the photo with one gnarled finger, her touch lingering on Harvey Neff's then handsome face. "Wonder what ever happened to him?" she murmured.

"Harvey? He's living in Lubbock. I talked to him."

She stared at me. "He is? You did?"

"Yes, right after my visit with Dinah Tucker." I told her a little about my chat with Harvey, leaving out his changed appearance and the fright he'd given me just before I left.

"I had no idea. Guess I thought he'd high-tailed it back to the East coast."

I couldn't miss the open yearning on her face as she gazed down at his picture. How could I not have noticed before that her voice grew soft when she talked about him?

"Bo, this is none of my business..."

She chuckled. "I know what you're gonna ask, child. No, we didn't dance the horizontal polka."

I felt myself blush. "Bo, you don't have to tell me about that."

"Why shouldn't I? Don't get to talk about my lurid past very often these days."

"You loved him?"

"I could have, if things'd been different. By the time I got to know Harvey, Ralph had purt' near soured me on love, but Harvey made me feel—well, that's it. He made me feel. He was always bringin' me little gifts—a music box once, I remember. I had to hide it from Ralph, 'cause the only music he approved of was hymns. Anythin' else was the wailin' of the devil, he said. But Harvey understood.

"I'd never had a man treat me so nice before. I...I let him kiss me, just once, and it was so sweet, like nothin' I'd ever known." She lifted her chin, met my gaze squarely. "And, yeah, I wanted to bed him, but I just couldn't get past my marriage vows. Besides, I was a little scared that even though the kissin' was nice, sex with Harvey would end up bein' like sex with Ralph. I know better now, but back then I didn't."

"I take it Ralph wasn't, um, great in bed?"

"Honey, I was a virgin when I married Ralph, and all I felt the first time we did the deed was fear. Didn't help that he turned the whole process into some kind of ritual. Kept hollerin' stuff from the Bible about being fruitful and multiplying."

I bit back a helpless giggle, imagining that scenario for a wedding night. "Oh, Bo."

"Yeah, well, soon's I got pregnant with Faith, the sex stopped. He saw no point in squanderin' his seed."

"He *said* that?"

"In so many words. Anyway, I had some problems durin' Faith's birth, and Doc told me afterwards that I'd probably never be able to conceive another child. I'd wanted more kids, a heap of 'em, but I gotta admit it was a relief when Ralph said that there was no reason for us to lay together anymore."

"Because sex has no purpose beyond procreation, right?"

"Right in one guess." Her voice softened. "But when I was around Harvey, I couldn't help it. I wondered what it'd be like with someone who...it wasn't sex so much. I was just so lonely for a human touch, you know?" Dropping the album to the floor, she yanked off her reading glasses and massaged the bridge of her nose. "We're wanderin' off the subject. Look here, sweetie, I want you to know how much I appreciate all you've been doin' on my behalf, but this thing's gonna blow up in our faces, and there's not a thing you can do to stop it."

"Hey, you're not throwing in the towel, are you?"

She sighed. "Tomorrow's Sunday, and Judge Prescott will be back in his office Tuesday morning. I'll betcha Underwood slaps that arrest warrant down for his signature before Prescott's coffee pot finishes perkin'." She lit a Camel and hissed the smoke out through her teeth. "I don't want to go to prison, Taylor, but I'll live through it, just like I have everythin' else."

I shook my head firmly. "You won't have to, Bo. Look, we'd better get some sleep, okay? Things'll look brighter in the morning."

"Sure they will."

My intent had been to give Bo my own bed and sleep in the smaller bedroom—accurately referred to as the junk room—myself, but she rebelled. Following a heated argument, I gave in, but only because I was getting too hoarse to shout her down.

Smug as a cat swimming in cream, she tucked herself into the foldout and was snoring before I'd pulled the drapes closed so dawn wouldn't wake her.

After prudently hiding the scotch bottle in case my guest experienced a wee-hour temptation, I sank into bed. Hazel climbed onto Cal's pillow—I smiled a little, wondering if Cal would be pleased that I now considered the spare pillow his—and bared her pink tongue in a yawn.

A half-hearted attempt to sort out the day's events proved futile. I drifted to sleep with unanswered questions floating around in my brain like random pieces from a dozen jigsaw puzzles.

Perhaps my subconscious assembled a few of those puzzle fragments in a dream because, when I jerked awake several hours later, I immediately switched on the lamp and reached for the bedside phone.

Eight rings later, Cal answered with a grumpy, "What?"

"It's me." I spoke in a whisper to avoid disturbing Bo in the next room, then realized I'd have to speak up in order to hear my own voice above her snores, which were rattling the glass in my windows.

"What?" Cal repeated, his voice raspy with interrupted sleep.

Now, I'm very much aware that Cal's only phone is located in his tiny living/dining combination room, so I could picture him standing there, goosebumpy from the chilly air, dressed only in a pair of boxers—or maybe in nothing at all. Such a vision started the blood pounding in my ears.

"Cal," I said sharply. "Go put your robe on."

"Why?"

"So I can talk to you without...just *do* it."

"I'll do it," he muttered. "Not because you told me to, but because I'm freezin'. Hang on."

I used his temporary absence to rein in my lustful fantasies and focus on why I'd called him.

"This'd better be important," Cal said when he came back on the line. "I was havin' a hell of a dream. Wish you were here," he added under his breath.

So did I, but I pushed the thought firmly to the back of my mind.

"I've been thinking—" I began.

"Normal folks don't think at this unholy hour of the morning," Cal muttered. "Normal folks are busy sleeping."

I let that pass. "Cal, if I was right, and the reason Keron didn't see that other car sooner is because it was pulled to the side of the road with its lights off—then there's no way this can be chalked up to an accident, or even to a bunch of stupid kids out joyriding."

"Yep."

"Yep? What do you mean, yep?"

"Means yes. Chrissake, Taylor, you're a native Texan. Don't they say yep in Houston, too?"

"Stop messing with my mind, Arnette. Are you telling me you already came to that conclusion?"

"Hard not to."

"Then why didn't you say so?"

"Thought you'd already figured it out." He squeaked a yawn. "Couldn't you pick a more decent time of day to yell at me?"

"I'm not yelling." Actually, I was, but only so I could make myself heard above Bo's snores, which were beginning to blister the paint on my bedroom walls. "I just don't get it. Who on earth would deliberately try to hurt Keron?"

He was silent for so long I thought he'd fallen asleep.

"Cal?"

"No one I can think of"

"Then why—oh. Oh." The obvious answer chilled me like an injection of ice water. "My God. Bo. They were after Bo."

"Sounds that way to me," he drawled. "I'm surprised it took the famous mystery writer so long to catch on."

"She's sure caught on now." I leaned back against the headboard and closed my eyes. "Question is, who? Why?"

"That's two questions."

"Here's a third. How? I mean, how did whoever it was know to lay in wait for her on that road, during that particular time frame? And it was dark—how could the other driver be sure it was Bo's truck he went after? No, wait, I've got that one pegged. The damned droopy headlight. Her trademark."

"I always said you were quick. As to how he—or she—knew to watch for Bo, I'll have to question Keron a little more before I can try to answer that."

"Yeah, I see what you mean. It had to be someone who saw Bo in town this afternoon." I glanced at the clock. "Make that yesterday afternoon."

I heard his jaw creak as he yawned again. "I'll pay her another visit this mornin' before Doc releases her. Now try and get some sleep, huh?"

"Sure, you, too. But, Cal, you *will* fill me in on what you find out from Keron, right?"

"You bet."

I stared at the phone for a minute after I hung up. He hadn't exactly lied, but I knew Cal Arnette well enough to suspect he'd run whatever information he shared with me through the protect-Taylor-filter first. No problem. Keron had already told me where she and Bo had been yesterday, and I was quite capable of doing my own snooping...er...detective work.

Despite spending most of the night juggling questions in my head, I awoke with the birds. To be literal, the birds woke me. They'd become accustomed to an overflowing feeder, and lately I'd neglected my end of the bargain.

I wrapped myself in a chenille robe—the warmest clothing I owned, and one I might have to start using as outerwear if I didn't hurry up and buy a coat—and staggered out into the backyard with a ten-pound sack of seed.

Everyone thanked me with little birdie chirps and dug in while I made my bleary way back inside and started a pot of coffee.

Hazel crunched cat food with vigor and Bo's snores still shook the foundation. I fixed myself a bowl of granola and added my own loud munching to the din. Instead of being an annoyance, the racket served as a kind of white noise, shutting out distractions as I replayed my witching hour conversation with Cal.

Whoever had rammed Bo's truck, unaware that Keron was the driver, had certainly done so to either frighten Bo or to get permanently rid of her. The fact that someone was willing to go to such extreme measures was both good news and bad. Bad because Keron could have been badly injured or killed, and because both she and Bo were in danger of another attack.

The other driver's motive was clear. If Bo died, the investigation into Ralph Posey's murder would certainly die along with her, and this seemed to confirm that I was getting close to uncovering the real murderer. Good news, of a sort, except for one little problem. Although I had obviously stumbled across some vital information, I had no idea what it was.

I think better on paper, a gentle way of saying that sometimes my brain doesn't function properly unless I write down my thoughts. My house is littered with scraps of paper containing scribbled ideas for my latest chapter, shopping lists, reminder lists, and reminders to look at the reminder lists. I pulled a magnetic notepad from the refrigerator door and a pen from the pocket of my robe.

Hazel climbed up onto the tabletop and settled in for a round of her favorite game. It's called Watch Taylor's Pen and Try to Bat it Out of Her Hand. Two points if she makes me drop the pen, and three points if she manages to knock it all the way to the floor. Watching me crawl around under the table in search of the pen adds excitement.

"This is serious," I warned her. She chattered in agreement, but her gaze never wavered from the pen.

Trying to ignore her, I set to work, first jotting down the places Keron and Bo had gone yesterday during their little excursion to town. Let's see, delivered cookies to Lewis, stopped by pharmacy for refill of Bo's medication, meal at the diner. Unfortunately, I soon realized that naming the places did little good. In Perdue, they could have met two-dozen people during the course of their errands, and—being Perdue—each would have stopped to chat.

What I really needed was a list of people they'd spoken to, and exactly what had been said to whom. The only thing I was sure of was whoever had been driving that other car couldn't have been present at Lucy's Café when Keron and Bo parted company and Doc announced he would drive Bo home. Unfortunately, such a list would be impossible to compile. Neither Bo nor Keron were likely to remember the names of everyone they'd encountered, and even if they did, it wouldn't preclude someone eavesdropping while they were having lunch.

I suddenly became aware someone was leaning on my front doorbell. Hazel, taking advantage of my lapse in concentration, whacked the pen, which skittered off the table, across the linoleum, and under the stove.

"Good one," I told her. "Five points."

Gertrude Snell proved to be my early morning visitor. She huddled, shivering, on the porch, wrapped up in a thick (gray, naturally) cloth coat.

Bo was still snoring, so I felt safe to invite her in.

"No, thank you. I'm on my way to church. Just came by to pick up the album."

"Oh?"

"I know I said you could look through it and pick out a good picture of Duke for your article. Uh...have you?"

"Not yet, I've been busy—"

She looked relieved. "Good, 'cause I decided I should be the one to choose just the right picture. Is that all right? After all, I knew him best."

"Well, sure, but—"

"Could I have it now, please? I don't want to be late for church."

I fetched the heavy album and offered to carry it to the car for her, but she refused.

"I can manage." She staggered a little under the tome's weight as she tottered off down the sidewalk.

"Who was that?" inquired a grumpy voice from behind me.

Bo looked like she'd encountered a tornado somewhere along the way to my living room. Her gray hair stood out in spikes, and the nightgown I'd loaned to her was bunched in the back.

"No one you'd want to wish a good morning," I told her. "Gertrude Snell, on her way to church."

Bo looked at the clock on my mantel and one grizzled eyebrow lifted. "At eight a.m. ?"

I shrugged, watching through the window as Gertrude drove away, keeping her car in the exact center of the street. "An early service, maybe?"

"No such thing in Perdue. All three pastors start preachin' at ten sharp." She yawned hugely. "Where's the coffee? And how 'bout a nip of that awful scotch in mine? The coffee'll kill the taste."

I left the scotch bottle in its hiding place, but did allow her a mug of "real" coffee.

"Ah, caffeine," she said with a grateful sigh. "I'm outta cigs, though, so let me bum one of yours, huh?"

As I'd expected, she bitched about my "fake," low-tar cigarettes, but the coffee cheered her up. While she leaned against the counter and sipped, watching the birds through the glass in my back door, I hid my notes in the breadbox. Hopefully, I'd find a way to get the information I needed without frightening her.

A twang against the front window screen told me the *Derrick Gazette* had arrived. The neighborhood paperboy, Freddie, aims for the same spot on my porch every week, and every week hits the same spot on my window. Luckily, the house sports old-fashioned metal screens instead of the nylon variety everyone uses in Houston.

I didn't even have to unfold the little newspaper in order to read most of the blaring headline, and I tried, too late, to conceal it from Bo, who'd followed me out to the porch. She took one look at my face and snatched the *Gazette*.

"Old black crow," was her first comment as we settled back at the kitchen table. "I always told him that's what he looked like."

I peered over her shoulder at the photo and had to agree. Some people shouldn't be caught dead—pardon the pun—in a black turtleneck. I was more concerned with the story itself than I was by an old picture of Ralph. After Bo read it through once, she wordlessly placed the paper to one side, fetched herself a second cup of coffee and went out into the backyard. "To get some fresh air," was all she said, but her expression spoke volumes—worry, anger, fear, futility.

Body of Minister Found in Chimney, the headline screamed. Below that, in smaller type: *Conspiracy to Protect Murderer?*

My blood froze. Conspiracy?

I skimmed through the first couple of paragraphs, which explained who Ralph Posey was and described the discovery of his skeleton. Omitted were references to the suspected murder weapon and a few other details which, I knew, the police would keep quiet for as long as possible. Cause of death was listed as a fractured skull.

When asked to comment on the investigation, Cal was quoted as saying, "We're working on it."I had to smile. Succinct and to the point—typical Cal Arnette. I sometimes wondered if he was a descendent of Calvin Coolidge, who had once limited a speech to two words. Cal would probably be peeved if I asked him, so I made a mental note to do just that, which would likely lead to another discussion about his first name. He insisted that it wasn't short for Calvin, but refused to tell me the unabbreviated version.

My smile faded as I read on. Dave Underwood could be called many things, but reticent wasn't one of them. His comments regarding the Posey case filled the remaining space on page one and were continued on page four. A true politician, he managed to imply all manner of dire possibilities while skillfully avoiding any potential grounds for a libel suit.

To my utter horror, I saw that the story had been picked up by the Associated Press, which meant that it wasn't only *Derrick Gazette* subscribers who were reading—between Underwood's oh-so-carefully constructed lines—that Bo Posey was guilty of murder and that Deputy Cal Arnette was trying to cover up her crime.

Shaking with anger, I folded the hateful newspaper and tucked it into my backpack.

"I know where you live, Jesse," I muttered.

The phone rang—Keron, wanting to know if I'd mind springing her from the clinic.

"Has Doc released you?" I asked.

"Reluctantly. I'm going to take a quick shower and then I have to fill out some paperwork."

"Okay. See you in about an hour then. Hey, has Cal stopped by this morning?"

"Yes, crack of dawn. He arrived at the same time the nurse delivered my morning gruel, so I had a good excuse not to eat it. I don't know how much help I was to him, though." She sighed. "Then Mother came storming in. Honestly, Taylor, the grapevine in this town could choke a herd of elephants—I have no idea how she found out about my accident."

"What did she say?"

"What do you think? She was insisting we both pack up and get out of Perdue immediately. I told her she was welcome to hop a plane whenever she liked, but I intended to stay with Grandma until we get this ball of worms unsnarled."

"You're a crown jewel, Keron. See you soon."

I informed Bo of Keron's call and we went to our respective rooms to dress.

"You want to come along this time?" I asked Hazel as she watched me pull on a pair of jeans. The morning was already warming, leading me to expect an Indian summer day, and I hoped my furry pal would take a break from her chill-induced near-hibernation. She scampered from the room, so I assumed the answer was no. But when I retrieved my backpack from the kitchen table, a small nose poked out from beneath the flap.

"Good for you!" I said.

Bo preceded me out the front door, and I nearly collided with her when she came to a sudden stop.

Following her gaze, I saw that Dorothy and Faith had decided to enjoy their morning coffee on Dorothy's front porch swing.

"Hi!" I called out. "Beautiful weather for porch sitting."

Dorothy waved and nodded. Faith didn't move a muscle, not even to fake a smile.

"Come join us!" Dorothy shouted.

At that, Faith turned her head, and I could only hope Dorothy was wearing armored earrings because the look she got would have otherwise scrambled her brains.

My heart ached for Bo. As she took a faltering step toward the street, Faith stood up, turned her back on us and disappeared into Dorothy's house, the screen door slamming behind her.

Dorothy gave an apologetic shrug. She picked up Misty, who'd been rolling in the grass, and followed her houseguest inside.

Chapter Eleven

BO SAGGED AGAINST me.

"I'm so sorry," I murmured. "C'mon, sit for a while. We've got time."

We headed for the white wicker chairs at the far end of my porch. A row of tall shrubbery shielded us from the street, giving Bo the privacy to regain her composure.

"I'm fine." She bummed a cigarette and lit it with trembling fingers. "You don't have to look so worried, kiddo. I'm not gonna stroke out on you."

"That's a relief, but it was awful of Faith to act that way."

Bo took a deep drag and aimed a plume of smoke at the sky. "Keron says it could be typical mother-daughter stuff."

"Maybe it is." My own mother-daughter stuff would have filled a psych textbook.

"Naw, I don't believe it, and I don't think Keron does either. She's just tryin' to spare my feelings." Bo took another drag, looking thoughtful.

"Keron told me she asked you when, exactly, Faith started freezing you out."

Bo stiffened. "Yeah, she asked me."

"And you said you couldn't remember. But she didn't believe you, Bo, and neither do I."

She gazed blankly at the overgrown hedge for a time, then sighed and looked me in the eye. "What I said last night about Harvey kissing me that one time. Faith saw it."

"Oh."

"She was fit to be tied. I don't think she ever forgave me."

"That's a little odd," I said. "I mean that it would traumatize her to that extent. I guess it'd be a shock for a kid to see one of her parents kissing someone, but as much as Faith hated Ralph..."

"I only know that's when it started. She'd barely speak to me afterwards, and she moved to that nasty apartment in Lubbock the day after graduatin' high school. I kept tellin' her it'd be cheaper for her to live at home and just commute, but she couldn't stand to be around me, even only for a few hours every day." Bo ground the butt of her cigarette out in the terracotta ashtray I keep on the porch. "'Course, she was actin' funny even before that, but I passed it off as growin' pains. I knew the hell she went through in school.

"Faith was what you'd call a late bloomer. Straight as a stick and covered with acne until she hit seventeen and then, seems like overnight, she filled out and her face cleared up. Bein' poor and wearing hand-me-downs didn't matter so much when she wanted to fade into the woodwork, but when she looked in the mirror one day and saw a pretty girl lookin' back at her, everything changed. She wanted to wear lipstick and nice clothes and throw parties—all forbidden, of course, by Ralph's private brand of religion."

Bo's face darkened. "I can't count how many times I've wished I'd just divorced that bastard. Hard to believe I was ever that cowardly, lettin' my little girl suffer because her mother was too scared of scandal to leave a bad marriage."

"Don't be so hard on yourself, Bo. You did what you felt was best at the time. Besides, Dorothy told me that you and your daughter used to be really close—best friends, in fact."

Bo barked a laugh. "Comrades in arms is what we were. You know how men—and women, too, these days, I guess—start feelin' a sort of kinship when they serve in the armed forces together? That's 'cause fighting a common enemy forges a pretty tight bond. Faith and me, we spent a lot of time outfoxing Ralph. Like, for instance, her clothes. I made most of 'em myself since Ralph was too tight-fisted to buy her any. Problem was, he insisted that all her dresses be plain white."

"Why?" I asked, and then answered my own question. "Oh, I get it. Pure and virginal."

"Yeah. Well, it was bad enough that all I could afford on the pittance Ralph doled out was cheap fabric—bleached muslin, mostly—but I'd be hanged if my baby would go to school every day dressed like a cross between Saint Bernadette and Casper the Friendly Ghost. So I cheated by raiding the clothing donation barrel Ralph kept in the church parking lot. I cut the most colorful castaways into pieces and made her little patchwork vests and scarves and sashes. That way, she could smuggle 'em to school in her lunch box, wear 'em all day, then take 'em off before she came home. He never caught on."

While I found it sad to imagine a mother and child forced into such subterfuge, I found the story touching. Neither the woman who raised me nor my recently discovered birth mother would work up a good spit to put me out if I was on fire.

The subject reminded me of something that had been niggling at the back of my mind since my dinner with Dorothy and Faith.

"Bo, how on earth did you manage to buy Faith an expensive silk dress for her senior prom?"

She blinked at me through the smoke of a second pilfered cigarette. "Come again?"

"The pink silk dress. How could you afford it?"

"Taylor, you're speakin' Greek."

She'd remembered everything so clearly up until now, I found it strange she needed a memory jog about the dress but, after all, several decades had passed since that fateful night. I filled her in on my dinner with Dorothy and Faith, describing the dress Dorothy had stored in her attic all this time.

Bo snorted. "Dorothy's gettin' senile. I recall plain as day the dress I made Faith for that prom. It was pale yellow broadcloth, and I spent weeks embroidering little daisies all over the skirt so's it wouldn't look so ordinary. That's why Faith went over to Dorothy's to change. Ralph would've pitched a double fit—a yellow dress *and* a dance? Two sins for the price of one."

It was past time for us to go get Keron, so we continued the discussion on our way to Doc's clinic.

"I don't know what happened to the dress you made, Bo," I said. "But Faith definitely wore pink silk on prom night."

"Well, I can't say I blame her. Store bought silk beats out homemade cotton any day. Only...where do you reckon she got it?"

"Beats me." *But I intend to find out*, I added silently as we pulled into the clinic's parking lot. A horrible suspicion was creeping into my mind. What if Faith had taken money from the church safe in order to buy her prom dress, and Ralph had found out? I could only imagine the scene. Could she have killed him herself—maybe in self-defense?

Okay, so I was grasping at straws. But that damned dress played a major part in this mystery. I just knew it did.

Keron sat in a waiting room chair, listening patiently as Doc lectured her.

"Rest. Lots of it," he said. "No bending over or lifting...you'll strain that rib. Eat. You're too skinny for my liking. Don't—"

"Ready, Keron?" I broke in.

"Am I ever." She gave Doc a sweet smile, thanked him for his excellent care and hurried out the door.

"I shouldn't complain to someone who's doing me a favor, but what kept you?" she asked, squeezing into the minuscule back seat of my Bug.

I let Bo explain about the pink dress as I navigated the streets of Perdue.

"Weird," Keron said when her grandmother had finished.

"Did you see the *Gazette* this morning?" I asked as I made the turn onto the long stretch of road leading to Bo's house. "It's in my backpack. Careful digging it out, 'cause we have an extra passenger."

"Who? Oh, hi, Hazel." Keron chuckled and I heard paper rustling.

"Old crow," Bo muttered.

"Did you say something, Grandma?"

"She's grumbling about Ralph's picture in the paper," I translated. "Bo says he always dressed in black, and she used to tell him he looked like a crow."

"How'd you ever talk him into that red shirt, Grandma?" Keron asked.

Bo twisted around in her seat. "What are you talking about, child? What red shirt?"

"He was wearing a bright red shirt in that studio portrait I saw in the picture album last night. Remember, Taylor?"

"Gertrude's album," I said. "Yeah, I remember you mentioning it."

"Did you see this picture, too?" Bo asked me.

"No, but—"

"Then my granddaughter's havin' delusions. Ralph Posey never once wore anything but black in all the years I was married to him. And as far as lettin' a real photographer take his picture?"

"Hardly a real photographer," Keron put in. "I think at Discount King the stock boys take turns manning the portrait booth."

"It's still baloney. Ralph purt' near went into spasms if someone even aimed a Kodak at him. You probably just dreamed it, honey, after that nasty noggin bump."

"I'm sure you're right, Grandma," Keron agreed, but she caught my eye in the rearview mirror and shook her head.

I dropped them off at the house, declining their invitation to stay for coffee and muffins.

"Things to do," I said. "I'll call later."

Hazel was happy when I moved her backpack into the front seat where it belonged. She crawled out and stretched to peer through the passenger window.

"Our first stop won't be pleasant, girl," I warned her. "Cover your delicate ears."

The esteemed editor of the *Derrick County Gazette* doesn't believe in taking days off, not even the Sabbath, so I found him exactly where I knew he'd be—hunching in front of his elderly typewriter. The man has probably built up enough calluses on his fingertips from pounding those stiff keys to play a guitar strung with razor wire.

I longed for a strip of razor wire as I pushed through the door to his office.

"I was wondering when you'd show up," he said.

"How *could* you print all those lies, Jesse?"

He took a copy of the paper from a stack by his elbow and flipped it across the desk to me. "You point out a single lie and I'll be happy to retract it. With apologies."

He had me there, and I knew it. Underwood was coated with the William Jefferson Clinton brand of Teflon—bullshit refused to stick to him.

My rage deflated like a punctured beach ball, leaving me weak-kneed. I sank into the chair across from him. Sensing that the yelling had ended, Hazel dislodged herself from the backpack and sat on my shoulder.

Jesse's eyes widened to dinner plate size. "*Madre de Díos*, Taylor, don't bring that rat in here!"

"She's not a rat, she's a ferret," I told him for the zillionth time. Jesse's one flaw is his phobia of rodents, or anything resembling a rodent. The first time he'd come to my house for drinks, Hazel had chased him into the bathroom.

"Well, just keep her over there."

"Fine."

He pushed his chair against the wall, distancing himself from my vicious pet. "As I was saying, I don't print lies. But I do quote the people I interview, usually verbatim."

"Usually?"

"If I'd printed half of what Underwood actually said, you'd have burst through that door wielding a pickax."

"That bad, huh?"

"That bad. He said, for example, that the suspect in the Posey case somehow obtained information regarding the evidence against her."

"Oh, Lord."

"It's true? Arnette was that stupid?"

"No, not Cal. Me. I was trying to help."

Jesse shook his head, one wary eye still on Hazel, who was busy chewing a lock of my hair. "Not good, Taylor."

"Tell me about it. Cal was...peeved."

"More likely, Cal was royally pissed off, and I don't blame him." He picked up a paper clip and started bending the wire into intriguing shapes. "Look, Taylor, I'll let you in on a little secret. I've been doing some digging of my own, and I've come to the conclusion Underwood's reason for hiring an outsider like Burke is that he's trying to find a way to get rid of Cal."

Having reached the same conclusion myself, I nodded. "And I helped spring the trap, damn it."

"Well, I don't know if the jaws of that trap are biting into Cal quite yet, but they might be soon."

"I don't get it, though. What does Underwood have against Cal?"

Jesse shook his head. "You're gonna make me say something good about my rival for your affections, huh? Okay, then. Despite his many flaws, Arnette is nobody's flunky, and that's what Underwood wants—someone who'll dangle quietly on the end of a leash and live to serve his master. It's a power game, Taylor, that's all."

"Power," I repeated thoughtfully. Sure, power plays were common in big city government or among board members of major corporations, but it had never occurred to me that such cutthroat tactics would extend to a minuscule county in West Texas.

As if he'd read my thoughts, Jesse said, "Derrick County may be a small pond, but Underwood wants to be the biggest fish in it."

"He's one of only two county commissioners—how much more powerful can he expect to be out here in the boonies?"

"Ah, but you're forgetting who the second county commissioner is. Bo pulls the reins on him pretty often."

A thought blasted into my head with such force that I nearly tumbled out of the chair. "My God, Jess, do you think he set Bo up?"

"Much as I like the idea, I don't see how he could have. Even if he had known something about Ralph's body being stuffed in that chimney, Bo decided on her own to clear out the cottage, and nobody forced you and Cal to poke the skeleton out of hiding. Nope, this mess with Bo is just icing on the cake."

"You're right, of course. But if things go his way, he'll get rid of both the thorns in his side with a single tweezer tug." I stood up. "And the only way to stop him is by doing what I've been trying to do all along—prove Bo's innocence."

Time was chasing me like a rabid skunk. In less than forty-eight hours, Judge Prescott would be back in his office, signing a warrant for

Bo's arrest. I sat in my car, thinking and scrawling notes to myself on the pad I kept in the glove compartment.

"Don't even consider it," I growled at Hazel, who was watching the moving pencil with intensity.

Harvey Neff, I wrote. What Bo had told me last night changed my perception of the man. Maybe the reason he'd become so angry near the end of my visit had been because he was afraid I was snooping around in an attempt to confirm Bo's guilt. I only hoped I could figure out an excuse to see him again, because he'd known both Ralph and Bo from the beginning of their marriage and could probably answer questions no one else could. It was possible he might even know why Faith had changed so abruptly from her mother's pal to her bitter enemy. In the meantime, two enigmas had surfaced this morning.

Pink dress, I scribbled. Red shirt.

Red shirt. I wondered if Ralph had, for some reason, sneaked over to the Discount King in Lubbock for his mini photo session. If so, why would he keep it a secret from Bo? He didn't sound the type to surprise her with a picture of himself for her birthday.

Discount King, dang it, what was bothering me about Discount King? My jaw dropped as realization struck.

A glance at the courthouse clock told me that Gertrude was, at this moment, attending church services. I started the car and floored it, hoping Burke wasn't waiting around the nearest corner, ticket pad in hand.

Although I suspected Cal would strongly disagree, I convinced myself that what I was planning couldn't really be called breaking and entering if the house in question was unlocked. I sure hoped Gertrude followed one particular small town custom.

After parking my VW two blocks away, I cut through unfenced backyards until I came to hers. The kitchen door was not only unsecured, it stood wide open, as did all the rear windows. Airing the house out, was she? Hooray for Indian summer!

"Hello?" I called, not expecting—or wanting—an answer, but also not keen on startling Gertrude into a heart attack.

The house remained silent. I crept through the kitchen and into the living room, Hazel chattering from her nest in my backpack.

"Hush," I cautioned her, crouching to rummage through the stacks of photo albums in Gertrude's bookcase.

Damn. The silver album with red trim was conspicuously absent. Clearly, Gertrude had not returned home with her prize before going to church.

This would make things harder, for sure. I'd either have to come up with a valid reason for a return visit, or keep watch on her house and wait for her to leave again—which, according to Jesse, might well be next Sunday morning.

I was trying to think of a few credible questions for a follow-up interview when the front door creaked open.

"*Shhh!*" I hissed at Hazel as I scurried on hands and knees behind the sofa.

Gertrude was humming "Onward, Christian Soldiers" under her breath. I heard a thump, then the slither of cloth as—I surmised—she removed her coat. The tune changed to "Rock of Ages" and her humming grew fainter.

I risked a peek in time to see the hem of her skirt vanish into the kitchen. Craning my neck, I saw that the silver album had been deposited on the coffee table. From my current hiding place, it was a few maddening inches beyond my reach.

I could grab it and make a mad dash for the outside but, as I'd just been reminded, the hinges on Gertrude's front door needed oiling. I couldn't exit through the kitchen because she was still in there—from the swish of running water and various clankings, I assumed she was brewing up a pot of her tasteless tea. I'd have to pass by the open kitchen doorway in order to reach a back room and leave via a window, so that was out.

Hazel was making the little squeaking noises that mean she's nervous. I groped behind me to give her a reassuring pat, then nearly jumped out of my skin when Gertrude's phone rang.

So much for a career in cat burglary. My nerves of steel had proved to be nerves of overcooked spaghetti. Which reminded me that I still owed Lewis a spaghetti dinner. I wondered if I was out of oregano. Okay, reason number-two I could never be a successful cat burglar—my mind wanders.

"Hi, sweetheart!" Gertrude's voice burbled from the kitchen. "You are? You did? Yes, I'd love to see your new dolly. Grammy loves you, too."

Like many people of her generation, Gertrude seemed convinced that long distance phone calls require speaking in shouts. Lucky for me, since I doubted she'd detect a hinge squeak over that high volume conversation.

I had no intention of being foolish enough to take the entire album, thus pointing the accusing finger straight at my own head. Crawling around the opposite end of the sofa, I peered through the kitchen door. Gertrude's left side was visible, but she was seated at the table, her back to me. I pulled the album into my lap and scooted out of sight.

I remembered that Keron had been going through the loose photos when she found the disputed shot of Ralph, so I started there. Kids and dogs and nature shots and...yep, sure enough, Ralph Posey dressed in a fire engine red shirt. I tucked the picture into my backpack, close to Hazel's quivering body.

Gertrude's voice was still booming off the walls as I crawled to the front door and raised a hand to turn the knob. "I'll be comin' to visit you soon, sweetheart, and I'll see your dolly and your wagon and...no, honey, you can't come stay in Grammy's house, I'm sorry. Put your daddy on the phone, okay?"

I was out the door and sprinting for my car before the earsplitting conversation reached new decibels.

My heart was pumping as if I'd just run a marathon, so I drove to the park and let Hazel play in a patch of dying grass while I stared at the stolen photo and tried to make sense of this new discovery.

I would have defied Bo, seeing this picture in living color, to deny that the man snarling into the camera was her late husband—even though he wasn't.

Chapter Twelve

SUDDENLY, I HAD A valid suspect for Ralph's murder. Maybe even two suspects. To prove I'd learned my lesson, I took the information straight to Cal. At least, I tried to.

"He went to Lubbock," Paula informed me. "Took that Molly to lunch. Again."

"Again? What does that mean?"

"Well, I shouldn't gossip, but he's been seeing a lot of her lately. I think it's time you knew."

Anyone else would have sounded catty, but Paula just sounded concerned—for me. I tried to take it with a grain of salt, aware she trusted men about as far as Hazel can spit. At any rate, I decided there'd be time to confront Cal—and murder Molly, if necessary—later on. Right then I was bursting to share my newest discovery. Unfortunately, when I get excited, I tend to blather.

"Stop!" Paula ordered after a minute or so.

I shut my mouth and waited for a reprimand on the subject of a deputy's girlfriend burglarizing a citizen's house. I should have given Paula more credit.

"How can you be so sure this isn't a picture of Ralph Posey?" she asked. "I get that he usually wore black, but..."

I flipped the picture over and pointed out the distinctive logo in the lower right corner—the letters DK in entwined script, topped by a crown.

"Yeah, Discount King. I shop there all the time. So?"

"So," I said triumphantly, "Discount King went into business in 1995. I know, because their nationwide grand opening coincided with the release of my first paperback novel. I did signings in both of their brand new Houston stores."

Paula gaped at me. "You mean—"

"—that Ralph Posey had been dead for more than two decades before Discount King was a glimmer in its founder's eye."

She picked up the picture again. "Then who on earth is this?"

"All things considered, I'd say you're looking at the son of Ralph Posey and Gertrude Mason Snell. If, indeed, she ever actually married a man named Snell. More likely, she moved away after Ralph disappeared to avoid gossip and condemnation. Unwed mothers weren't popular back then, especially in small towns like Perdue. And if you add in the fact she was pregnant by a married minister...well."

"So the new suspects are—"

"Gertrude, for one. Maybe because he refused to acknowledge the baby was his, maybe out of shame. Or Sheriff Mason himself—I can see him finding out and flying into a rage against his sister's illicit lover."

Paula wanted to play a few more rounds of the speculation game, but I had places to go and people to see.

"Hold your horses, gal," she said before I could make it out the door. "I've got the scoop on Burke. You want it now, or later when you're not so all-fired busy?"

"Now, please," I said meekly.

"Burke was fired—no, make that 'asked to resign' from Dallas P.D."

"Yeah?"

"Yep. Seems our Ollie was paddin' his bank account with a little bribe money."

I sat back down and stared at her. "From who?"

"You're the writer, but shouldn't that be 'whom?' Anyway, I don't know the details, but rumor has it he was paid to look the other way while some kind of illegal activity was going on."

"So why wasn't he prosecuted?" I demanded.

She shrugged. "From what I understand, the P.D. was trying to avoid media exposure. They offered him a choice—stay and get dragged through an investigation, or quietly resign."

I shook my head. "Paula, Underwood has to know this. Why would he hire someone who...? Oh, I see. Burke's exactly the type Underwood would seek out, someone who'll do most anything for money."

"You got it. Question is, will the information do you any good?"

"Dunno, but the news will make Cal smile, so that's something. He's not smiling a lot these days. You'll fill him in on Gertrude, right?"

"Sure." She made a shooing motion. "Go—uncover a few more secrets. Save our Bo. Whoops! Don't want the initials of *that* slogan on a poster, do we?"

AS OFTEN HAPPENS, the process of spelling it out for another person had exposed the weak spots in my theory, and by the time I got back to my car, I was already doubting my hastily reached conclusions. Duke Mason had been, by all accounts, a good sheriff and a decent, law-abiding man. Sure, cops committed crimes every day—Oliver Burke was a perfect example of that—but from what I'd learned about Sheriff Mason, he'd have been more likely to run Ralph out of town than to kill him. And although Gertrude's son was definitely the child of either Ralph Posey or his clone, that didn't automatically make her his killer. In fact, even after all these years she seemed to still think of him as a god among mortals.

I wouldn't know the details unless I confronted her, and I was champing at the bit to do just that until I considered how mad Cal was going to be about my...unauthorized entrance into her home. I figured I'd let him find a way to approach her while I concentrated on other unanswered questions. Bo's freedom hung in the balance. Leaping to pin the crime on the first suspect to come along would be stupid and irresponsible.

After a discussion with Hazel (I talk, she listens) I decided I had to approach Harvey Neff again. He'd been close to the Posey family, and also knew all the church members, so he'd be a font of information if I could just get him to open up. Problem was, how? A few moments of painful brain wracking gave me a tentative plan. Since he was convinced I was a reporter, I'd simply use that cover to my advantage. No one can resist being interviewed when the subject is his or her own personal obsession.

Again cursing my dead modem—this would be so much easier if I could just surf the Internet—I headed for the library. Being Sunday, it was closed, but I knew that Sadie Klune's tiny apartment was around back.

Sadie answered her door dressed in a sapphire blue satin robe with matching slippers. Half-moon reading glasses, perched at the tip of her sharp nose, somewhat diluted the outfit's glamour.

She blushed. "You caught me," she said in her perpetual whisper. "Sunday decadence."

"Decadence?" I sneaked a glance over her shoulder, wondering if I'd interrupted a tryst with the butcher or the mailman. All I saw was an old-fashioned chaise lounge. On the table nearby rested a china cup and a thick paperback.

Sadie dropped her voice even further, so I had to lean forward to hear her.

"Historical romance novels," she confessed. "A box of Godiva chocolates, a cup of Earl Grey, and a slithery robe. What could be more decadent than that?"

I could think of a few possibilities, but decided we weren't really close enough friends for me to wander into such topics.

"Sorry to bother you," I said. "It's sort of an emergency. Could I please get into the library for just a little while?"

She grinned, transforming a rather plain face into quite a pretty one. "A library emergency, huh? That's a new one. Come on in. You can use my private entrance."

A door in the corner of her living room led to the alcove where she repaired torn covers and entered inventory into a spanking new computer. I'd have to remember to tell Jesse that, if Sadie Klune could move Perdue's crumbling library into the computer age, he could surely do the same for the weekly rag.

"You can let yourself out through the front door," Sadie whispered in parting. "It'll automatically lock behind you."

I've always loved libraries, and if I hadn't been on a mission, the countdown clock to Bo's impending arrest ticking loudly in the background, I would have reveled in having one all to myself. As things stood, though, I ignored the intoxicating scent of all those unread books and headed for the card catalogue—a relic from the past in most modern, fully computerized libraries. The cards obligingly pointed me toward the proper shelves, and soon my arms were full of books about ballet. I settled at a long table, my research tools spread about me. Hazel squeezed out of the backpack and circled a three-hole paper punch, deciding whether to bite it or try to crawl inside it.

Not being an aficionado of the graceful dance—though I did prefer ballet to opera—I found it hard to concentrate. The manner in which Isadora Duncan had met her death held my interest, but only because I found myself wondering if I could incorporate the bizarre accident into a future murder mystery.

Ballet costumes had certainly changed throughout the years, I noted. Short tutus, long tutus, sheer and flowing gowns—sometimes a combination gown/tutu with a little netting gathered at the hips. The slippers remained pretty much the same, although Isadora had blown the minds of her audiences by dancing in bare feet. My vision was beginning to blur, and I realized how spoiled I'd become conducting research via the Internet. A good search engine, a few clicks of the mouse, and voila! The very fact I was seeking appeared onscreen.

Sighing wearily, I flipped through a few more pages. A painting by Degas caught my eye, and I studied it for a moment, intrigued by his ability to capture the body in motion. No wonder he'd focused so much of his work on ballerinas, the most fluid human form in existence.

Giving up, I replaced the books on their shelves, wondering how frail, little Sadie hauled these tomes around on a daily basis—she must have the shoulder muscles of a weight lifter. I could only hope I'd gleaned enough information to entice Harvey into an interview. When Hazel and I emerged into the sunlit garden at the library's entrance, I set her down and she scampered behind a rose bush to do her business while I stretched the kinks out of my neck, looking through my scanty notes. Something itched at the back of my mind, but I couldn't decide what it was.

A harsh cry erupted from somewhere above me, and I craned my neck to try and determine its source while Hazel, spooked, did her best to climb my pant leg. I had just scooped her up when the cry was repeated, and I smiled in sudden understanding. The pharmacy building abuts the library, and the windows of Lewis's upstairs apartment stood open to the mild weather. Cecilia the cockatoo was testing her lungpower.

The thought of Lewis pricked me with guilt. I still hadn't carried through on my promise of cooking him dinner. I'd checked the directory the day before, but his phone number was unlisted (probably the only unlisted number in Perdue) so I decided that, while I was in the neighborhood, I might as well climb the stairs and explain.

As I put my foot on the top step, I heard him laugh. At least he was in a good mood, and perhaps wouldn't mind me dropping by unannounced. He pulled the door open, saw me, gave a tentative smile. "Ms. Madison?"

"Taylor, please. I was wondering if..." A movement from within the apartment caught my eye and I looked past him to see a woman turn to face me.

"Hi, Faith," I said. She was still wearing her coat, so I didn't know if she'd recently arrived or was on the verge of leaving.

She nodded wordlessly and scooted past me, dashing down the steps.

"I didn't mean to interrupt," I told Lewis. "Just wanted to discuss that meal I promised to cook for you."

"I'd forgotten all about it," he said.

So much for my misplaced guilt. I had planned on suggesting that we put it off for a few days, so I could concentrate on Bo's problem, but Faith's presence reminded me of all the oddities in her behavior, both present and past tense, and since Faith wouldn't even speak to me, perhaps Lewis could shed some light.

"How about this evening?" I asked.

"Fine. The single burner in my kitchen is all yours."

"Okay, then, I'll see you about seven."

This threw a kink into my plans for the day, but I should still have time to see Harvey and get a few other things accomplished before seven. I made a quick stop at Posey's Grocery, evading questions from Arnold, then headed by the house to stash the spaghetti fixings in my fridge and feed Hazel.

I was still considering how best to approach Harvey Neff. Gushing about his ballet memorabilia might work on its own, but maybe he'd be even more receptive to an interview if I promised a full-page article, complete with pictures. Jesse probably wouldn't balk.

When I'd bought a new computer system a few months back after the hard drive in my laptop crashed, the package had included a digital camera. I'd only used it a few times, mostly to snap photos of Hazel. I had taken one of Cal, which I sent by email to my agent. She pronounced him "dreamy" and said that if all guys in Texas looked like him, she'd almost be willing to give up New York.

I found the camera in a desk drawer and replaced the batteries, then took a few practice shots of my living room, all of which turned out too dark. Muttering under my breath, I located the instruction manual and forced myself to skim it until I located directions for turning on the flash. I also learned about the portrait setting versus the landscape setting, and practiced some more so I could find out which worked best for objects. A picture of the lamp beside my sofa turned out clear, as did the horrid snake-head-in-a-glass-globe paperweight that Billy had given me—and that I kept on display so as not to hurt his feelings. The M.C. Escher poster behind my desk blurred, though. I was adjusting the settings to take another when a thought slammed into my brain like a stray bullet.

Slowly lowering the camera, I stared at the poster for a moment. My God. If I was right, it might be dangerous to question Harvey...but I did need to get into his house.

"You need to stay home this time," I told Hazel, who had finished her lunch and was ready to go again.

TO MY SURPRISE, Harvey didn't fly into a rage the moment he discovered who was knocking on his door. Not that he was glad to see me.

"What is it you want?" The fake British accent was tinged with ice.

"You were right, Mr. Neff," I said crisply. "The other day, I really was sniffing around for information about Bo Posey, but my editor ended up snatching that story for himself. He assigned me to come up with a human interest piece we can run when this Posey stuff hits a lull, and right away I thought about you and your amazing collection."

Apparently, my pushy, *National Enquirer* shtick was doing its job. Harvey hadn't managed more than a couple of indignant squeaks and, during my nonstop diatribe I'd been able to squeeze past him.

"Truly awesome!" I shouted back over my shoulder. A brisk trot had delivered me to his living room and, while he was still wheezing to catch up, I whipped out my camera and began photographing the room.

"What are you doing? Stop that!"

"When did you begin collecting?" I asked, still clicking away.

"I said stop!" he roared, grabbing my camera. He fumbled with it and finally got a compartment to swing open. Clearly, his intention was to confiscate the film, but since digital cameras don't use film, he only succeeded in dislodging its batteries. One struck him on the toe before rolling under the sofa.

I took the camera from his hand while he was still staring at it in confusion.

"Really, sir, if you'd rather not be interviewed, just say so. You don't have to break an expensive piece of equipment."

"Out," he said, pointing toward the front door.

"Mr. Neff, please reconsider. People would love to read about—"

"Get out," he repeated. "Before I call the police."

More than willing to comply, now that I'd gotten what I came for, I sidestepped as one of his beefy hands reached for me and sprinted for the door.

Just as I reached my car, he called out to me. Reluctantly, I turned around.

He stood on his porch, still wheezing. "Does it really look bad for Bonita?" he asked.

"It sure looks bad for her right now," I answered honestly, and was surprised to see his heavy shoulders slump as he turned to go back into the house.

Could my newest suspicion be wrong? Surely if he cared about Bo, he wouldn't have...but there was no use speculating until I did some research. And this time I'd use twenty-first century methods.

I headed to the nearest mall, found a computer store and bought a new modem—for once, not even taking the time to compare prices.

Back home, it took me longer than I would have liked to get the new hardware installed and operational, but within thirty minutes I was online and surfing. I had uploaded the photos from Harvey's living room into a new folder and alternated between studying them and searching art sites, museum sites, collector sites and auction sites.

I sat back in my chair, stunned. I'd suspected Harvey's collection might be more valuable than it appeared, but I'd had no idea that his unassuming, little tract house contained items worth several hundred thousand dollars. The Degas alone, hung so casually near his fireplace, would likely fetch at least a quarter-million at auction, and the cute, little ballerina doll on the mantel was a Lazenby original—Sotheby's had just sold a Lazenby doll, in much poorer condition than Harvey's, for ninety-six thousands dollars.

While one puzzle piece clicked into place, though, others scattered. Testing the camera with photos of my Escher poster had made me think of the painting at Harvey's house and connect it with the samples of Degas' work I'd studied at the library. It had also led me to surmise that Harvey might have been responsible for stealing the money from Ralph's church safe.

But although Bo had stressed how five thousand dollars was worth a lot more thirty-five years ago, unless Harvey had invested every penny in the equivalent of Apple Computer, I didn't see how he'd gone from a few grand to pushing—if not exceeding—the millionaire mark.

I also wondered why on earth he was living in a section of Lubbock barely above trashy trailer park status.

What was it Cal had told me Harvey Neff did for a living before he retired? Oh, yeah. Real estate.

Back online, I managed to locate the Texas Board of Realtors and several other real estate related websites, but could find no mention of Harvey Neff on any member list. Which told me exactly nothing. I had no way of knowing how long an agent or broker remained on such rosters after leaving the business, and I wasn't sure exactly when Harvey had retired.

But for a six or seven percent sales commission to pull in that kind of wealth, he would have had to sell a few mansions along the way. I stopped myself. So? Maybe he had done just that. Maybe I was way off base. I remembered his dejected slump when I confirmed how much trouble Bo was in, and she, after all, had nothing but good memories of him.

Someone knocked—make that pounded—on my front door, then swung it open without waiting for me to answer.

I'd been wondering if Paula had filled Cal in on the situation with Gertrude yet, and half expected him to be the one barging in to yell at me about my (alleged) break-in at Gertrude's house, but it was Faith who stood wild-eyed in my entryway, her usually impeccably groomed hair disheveled.

"Stay away from Lewis Tucker!" she rasped, then turned on her heel and left.

Chapter Thirteen

I STOOD AT my door, watching her stomp across the street.

Dorothy, shelling peas on her front porch, stared after her guest, who slammed the door so hard it sounded like a gunshot. Setting her bowl aside, Dorothy hurried over to my place.

"What on earth is wrong with that girl?" she demanded.

"I was about to ask you the same thing. C'mon in, and we'll try to figure it out."

I seated her at my kitchen table with a glass of iced tea and started chopping tomatoes for my spaghetti sauce.

"Hand me a knife, child, and I'll dice those onions for you," Dorothy said. "Special dinner for Cal?"

"No, for Lewis Tucker. Speaking of Lewis—why exactly did he and Faith break up? Was it her idea or his?"

"I don't rightly know for sure." Dorothy never lifted her eyes from the onion on the cutting board.

"Don't give me that, Dorothy Stenson. For one thing, you know enough details about folks in Perdue to write a gossip column and, for another, you and Faith were best friends." I dumped a cupful of tomato chunks into a large pot then slid into the chair across from her. "I'm not just being nosy—I'm trying to help Bo."

She sighed. "I still don't know, Taylor, and that's the truth. Faith wouldn't tell me anything about what happened that evening."

"Do you think they had an argument on the night of the prom?" I asked, remembering the torn seam in Faith's dress.

Dorothy shrugged. "Could be. She was sure upset when Lewis dropped her off at my house."

My knife stilled as I thought back to what Keron had said about her mother's aversion to physical contact by men. Faith's dress had been ripped, and she'd been in tears that night. I stared through Dorothy, who was still chopping away. Had Lewis raped her? Or attempted to? He seemed such a nice, intelligent man, but that's what acquaintances said about Ted Bundy, too.

Had Faith's visit to Lewis today been one of confrontation and closure? Rape victims often attempted to conceal the act out of misplaced shame. Did she want me to stay away from Lewis because she was afraid I'd discover her secret?

"I wish I knew what happened that night," I mumbled. "It might be important."

Dorothy stood up and scraped the diced onion into my saucepan. "Okay, you don't have to come up with a way to ask me—I'll find out what I can from Faith." She winked at me knowingly. "But I 'spect you'll be working on Lewis over dinner tonight, too."

I sure would.

SINCE LEWIS WAS clearly an animal lover, I figured he'd get a kick out of meeting Hazel, so I took her along. Loaded down as I was with the full saucepan, an extra pot for the pasta (which I'd cook in his tiny kitchen), a loaf of garlic bread and a Tupperware bowl of green salad, it was tricky climbing the stairs to his apartment.

He apologized as he rolled his chair backwards to allow me entry. "Gosh, Ms. Madison, I didn't mean to cause you so much trouble." His smile was as sweet as ever, but his eyes were wary. I wondered if Faith had said something to him about me. I would have given a lot to know exactly what the two of them talked about—maybe Dorothy would find out.

"Not a problem," I puffed, shoving everything onto a kitchen counter.

He was, indeed, enchanted by Hazel, who immediately climbed into his lap. The same could not be said for Cecilia.

"Cat!" she screamed the moment her beady eyes alighted on Hazel. "Cat! Cat!"

I went to her perch and stroked her, smoothing the ruffled feathers. "Calm down, sweetheart."

Hazel made a chittering noise and Cecilia's white comb twitched forward.

"See?" I said. "Ca—um, those animals you don't like say meow. Hazel doesn't say meow, does she?"

Cecilia cocked her head doubtfully, but at least she stopped screeching. Nigel meandered out from beneath the day bed where he'd been napping, stretched, and gazed inquiringly at Hazel (who probably looked, through cat eyes, like an overfed rat). My flicker of alarm didn't last long. With a final glance at the uninvited visitor, Nigel bounded up onto a padded window seat, curled into a large ball, and went back to sleep.

"He's learned to live and let live," Lewis said.

"Glad to hear it, and I'll bet Hazel is, too."

I put a pot of water on to boil for the pasta, then produced a small jug of chianti from the depths of my backpack and encouraged Lewis to have a nip before dinner.

Patience is not among my dubious virtues, but I forced myself to exercise it, hoping a full tummy and sufficient wine might make the questions I needed to ask more palatable.

Lewis ate like a man just rescued from a desert island, requesting seconds of the spaghetti and thirds of the bread. I wondered if the poor guy lived on Spam and Ritz crackers, but discovered a hint of exasperation seeping through my sympathy. Bo was right, however harshly she'd stated her opinion. Lewis' prison was of his own making. He had free access to the outside world and the arm muscles to propel his chair to any corner of it—at least to Lucy's Café now and again for a decent meal.

I poured the last of the chianti into his tumbler and let him sip as I tidied the kitchen. Gazing at him as I dried my hands, I thought, *Mellow or not, here I come.*

"So what brought Faith here this afternoon?" I asked, sitting down across from him and getting to the point with swift bluntness. "Did you know she was in town? I'll bet it was a surprise when she turned up on your doorstep after all these years, wasn't it?"

He blinked, and I could almost see the rapid series of questions buzzing confusedly around his head like a swarm of drunken bees.

"Yes," he said. "Uh, I mean, no. I didn't know she was in Perdue, and—"

"Y'all were quite an item back in high school, or so I hear," I continued before he could sort out his response. "It's a shame you broke up, but that happens a lot with teenage romances."

"I guess so."

"What made you break up?" I leaned forward, inviting confidentiality. "Another girl?"

"Huh? No!"

"Oh. Another guy then."

He started to shake his head, but stopped.

"It *was* another guy? Damn, that must've hurt. When did she tell you? On prom night?"

He backed his chair away a little. "What makes you say that?"

"Heck, Lewis, you know how small towns are. Gossip has it that y'all were fighting on prom night."

"We weren't fighting. Who told you that we were?"

"I saw the dress she wore that night, and a seam was ripped." I held his gaze. "Lewis, did you rape her?"

"What? God, no!"

"The dress was torn and she was very upset—"

"You've got to believe me. I would never have done something like that! I was in love with Faith. I wanted to marry her."

He was on the verge of tears and I found that I really did believe him. "Okay, Lewis, sorry. I'd just heard something that made me think...so how did her dress get torn?"

"It was an accident." He rubbed his eyes like a child in need of a nap. "I...I grabbed her shoulder. I was just trying to make her look at me. She was crying."

"Because she was dumping you for someone else?"

"No, she didn't dump me."

"But you said there was another guy."

He lowered his head and I saw a tear trickle down his cheek. "Damn him. She's still such a mess, even all these years later. How could a grown man do that to a seventeen-year-old girl?"

This was turning in a direction I hadn't expected, and I found myself as confused as Lewis was, despite having indulged in only a few sips of wine.

"What man, Lewis? Did he—?"

"She wouldn't tell me who. She was babbling and I couldn't make sense out of half the things she said. But, yeah, someone raped her."

He went silent after that, and I decided it was time for me to leave him alone. My mind was racing, and I couldn't face going home to an empty house, so I drove around Perdue for a bit.

"You like him, don't you, Hazel?" I asked her as she curled up in the empty spaghetti pot and yawned. "So do I. But I can't help feeling there's something he's not telling me."

I found myself cruising past the old Tucker mansion. I'd learned that it had been partitioned into several apartment units, since obviously no one in Perdue could afford to maintain it as a single residence. With light blazing through most of the windows and cars parked neatly on an asphalt lot that had replaced most of the front lawn, it looked like a nice place to live.

But I wondered what kind of home it might have been for a little boy. Did he revel in the space, playing pirate on the widow's walk and knight in the turret? Or did the vast expanses make him feel small and lonely? At least he'd had a mother like Dinah. I had no doubt she'd been the type who would have listened to childhood woes, suggested rainy-day games, read fairy tales aloud at bedtime. I wondered if he had talked to her about his prom date with Faith. Would a seventeen-year-old boy approach his mother with problems of that nature, or would he consider himself man enough to handle it on his own? Would he try to find out who the rapist was and seek vengeance, or would he...

My mouth dropped open.

Ten minutes later, I was pounding on Lewis's door.

"Not to be rude, Ms. Madison, but please go away," he said when he saw me. "I'm tired and—"

I ignored him. "It was Ralph, wasn't it?"

He looked at me for a moment, then his head drooped and he turned the chair around.

I followed him inside. "Lewis?"

"Yes," he said.

"She told you?"

"She didn't have to. I was smart enough to put everything together." He wheeled himself into a corner near his front window, as if retreating to a safe cocoon.

"What did you put together?" I asked, sitting cross-legged on the floor in front of him.

"She was always trying to avoid her father," he said. "Yeah, I know he was crazy and all, but the night of the prom I figured out she had more reason than that. She asked me to pick her up after school and drive her out to Dorothy's to get ready for the dance, and I said I would. Then my mother asked me to run a couple of errands, so I called Faith and told her she'd have to get ready at home and I'd pick her up there.

"She went ballistic. I mean it, Ms. Madison. She started yelling about how she couldn't get dressed at home. I thought that was weird at the time, but she was so frantic I finally just begged off Mom's errands and went to get her." He shot me a puzzled look. "How did you figure all this out?"

"After I left here tonight, I drove by and looked at the Tucker mansion, and it dawned on me that you must have gone to confront Ralph after you dropped Faith off at Dorothy's house. From what Doc told me, you smashed up your car somewhere between the Posey ranch and Perdue's city limits, and since your parents' old house is on the opposite side of Perdue, you couldn't have been on your way home." I reached to touch his hand. "Lewis, did you kill Ralph?"

"No!"

"But—"

"Look, you're right. I went out there, and yeah, I might've hit him or something. I was sure mad enough. Mostly, though, I went to tell him that I was taking Faith away, and if he tried to come after us, I'd turn him in for what he'd done. Then when I got there, I...I chickened out." He hung his head. "I know how cowardly that sounds, but he was a scary man. I decided I'd just take Faith and leave without sayin' anything to him at all."

"But you never made it home." I chewed on a fingernail, a childhood habit that reasserts itself when I've gone too long without nicotine. "So after all that, why did you and Faith break up?"

He was silent for a moment, gazing down at his legs.

"Oh, I get it," I said grimly. "Male pride. The old I-don't-want-to-saddle-her-with-half-a-man routine."

"You're right, I didn't."

"But you'd been so determined to take her away."

"By the time I came out of the coma, Ralph was gone. She was safe from him, so I didn't have to worry. I...I knew she could do better for herself."

"She still needed you, Lewis, especially after what she'd been through. Did it never occur to you that she'd think you'd thrown her away because she'd been violated and was somehow unworthy of you?" I got to my feet and stood glaring down at him. "I swear, sometimes I think testosterone is a stupidity drug."

Chapter Fourteen

PULLING INTO MY own driveway, I spotted Cal on the front porch. Sprawled in one wicker chair with his booted feet propped in the other one, his Stetson was tipped low over his eyes and, as I approached, I heard snores issuing from beneath its brim.

My hands were full, so I kicked him. Gently, of course.

He tipped the hat back and stretched, peering up at me.

"You have a key, you numbskull," I reminded him.

"Just thought I'd enjoy the night air," he said through a yawn. "Didn't intend to doze off."

Standing up, he eyed my collection of kitchenware. "You've been cooking," he accused in the same tone he'd use to someone he caught shoplifting.

"Yes, I have."

"You never cook for me."

"Cal, this is a fascinating subject, but could we discuss it at a later time? This stuff's heavy, and Hazel is scratching the back of my neck because she wants down. I'm afraid she's about to use my backpack for a potty."

"Sorry." He dug my spare key from his pocket and opened the door, then relieved me of half my burden. "Gossip has it that you lock your doors because you don't want anyone coming in and reading your racy manuscripts."

"Racy?" I sprinted for the kitchen, threw everything down, and planted Hazel in her litter box.

"Yeah, you know—heaving bosoms and shirtless men."

I stared at him. "Whose novels have they been reading? I've never heaved a bosom in my life, either in person or on paper."

"Doesn't matter. You're our local celebrity, and what's a celebrity without myth?"

"I guess someone's gotta keep the supermarket tabloids in business," I muttered. "Want some coffee?"

"Sure." He watched me wrestle the tin pot into submission and adjust the burner's flame. "It's later."

"What?" I was rummaging in the pantry for powdered creamer, having discovered that the milk in my fridge smelled like day-old road kill.

"You were going to explain 'later' why you cooked for someone else when you never cook for me."

"Because I love you," I said absently, still shuffling through the pantry's cans and jars in search of the elusive creamer.

The words echoed in my ears, and it slowly sank in what I'd uttered.

"What did you say?" Cal sounded as stunned as I felt.

My cheeks grew hot, and I avoided turning to face him right away.

"You're a nice guy," I said with feigned lightness. "I'd hate to take a chance on poisoning you."

I heard his chair scrape back along the linoleum, felt his hands on my shoulders.

"Taylor?"

Was it trepidation or longing that I heard in his voice? I was afraid to look into his eyes.

"I love you, too," he said, so tenderly that my heart did a little flip as he spun me around and pulled me into his arms.

SOMETIMES I FANCY that God must have rigged a gargantuan magnifying glass over the state of Texas, because—to paraphrase the song lyrics—the stars here at night do seem bigger and brighter. Out away from the city lights, they almost shed enough light to read by. Almost. I squinted at my notes and wished I'd thought to grab the flashlight from my bedside table drawer.

Indian summer's reprieve was waning, and I shivered despite my robe and slippers as I sat on the back steps and smoked.

"Do you know what time it is?" grumbled Cal's sleepy voice from the darkness of the kitchen behind me.

I smiled. "About two a.m., I think."

He sat down beside me, all warm and rumpled from my bed, and slid an arm around my shoulders.

"I love you," he said for what must have been the seventy-sixth time since the dam had broken and those amazing words had first rushed out.

"I love you, too," I told him, wondering if the tingle in the pit of my stomach was now a permanent condition.

He kissed my earlobe, the nape of my neck, my shoulder.

"I really don't want you to stop," I murmured, "but we need to talk."

"Yeah, we do," he agreed. "That's why I came over in the first place. Wasn't expecting to get seduced."

"Who seduced whom?"

"Does it matter?" His lips found mine and, for a moment, nothing at all mattered.

"Wait," I said suddenly, pushing him away. "I have a bone to pick with you."

"Well, I've never heard it called that," he drawled, "but whatever you say. Does this variation involve handcuffs? I happen to have a pair with me..."

I scooted away from him a little. "Matter of fact, it might involve handcuffs, since we're discussing a pair of cops. What's the deal with Molly?"

"Huh? Molly Sullivan?"

"How many Mollies do you know?"

He leaned back on his elbows, studying the sky. "What about her?"

"Stop being coy with me, Arnette. I know you've been seeing a lot of her lately. Damn, I didn't mean to phrase it quite like that..."

"You're jealous." He sounded so pleased I wanted to swat him.

"I'm not jealous. I'm...I'm curious."

"Curious?"

"Make that concerned. Annoyed, even." I struggled for composure. "After all, a good friend of ours is up to her neck in a mound of bullshit, and you're supposed to be helping her, not running off to Lubbock every five seconds for a quickie with some female cop. Is it the uniform? I still have my badge from when I was a temporary deputy, you know."

I realized I was babbling and shut up.

Cal turned his head to look at me, and the emotion I saw in his warm, brown eyes brought a lump to my throat.

"It's sorta nice that you're jealous," he said softly. "And I'll admit I'm tempted to tease you so I can have the fun of watching you get your dander up. But this is too important." He took my hands. "I've waited a long time to hear those three words come out of your mouth, and I'm not gonna screw it up.

"Molly's been helping me with the case. We've been tryin' various methods of detecting any prints that might have been left on that shovel handle after the mud dried—no luck, so far.

"We've also contacted a couple of experts to examine the skull, hoping to determine the direction and force of the shovel's impact. Still waitin' on the results, but fingers crossed that we can throw a hitch into the prosecution's case, if it comes to that. If an expert can testify that the fatal blow was made by someone taller than Bo, or left-handed instead of right, then the defense'll have a good shot at reasonable doubt."

"Oh, Cal." I couldn't say more past the lump in my throat. I knew very well what a fine and dangerous line he was treading. It's not a cop's job to try and prove innocence or guilt—that's the defense attorney's venue—and I shuddered to think how fast Cal would lose his badge if Underwood or Burke found out what he'd been up to.

"Molly's also been advising me about fitting out Derrick County's S.O. with a decent crime scene kit, and she's making a list of forensic classes our deputies need to attend," Cal concluded. "That, Taylor, is the sum total of my relationship with Sergeant Sullivan."

A knot in the area of my heart dissolved into dancing sunbeams. "Really?" I asked meekly.

"Really. Now, what about you and Zorro the magnificent editor?"

"You're just pretending to be jealous so I won't feel so stupid, aren't you?"

"Sure. That's why I put a rattlesnake in his suggestion box."

"You didn't!"

His lips twitched. "I did. Don't worry. It was dead. Flat, too—I found it out on the highway. Made it right easy to slip the critter through the little slot."

I had to laugh, imagining Jesse's face when he discovered that particular suggestion. "God, Cal, how old *are* you? Twelve?"

"Nah, at least thirteen. I didn't like girls yet when I was twelve." He shrugged. "Hey, it was a legitimate suggestion."

"How do you figure?"

"I was suggestin' he stretch out on the highway and wait for an eighteen-wheeler." He helped me to my feet and led me into the kitchen, switching on a light. "How about some hot chocolate?"

"If you're making it."

"Since your milk's gone sour, I'll have to use this instant stuff." He lit a burner and put the kettle on to boil while I retrieved mugs.

We sat down across from each other at the table, and I saw my lover transform into a cop just as surely as if he'd taken off one costume and donned another.

"About Gertrude Mason," he began in a deceptively soft voice, and then I was subjected to a blistering account of the penalties awaiting those who break and enter.

"I didn't break in," I protested. "Her door was standing wide open."

"Obviously, you need to study up on the Texas Penal Code," he drawled.

"Okay, okay. I give up. Slap the cuffs on me, Deputy."

I glimpsed Cal-the-lover in his eye for a brief second, but he visibly shook the thought away. "This is serious, Taylor."

"I know." I also knew what his response would be if I told him about my little ploy that had gained me entrance into Harvey Neff's living room. "If you're through yelling at me regarding my methods, let's talk about my results."

He took a sip of cocoa. "Results?"

"C'mon, if Paula told you about my...er...visit to Gertrude's house, she told you what I found out. So?"

"So?"

"Damn it, Cal, you sound like Cecilia."

"Who?"

"Forget it, let's stick to the subject. What did Gertrude say when you confronted her?"

"Confronted her with what? Gossip? Because that's all this is, Taylor. So she had a kid out of wedlock—"

"Ralph Posey's kid!" I reminded him. "Didn't Paula show you the picture?"

"Yeah, but that's hardly a crime. We don't arrest folks for moral turpitude anymore, you know."

"But it gave her a motive to kill him," I protested.

"Look, I haven't been sitting on my hands here, I've been asking questions. From what I've been told, Gertrude Mason thought—and still thinks—that Ralph Posey gave the Almighty a hand when He was constructing the universe. She was probably convinced that being pregnant by Reverend Perfect was an honor, and expected to deliver the Second Coming into the world."

I couldn't argue with that. "Okay, then, if not Gertrude, then what about Duke Mason?"

He shook his head. "Paula filled me in on that little theory, too. So Duke Mason murdered a local minister in order to protect his sister's reputation? Pretty lame."

"Maybe in this day and age, but back then—"

"Back then he might've run Posey out of town or, less dramatic, suggested that he leave. But more likely he would've sent Sis off to relatives so she could give birth without the prying eyes of Perdue watching the process. And from what I understand, that's exactly what happened."

"So explain why he conducted such a half-assed investigation into Ralph's disappearance."

"It's possible I just did explain that. He was glad to see Ralph gone, so why waste manpower to find him? Maybe he even figured that Ralph had left because of Gertrude's situation. He sure wouldn't have wanted to put that in his report, so he just wrote up what he had to for the record and let the rest slide."

"I hate it when you're logical to the point of idiocy."

He grunted. "You're callin' me an idiot now?"

"Yes. No. I'm just frustrated. I think you're only seeing the surface, and you think I'm digging too deep."

Cal reached to take my hand. "I'm sorry, hon. I know how worried you are about Bo, but linin' up false suspects isn't going to help her. You can speculate all you want to, but it's gonna come down to evidence, and I'm sorry to say that, so far, all the evidence in this case points to Bo Posey. Besides," he added, "there's something you're not considering."

"What's that?"

"If Bo knew that another woman was carryin' Ralph's child, seems to me that makes her motive for killing him even stronger."

I laid my head down on the table like a tired little girl in nursery school who needs a nap, considering whether to tell him about Harvey Neff's unexplained wealth and about Lewis's hatred of Ralph Posey.

"Look, I'll find a way to talk to Gertrude if it'll make you feel any better. Who knows? Maybe you're onto somethin'. But for now, let's go back to bed."

CAL WAS GONE by the time I woke up the next morning. A wilted morning glory rested on his pillow, alongside a note. "Later" was all it said, but he'd drawn a heart next to the word. My own heart did a little leap.

In the cold light of day, I was glad I'd resisted the temptation to tell him about Lewis's revelation. He might suggest that, if Bo had known about what Ralph did to Faith, she would had motive to spare for murdering her husband. I sighed. Cal, unfortunately, was right about one thing. Every shred of new evidence that I uncovered pointed more firmly to Bo.

A glance at the clock informed me that I had overslept. Only twenty-four hours remained before the hanging judge got back to town and signed the warrant for Bo's arrest. For a moment, I felt like I was living in a bad Italian western, and almost picked up the phone to call and tell Bo she might oughta catch the noon stage out of town.

I made coffee, fed Hazel, then sat down to think. While sipping my third mug of caffeine and smoking my second cigarette of the morning, I came to a decision. Hazel climbed into my lap and watched me dial the phone.

"Bo, has your new truck been delivered yet? Good. No, you don't have to tell me about it, you can show me. I need for you and Keron to get over here right away. It's important."

I hung up on her questions and went to throw on jeans and a sweatshirt, then spent the next fifteen minutes on my porch, watching Dorothy's car across the street to make sure Faith didn't take off in it. If necessary, I was willing to throw myself in its path.

Bo and her granddaughter arrived in a shiny, royal blue Chevy pickup, which Bo parked haphazardly across the dying grass in my front yard.

"Ain't she a beaut'?" she crowed as she jumped down from the high cab as easily as a girl of fifteen might have done.

Keron made use of the fold-down step on the passenger side and alighted more gracefully. "What's up, Taylor?" she asked immediately, scanning my face like someone examining a nasty thundercloud.

"Come on, both of you." I gripped Keron's hand and Bo's upper arm and marched both of them across the street.

"What the hell?" Bo sputtered, trying to pry herself loose when she saw where we were headed.

"Stop it," I ordered. "This is long overdue."

Not willing to release my hold on either of them, I tapped on the door's base with the toe of my Reebok. Inside, Misty started yapping.

"Taylor, damn it—"

"Shut up, Bo," I said.

Dorothy opened the door and looked pleased to see me for an instant before her gaze took in my companions.

"Excuse me, Dorothy," I said and brushed past her, my captives still in tow and Bo still cursing. "Where's Faith?"

"Why, she's...she's in the kitchen," Dorothy stammered, snatching Misty up from the vicinity of our trampling feet.

Again using my foot, and feeling like a S.W.A.T. team member with a battering ram, I pushed through the swinging door that led to Dorothy's kitchen.

Faith, still in her sleepwear and looking bleary-eyed, was hunched over a cup of coffee. Her eyes widened as I stormed into the room, then hardened when she saw Bo. She stood abruptly, catching her sleeve on the saucer and sending brown liquid cascading over the table's edge.

Letting go of Keron, but maintaining my grip on Bo's arm, I grabbed the belt of Faith's robe before she could bolt out the back door.

"Don't even think about it," I growled. "Sit. All of you. Dorothy, stop eavesdropping and come on in. I owe you that much, since I'm turning your house into a battleground."

The women sat, each wearing a different expression. Dorothy looked baffled, Bo nervous, Faith rabid. Keron appeared rather pleased.

There were only four chairs in the kitchen, so I perched on a countertop and lit a cigarette.

"Don't worry, Dorothy, I'll flick ashes into the sink," I said. "Okay, time for a poll. How many of you have watched daytime soap operas? Let's have a show of hands. C'mon now, don't be embarrassed. We've all taken a peek at them."

Three hands went up. Faith crossed her arms and continued to glare at me.

"Fine. Three admit it, and one is playing deaf. Personally, I get a kick out of some of the soaps, but there's one thing that's always bugged me about their storylines. Have you ever noticed that ninety-eight percent of the plot conflicts could be resolved—or even avoided entirely—if the characters would only talk to each other?"

Keron tried to hide a smile.

"So that's what we're gonna do right now," I informed them. "This has gone beyond ridiculous."

Faith shoved back her chair. "I don't have to listen to this lunacy."

"Interesting word choice," I said, "coming from someone who's lived on the edge of lunacy for thirty plus years. Must've been tough to lead a normal life with that terrible memory lurking in the recesses of your mind."

"I don't know what you're talking about!" she snapped, but her voice quivered a little and she stayed seated.

"I'll get to that in a minute." I dunked my cigarette butt in a cup of soapy water in the sink, then tossed it into Dorothy's wastebasket. "Ladies, we're fixing to let a few cats out of their bags, spill some moldy beans, and free skeletons from dark closets. In other words, no more secrets."

Bo lit a Camel with hands that trembled, but her voice was steady. "Go ahead, Taylor. I have a feelin' this is long overdue."

"Fine, Bo, then I'll start with you. Were you aware that Ralph cheated on you?"

Dorothy and Keron gasped, but Bo did the last thing I would have expected. She laughed.

"I may've been a little naïve back then," she said, "but my mama didn't raise no fool. Sure, I knew."

Keron gaped at her grandmother. "Who in her right mind would have sex with that awful man?" She pressed a hand to her mouth. "Oops! Sorry, Grandma, no offense."

"None taken, child. As to who, I'd have to make a list. For some reason, women found him sexy as all get out."

"One of his conquests was Gertrude Mason," I said. "And he got her pregnant."

Again, a series of gasps followed by laughter from Bo.

"Remember what I told you, Taylor—to be fruitful and multiply was Ralph's sole reason for indulging in the dirty deed. He sure as hell didn't get any pleasure out of the act itself. Took a scalding hot bath right after we got done every single time. Washing away the sinfulness of the filthy act, he said. Well, however he managed it, I'll bet Gertie was ecstatic to be blessed with carryin' the sacred fetus."

For the first time, Faith really looked at her mother. "Good Lord, how many women bore children for that demented man? Are you saying I might have more than one half-sibling out there?"

"Not likely. Ralph's will was a lot stronger than his way, if you get my drift. I reckon a doctor these days would figure out he had a low sperm count. Back then, all I knew was that it took him almost more tryin' than I could endure for him to get me with child."

I caught on. "Then all those other women—"

"Most of 'em were one night stands. I 'spect they woke up the mornin' after and high-tailed it back to their own husbands, wonderin' what on earth had possessed 'em. Didn't take long for Ralph's charm to wear thin." She shook her head. "Poor Gertie, though, she was different."

"Yeah," I said. "It wouldn't have been the sex that attracted Gertrude, but procreation in its purest form. For that matter, she might even have come to believe that it was Immaculate Conception."

"Wouldn't be surprised," Bo agreed.

I took a deep breath, regretting the pain my next words would cause. "Then I don't understand, unless his warped version of the Bible called for impregnating his own daughter, why he forced himself on Faith."

Dorothy clutched her chest, Keron's eyes threatened to pop from their sockets, Bo's mouth dropped open, and Faith shot to her feet.

"What?" It was a unified shout.

Bo reached for her daughter. "Oh, darlin', is that true? Why didn't you tell me? I would've torn that bastard's arms off and beat him to death with the bloody stumps!"

Faith jerked away from her mother's touch, her lip curled as if she'd encountered something slimy. She turned on me.

"You've lost your mind," she spat. "I'd have killed that pig myself before I let him lay a hand on me."

Bo's shoulders slumped in relief. "Thank God."

Faith whirled to face her, her cheeks purple with fury. "You hypocritical bitch! You have the gall to sit there and pretend concern after what you did to me?"

Bo stared at her for a moment then, quick as lightning, slapped her. Hard.

"You've got no call to speak to me that way," she said in a low voice. "I loved and protected you from the time I knew you were growin' inside me, and I've never done anything to warrant the way you've treated me all these years." She looked around at the rest of us. "I'll tell y'all again that I did not murder my husband, but if I'd thought for one second that he was hurtin' my daughter with more than his hateful words, I would've."

I was feeling like an actor who finds out mid-scene that the script has been rewritten. "So Lewis was wrong?"

Still rubbing her cheek, Faith narrowed her eyes at me. "What does Lewis have to do with this? I warned you to leave him alone."

"Yeah, and I ignored you. The two of us had dinner together last night. Sorry, Faith, no more secrets, remember?" I filled all of them in on what Lewis had told me. When I was finished, complete silence reigned for several minutes.

"He thought I was raped by my own father?" Faith's voice came out in a squeak. "No wonder he..." She stopped.

I jumped in. "No wonder he what? Damn it, Faith, now isn't the time to clam up. What exactly did you tell Lewis that night? Where did you get that silk dress? And why are you so mad at your mother?"

Faith cast a wild look about her as if she were an animal in a cage, being prodded through the bars by people wielding pointed sticks.

"Somebody give me a cigarette," she said, finally. "I quit smoking fifteen years ago, but I sure need one now. And Dorothy, dig the last bottle of wine out of my suitcase."

Chapter Fifteen

"I KNEW THAT Lewis went to see my father that night. He told me he was going to, and I couldn't talk him out of it." Faith took a mouthful of wine and poured more into her glass before she'd even swallowed. "And as far as I know, Taylor, he went for the reason he told you—to tell Ralph that he was taking me away from Perdue."

"But if Ralph didn't rape you..." I halted. "Look, let's start at the beginning. Why were you so frantic for Lewis to take you to Dorothy's house so you could dress there? He was sure it was because you were afraid to change clothes with Ralph around."

"I didn't want Ralph to know I was going to the dance. He wouldn't have approved, and might even have locked me in my room to stop me. And he would've demanded to know where I got a silk dress—a pink one, no less, not virginal white."

"So where *did* you get it?"

"Ma knows," she said. "Don't you, Ma? He was generous with his gifts, wasn't he?"

Bo gaped at her daughter as if she was an alien being who had landed in the midst of our mad tea party.

"Who?" I croaked, since no one else seemed able to.

"The man she set me up with," Faith replied. "Harvey Neff."

"Harvey? Set you up? Child, what on earth are you saying?" Bo's mouth kept moving even after the words stopped coming out.

"Oh, come off it, Ma." Faith gave a hiccup and looked accusingly at her wine glass. "He told me all about the arrangement."

"Why don't you fill the rest of us in?" I suggested, since Bo hadn't yet regained her power of speech.

Faith giggled a little, caught on a wave of fermented grapes. "Was it good for you, Ma? Can't say it was good for me."

Bo started shaking her head, and kept shaking it until I was afraid it would separate from her neck and roll across the floor.

"Faith, you're not making sense," I said.

"Did you feel like a pimp, Ma? Did you take money from him, or just sex and presents? He never said."

Bo found her voice. "Harvey Neff was...having sex with you?"

"With your permission, of course. Not with mine, but I guess that didn't matter."

The rest of us stared at each other in utter disbelief.

"You thought...you *think* I would prostitute my seventeen-year-old daughter?" Bo looked as if someone had kicked her in the stomach. "That's what he told you?" I heard her ancient knee joints protesting as she knelt by her daughter's chair and took Faith's face into her gnarled hands. "Never, do you hear me? I would never do such a thing. He tricked you, Faith."

Faith pulled away a little, but maintained eye contact with her mother. "I saw you with him."

"Honey, we need to talk this out." Bo glanced at the rest of us.

I beckoned to the others. "Let's leave them alone for a few minutes."

We staggered out into Dorothy's backyard like shell-shocked veterans. Keron sat down on a low-growing branch of a big mulberry tree, and stared into the middle distance.

"Some shrink I am," she murmured. "Why didn't sexual assault ever occur to me?"

"I can't believe that man was forcin' himself on her," Dorothy said. "We were best friends. We told each other everything, but she never said a word."

"That dress," I said suddenly. "Damn, I should've put it together. The ruffle of netting at the hips. Remember, Dorothy? Like a tutu."

Both women looked at me as if I'd gone completely around the bend.

"I'll explain later," I said. "Meanwhile, there are still some questions to be answered, so I'll give mother and daughter five more minutes and then I have to break it up."

"MAMA AND I have talked it out...some," Faith said as we came back inside. "But I think I owe all of you an explanation." She laid her head on Bo's shoulder. "Harvey had been working on me for months before he raped me. It all started when something happened at school—I don't remember what exactly, most likely a kid picking on me. That afternoon, I ran over to the church. Mama was supposed to be there pricing items for a rummage sale, but she'd gone somewhere.

"Harvey was there, though, and when he saw I'd been crying, he took me into his office, brought me lemonade and Kleenex. We talked for a long time." She gave a bitter smile. "He seemed to understand. Not only about the teasing at school, but about how weird Ralph was. It helped at the time."

"Harvey was a good listener, all right," Bo said sourly, and I remembered how she'd told me about all the times she had cried on his shoulder.

"He was so nice, and so handsome." Faith blushed. "He told me I was the prettiest girl he'd ever seen. Graceful and elegant, he said, like a ballerina."

"Aha!" I shouted, and everyone looked at me. "Sorry. Go on, Faith."

"I talked to him a lot after that, and when he said he'd get me a part time job at the radio station, I thought I'd gone to heaven. Not only because it meant I'd finally have a little money of my own, but because I'd be working with him three times a week."

"So you thought you'd fallen in love with him," I said gently.

"No," she interrupted. "No, it wasn't like that at all. I liked Harvey at first because he was easy to talk to and he made me feel like I was worth something, but that's all. I'd been in love with Lewis for half my life, even before he knew I existed, and I still loved him with all my heart."

Keron chimed in again. "Harvey was a substitute father figure. All children want their parents to love them, but Ralph wasn't capable of normal emotions, so you looked for that kind of fatherly love in Harvey. Which," she added under her breath, "may also be why you married Daddy."

Faith gazed at her. "My daughter, the shrink. That does make sense, I guess."

"Why didn't you tell me?" Dorothy wanted to know. "We were best buddies."

"Dot, you don't know how many times I nearly told you, but I was too ashamed."

"Which is the most effective weapon in an abuser's arsenal," Keron muttered. "Shame. It cuts their victims off from those who could provide help. But, Mother, what did Grandma have to do with any of this?"

Faith took a deep breath. "One evening, right after we'd finished a broadcast, Harvey pulled me into a vacant office at the radio station and locked the door. He had a present for me, and said I could wear it home under my clothes so Ralph wouldn't know."

"I'll bet it was a tutu," I put in.

She stared at me. "How on earth did you know that?"

"Long story."

"Yes, it was a tutu. A white one with sequins. I was delighted.

Harvey had been telling me for weeks that I should take dance lessons, and he'd pretty much convinced me. I'd even been saving my pay from the radio station so I could sign up at a class in Lubbock. Then he told me to try it on so he could make sure it fit me, and I realized he expected me to strip right there in front of him.

"I got scared and tried to get out of the room, but the key was in his pocket." She squeezed her eyes shut in remembered horror. "I don't have to go into detail about what happened next, do I?"

"No," Bo said, tears rolling down her face.

"Afterward," Faith went on, her voice trembling, "I was curled up in a ball on the floor, crying for Mama. Harvey snarled at me to get up and quit acting like a baby. 'Your mama knows all about it,' he said. 'Matter of fact, it was her idea. She wanted you to learn sex isn't dirty and sinful like your daddy's always tellin' you, and she knows from experience that I'd make a good teacher.'"

Bo's lips were set in an angry line. "That lyin' sack of donkey shit."

"I thought he was lying, too, at first. But he drove me home and told me to go up to my room and watch out the window. I did, and a little while later I saw him walk you out to the edge of the garden and take you in his arms. The two of you kissed for a long time. Then he gave you a little box, tied with ribbon." She looked at her mother.

"So you thought he was carryin' on with me and that I didn't mind if he had you, too. Is that it? Faith, darlin', how could you believe that?"

"I didn't know what to believe, I was so confused. I'm sorry, Mama."

She clutched her mother's hand and Bo leaned over to kiss her cheek. "Honey, you were just a little girl."

"I was seventeen," Faith countered bitterly.

"Mother, you were a shy, insecure child," Keron put in firmly. "One whose father made her dress in rags while he spouted dire warnings about sin from morning 'til night, and refused to allow any semblance of a normal social life. You didn't even have television for a reference to the outside world. Honestly, I'm amazed you didn't end up in a padded cell."

"Maybe that would have been a good place for me," Faith said glumly. "I was certainly crazy to fall for Harvey's lies." She tried to shrug it off. "After the first time, it got easier."

Bo looked like she'd just been kicked in the stomach. "The first time? You mean he kept on doin' it?"

"Yes, but after that first rape, my feelings went...numb. He always gave me a present afterward, and the awful truth is that, eventually, I started looking at it as just another job."

"Rationalization," Keron said. "A natural coping mechanism. It probably helped you maintain your sanity."

Faith lifted her chin. "Well, I never let him do it again after the night of the prom. Maybe Lewis coming so close to death snapped me out of whatever trance Harvey had me in, but I just quit my job and ran the other way if I saw him coming, which is what I should've done in the first place. I know, Keron...you don't have to say it. When we get home, I'll let you recommend a good psychologist."

Dorothy's kitchen clock told me that morning had scurried into afternoon.

"Excuse me," I said. "The two of you have a lot of cobwebs to clear, but I'm afraid we don't have time for the dusting process right now. Faith, earlier when we were talking about Lewis, you said something about understanding why he'd...why he'd what?"

She lowered her eyes.

"Faith, please! I'm sure when you woke up this morning, the thought of Bo going to prison didn't bother you, but you don't want that now."

"Of course not."

"Then start by telling me what happened the night of the prom."

"Lewis picked me up here," Faith began. "He looked so gorgeous in his tux, I almost died. Remember, Dorothy?"

Dorothy smiled. "He made my date look like a warthog by comparison, I remember. I was so jealous."

Faith's voice grew dreamy. "Funny thing. I know it was only a smelly high school gymnasium decorated with glitter paint and crepe paper, but that night it was fairyland and I was Cinderella. For hours, I didn't even think about Harvey or—" She glanced at her mother. "—anything. Lewis held me in his arms and we danced and nothing else mattered."

She took a small sip of wine. "After the dance, Lewis drove me out to Simm's Lane. Which, by the way, is exactly what I'd hoped he'd do. Harvey gave me that pink dress, specifically for the prom. He seemed to get a kick out of the thought of me acting like a typical high school senior, out for an evening with my beau. One of the reasons I was so determined to wear that dress—even though I hated the man who gave it to me—was so I could look my best for Lewis. I was hoping he'd propose to me that night."

"I can understand that," Keron said. "Marriage probably seemed the perfect escape from the hell your life had become."

"But I really did love Lewis, you know," Faith said softly. "And everything was going fine until he kissed me. Suddenly, it was Harvey's mouth on mine, and I felt like I was being smothered. I screamed at him to stop."

Keron patted her mother's hand.

"Lewis didn't understand why I was pushing him away, and I didn't want to explain it. I was afraid of what he'd think of me, afraid I'd lose him. But he kept asking and refused to drive me home until I told him what was going on." She gave a shuddering sigh. "I was pretty hysterical by that time, and I started blurting things out.

"I really have no idea what I said. I know I was struggling not to tell him too much. All of a sudden, he got this odd look on his face and told me not to worry, that he'd take care of everything. Then he drove me back to Dorothy's."

"You were so upset," Dorothy recalled. "But you wouldn't talk to me at all."

"Lewis said he was going to tell Ralph we were eloping. God, that scared me to death. Ralph was barely hanging onto sanity by a thread, and I didn't know what he might do to Lewis." She looked at me, clearly troubled. "Taylor, if what you say is true—if Lewis really got the idea Ralph was the one who was forcing me to have sex..."

She couldn't bring herself to finish that sentence, so I did it for her. "You think Lewis killed Ralph."

Her eyes filled with tears, but she nodded.

I jumped down off the counter. "Well, there's only one way to find out."

"I'm coming with you," Faith said quietly, and I didn't argue.

THE OTHERS CLAMORED to go along, but I made them stay put. Keron took me aside while her mother was changing out of her robe.

"Taylor, I don't think this is a good idea," she said in a low voice. "If the man really is a killer, it's foolish for you and Mother to confront him alone."

"Not to be cruel, Keron, but what's he going to do? Run us over with his wheelchair?"

"He could have a gun or something," she insisted.

"I doubt it. Look, we'll be careful, okay? But if it makes you feel any better, you can call Cal if we're not back in an hour."

"Thirty minutes," she countered.

"Forty-five."

Still looking worried, she waved from the porch as Faith and I started off down the street in my Volkswagen.

"I'm curious about something," I told Faith, who was gazing blankly out the window. "Why did you go to see Lewis yesterday?"

"To get an answer," she said.

"What was the question?"

She leaned back in her seat with a sigh. "After his accident, I tried every day to visit him in the hospital, but Harvey was always there." She frowned. "I never figured out why. Harvey wasn't exactly Mr. Compassion. Anyway, after Lewis was finally able to go home, I kept calling and stopping by, but he refused to see me. His parents made excuses, like he was resting or he was in pain, but I knew they were only trying to spare my feelings because his other friends went over all the time."

"Let me guess. When you asked him about it yesterday, he told you that he broke things off with you for your own good—so you wouldn't be stuck with a cripple."

"That's what he told me, all right." She looked at me. "But now, of course, I'm pretty sure of the real reason."

"Yeah," I said. "Hard to court a girl when you've just murdered her father." As I pulled into the alley behind the pharmacy building, I noticed a white car parked in the adjoining vacant lot, its hood partially obscured by an overhanging tree branch, but the emblem on its front license plate standing out like a brand. "Well, would you look at that?" I exhaled through clenched teeth.

"What?" Faith's gaze followed my pointing finger.

"A handicapped plate," I said. "Looks like Lewis decided to get a new toy. One with hand controls and a full gas tank, I presume. I guess my questions last night hit a little too close to home, and he figures I'm onto the truth."

Faith caught on. "Oh, Lewis," she murmured.

We climbed the wooden steps like two prisoners trudging their way to the gallows.

When Lewis answered our knock, he looked horrible—gaunt and hunched, as if recovering from a long illness. He didn't seem surprised to see me, but his eyes widened at the sight of Faith.

"Come in," he said resignedly.

I noticed right away that he hadn't done any packing, and wondered whether he'd changed his mind about running, or had merely decided there was nothing of his old life he wanted to take with him.

Faith and I sat on the daybed and watched him roll his chair into place across from us.

"What really happened that night, Lewis?" I asked bluntly, not knowing how to ease into the subject.

He kept his eyes on Faith. "I loved you so much," he told her. "When I found out what Ralph had done to you, I think I went a little nuts."

Faith opened her mouth and I knew she was going to tell him that Ralph wasn't the rapist. I nudged her and shook my head slightly, not wanting to veer off the subject at hand.

"After I dropped you off at Dorothy's," he went on, "I drove out there like a maniac. I wanted to—

"Kill him?" I supplied.

"No. Honestly. I wanted to hurt him like he'd hurt Faith, and tell him to his face that I was taking her away, but I never even considered killing him. I wasn't raised to think that way."

"I believe you," Faith said and, strangely, so did I.

"But when I got there, Ralph wasn't alone. His assistant was with him."

"Harvey Neff?" Faith squeaked.

He nodded. "As soon as I'd shut off the engine, I heard their voices. They were arguin' about something, but I couldn't make out the words. I slammed open the door. Mr. Neff looked surprised, but he didn't say anything. Ralph Posey was standin' by the fireplace. His fists were clenched and he was all red in the face."

Lewis's mouth tightened. "Soon as I caught sight of that sorry S.O.B., everything you'd told me came flooding back and, all of a sudden, I didn't care that Mr. Neff was there. I charged your father and hit him across the chest like a blocking lineman. He was a scrawny little guy, and he went down hard."

Faith swiped a tear from her eye. I knew it was for Lewis and not for her late father.

"I saw the blood start to trickle from the side of his head," Lewis whispered, "where he'd hit it against the brick hearth. Mr. Neff bent down and felt Ralph's neck for a pulse, then he looked up at me. 'Get out of here,' he said."

Faith and I exchanged a puzzled glance.

"He told you to leave?" I asked.

"Yeah. He said he knew I hadn't meant to kill Ralph, and that he'd take care of things for me if I'd just leave right that minute. I...I did what he told me. I ran out to my car and jumped in and drove away from that cottage as fast as I could." He looked down at his legs. "Too fast, as it turned out. I must've been going ninety when I hit that big curve."

"Lewis," I said, "I think you're leaving something out of the story."

"Huh?"

"The shovel," I reminded him. "When did you hit Ralph with the shovel?"

"What shovel? I didn't hit him with anything except my shoulder. I told you, I just knocked him off his feet."

I leaned forward and looked him in the eye. "There's no reason to lie anymore, Lewis. The police found the shovel, with traces of Ralph's blood and hair on its blade. You struck him with it hard enough to fracture his skull."

He looked from me to Faith, his jaw hanging. "I have no idea what you're talking about."

"Ms. Madison," said a voice behind us. "You are one nosy, damned, meddling troublemaker. Anyone ever tell you that?"

Chapter Sixteen

HARVEY NEFF'S BULK filled Lewis's front entrance so completely that not a sliver of afternoon sunlight made it past him. He closed the door behind him and I heard it latch with a gentle snick.

Nigel, who had been dozing by Faith's side, took one look at the huge man, hissed like a steam engine and bolted for the space behind Lewis's refrigerator.

Faith gasped and shrank back, but there was no place to retreat. She grabbed a pillow and clamped it across her stomach as if it would shield her.

Harvey snarled at me. "I see now that I should've tried to get rid of you instead of Bo."

"You're the one who ran Bo's truck off the road?" I asked.

"If she'd ended up dead, the police would have dropped the investigation. From what I hear, they're positive she's the one who killed that crazy Ralph." Harvey gave Lewis an insincere smile. "Like a good boy, Lewis called to inform me that Bo had stopped by here with some cookies while she was in town to run errands. He neglected to add that she wasn't alone."

"Keron stayed outside in the truck," I muttered. "Allergies." The word gave me a glimmering of a plan, but I'd have to work a few kinks out of it.

"Keron," Harvey repeated, lingering on the name. "So that delicious girl is your daughter, Faith? I checked Bo's truck after it ended up in the ditch. Imagine my surprise when I discovered Sleeping—make that unconscious—Beauty instead of Dead Hag." He smacked his blubbery lips. "Mmmm, wish I could've stuck around and gotten to know her better."

"You bastard," Faith said flatly.

"Oh, God," I said in sudden comprehension. "That's your car parked outside. When I saw the handicapped tag, I thought Lewis had bought himself an escape vehicle."

Harvey laughed. "As if Lewis'd have the gumption to learn how to drive. I got the special license plate when I started driving him to Lubbock every week to visit his mother. All I had to do was claim her as a handicapped passenger, even though I never really take her anywhere. Comes in handy—lets me park wherever I want to." His mouth drew into a hard line. "I've been keeping a close eye on your pal here, ever since he told me about your visit last night, Ms. Madison. I was sort of hoping you wouldn't figure things out, but when you showed up today, I knew you had."

Lewis looked completely baffled. "Harvey, I don't understand any of this."

All the puzzle pieces I'd been chasing locked into place at the same time. "I do."

Harvey chuckled. "I'll bet you do at that."

"The only thing I understand is that I'm leaving." Faith stood up and made a move toward the door.

Harvey pulled a small revolver from his coat pocket. "I don't think so." He examined her from head to toe. "You've held up pretty well, Faith, but you're hardly ballerina material anymore."

She sat back down. "Look who's talking."

"Will someone tell me what's going on?" Lewis pleaded.

"Sure," I said. "You didn't kill Ralph after all, Lewis. Harvey did."

Lewis's eyes grew round. "That's impossible. I told you everything—"

"You told us the part you know about," I interrupted. "Here's what I think really happened that night. Harvey, you'll stop me if I wander off course?"

He waved the gun and gave a sarcastic little bow.

"Lewis, Ralph didn't die when you pushed him. He was only knocked out."

"But Harvey couldn't find a pulse."

"So he told you. I'm betting Ralph still had a nice, strong pulse, and that's why Harvey wanted to get you out the door so fast. He didn't want you to be there when Ralph came to. I suspect Harvey had been waiting a long time to find a way to get rid of Ralph, and your attack presented the perfect opportunity."

"Not such a long time," Harvey demurred. "Only since he found out I'd been pocketing most of the donations from the radio broadcasts. Amazing how many people send cash through the mail."

"After you left, Lewis," I went on, "Harvey grabbed the shovel and finished the job on Ralph. I surmise he originally planned to run to the police and tell him he'd witnessed the murder. What could be easier? He'd gotten rid of his problem, and knew Lewis would confess once confronted by the police. But then another scheme occurred to him. Blackmail."

Faith spoke up. "Blackmail?"

"Sure," I said. "A rich, scared kid who thought he'd just killed a man—what an easy target. And the chimney made a perfect hiding place for the body, although I doubt he intended to leave it there permanently."

"I figured I'd bury it sometime in the next couple of days," Harvey agreed, "but I just never got around to it. Then I found out Bo had closed up the cottage for good, so there was really no reason to bother."

Lewis sat in stunned silence.

"Lewis's car wreck put a kink in Harvey's plans. If the kid died, blackmail was out. If he came to in the hospital and started spilling his guts about Ralph's death, again, no opportunity for blackmail. So once Harvey learned Lewis was going to live, he sat by the hospital bed around the clock."

"When I came out of the coma, he was there," Lewis said slowly. "He told me it would be a cryin' shame for someone as young as I was to spend the rest of his life in prison over something I hadn't meant to do. He said he'd hidden the body and that everyone thought Ralph had just skipped town with the church money because he'd set it up to look that way."

"Harvey took the church money," I said. "But he wanted more. And Lewis went along."

"I handed over all the cash I could," Lewis agreed in a small voice. "I had a pretty hefty bank account because my folks always gave me way more money than I needed. And when Pop died—"

"Your trust fund kicked in," I finished for him. "Which meant even more money for Harvey. He was probably delighted when you had to put your mother into a nursing facility because that meant you could sell the house and give him the profit from that, too."

"Would've been more," Harvey groused, "if he hadn't insisted on moving that batty old woman into the most expensive nursing home in the state."

"Only reason you gave in on that," Lewis reminded Harvey, "was because I said I'd rather get locked up than see Mom put in some awful place where she'd be abused or neglected." He hung his head.

Faith rose and moved to Lewis's side, sliding an arm around him. "Oh, you poor thing."

He ducked away from her, rolling his chair backwards. "I don't want your sympathy, Faith, and someone who's been as stupid as I have doesn't deserve it." He turned his head to look at me. "Ms. Madison, I just want you to know I couldn't have carried this off much longer. Harvey kept tellin' me there's no way a jury would send an eighty-year-old woman to prison, but if they had—hell, if she'd even been arrested—I would've spoken up."

"Why do you suppose I've been keeping such tight tabs on you?" Harvey said calmly. "I never knew when you might get an attack of conscience. You don't think I kept driving you to that nursing home out of the goodness of my heart, do you? Just couldn't take a chance on you baring your guilt to one of those pretty nurses." He gestured around the small room. "This place made a pretty good isolation cell. Pity it's all over now."

Harvey raised the gun. "Here's how it ends. Lewis panics because you discovered his long-buried secret and shoots both you ladies." He nodded toward Lewis's corner desk. "He'll then type out a confession on his computer—actually, I will, to save him the trouble—before turning the gun on himself. A gun, incidentally, that I picked out of the late Mr. Tucker's collection when Lewis was readying his parents' house for sale, so the police will have no trouble figuring out how Lewis got his hands on it.

"At least, Ms. Madison, you'll have the comfort of knowing your good pal Bo will not be arrested, though the death of her only daughter might knock the wind out of her sails."

"You can't shoot us," Faith blurted out. "This apartment is right above the drugstore, for heaven's sake. People will hear the shots."

"Good point, were it not for the pharmacist's habit of closing up shop at noon on Mondays so he can go fishing. And if a passerby does happen to hear a noise and rush to investigate—" Harvey's piggy little eyes widened innocently "—I came over to drive my good friend Lewis to visit his aging mother, and here's what I found. Awful! Blood everywhere!" The revolver's barrel pointed at each of us in turn. "Now we have that clear, who'd like to go first? Any volunteers? No? Then I'll choose."

"Wait. Satisfy my curiosity about something." I was desperate to keep him talking. Surely Faith and I had been gone for at least forty-five minutes—even now, Keron might be phoning Cal to fill him in on everything we'd learned. "You've obviously bilked Lewis out of thousands of dollars over the years—"

"Hundreds of thousands," Harvey corrected with a smirk.

"So why do you still live in that god-awful tiny house?"

"C'mon, mystery writer, you're smarter than that. I've filed income tax at the poverty level for decades—how would I explain a mansion to the IRS? Anyway, it doesn't matter what the outside looks like, as long as the things I love are inside."

"Love," Faith spat. "You don't know what the word means."

He barked a laugh. "I seem to remember giving you some pretty good lovin', little girl."

Lewis finally caught on. "My God," he said slowly. "You were the one who raped Faith."

"Rape? Is that what she called it? Trust me, Lewis, she couldn't get enough."

With a growl worthy of a Doberman, Lewis lunged forward, apparently forgetting in the heat of the moment that he couldn't walk. Faith caught him before he tumbled headfirst to the floor.

"Such bravery!" Harvey marveled. "As your reward, I'll dispose of you first."

I stood up, keeping my eyes on the gun as I slowly approached him. "I'd rather you kill me first. The sight of blood makes me squeamish. But I do have a last request."

"Cigarette and blindfold?" Harvey queried with a grin.

"No, just a little compassion on your part. Lewis's animals mean a lot to him, and I'm sure he'd appreciate knowing they'll be cared for. Especially the *cat*!"

I raised my voice to a shout on the last word and Cecilia, true to her nature, screamed like the victim of a torture rack. Startled, Harvey shot blindly in the direction of the sound and, while his attention was distracted, I made a dive for his knees.

When the plan had first occurred to me, I'd considered trying a shoulder block similar to the one Lewis had described using on Ralph, but Harvey's midsection was so well padded that I figured I'd bounce off him like a seagull encountering a hot air balloon. I remembered, though, that he'd been limping when I visited his house. Most obese people have trouble with their knees—the joints grow weak from trying to support too much weight. I was proven right when he crumpled to the floor (fortunately not crushing me in the process).

The revolver dropped from his hand as he made impact and I kicked it as hard as I could—it skittered under the day bed. Problem was, Harvey was already struggling to stand and my one hundred thirty pounds was no match for his bulk.

"Help me hold him!" I yelled.

Faith made a jump worthy of the Olympics and straddled both of us, whacking Harvey's forehead with the butt of her hand as he made another attempt to rise. Lewis's chair shot across the room like the ball from a cannon and came to a screeching halt beside Harvey's still-prone form. In one motion, Lewis tipped himself to one side and fell, chair and all, atop the three of us.

"Tie him up with something." Lewis had to shout to be heard above Cecilia's continued screaming and Harvey's bellows of rage.

"What do you suggest we use?" I panted. "I forgot to carry the usual coil of rope in my pocket today...sorry." Faith's elbow was in my ribs and one of Lewis's fingers hovered perilously close to poking out my left eye.

"How about the curtain pulls?" Faith breathed in my ear.

"Good idea, except that it's taking our combined weight to hold him down. Cecilia, *please* stop screaming! And, Harvey, if you don't shut up, I'm going to shift my very sharp tailbone to a part of your anatomy that will change your voice from bass to soprano. Lewis, where's your phone?"

"In the kitchen," Lewis puffed. "Too far."

"I have a cell phone," Faith squeaked. "Lewis, get your arm off my throat. I can't breathe. The phone's in my jacket pocket, Taylor. Can you reach it?"

"I can try." I couldn't see her pocket, so started groping and ended up with my hand down Lewis's pants.

And that, of course, is how Cal discovered us when he came bursting through the door, his .357 drawn and ready.

"Howdy, Taylor," he drawled after a moment. "I should've known you'd have things well in hand."

Epilogue

BY THE NEXT weekend, summer (Indian or otherwise) was officially past, as was autumn, but that didn't stop Bo from throwing a massive barbecue out at her ranch. Half the town showed up, everyone bringing at least one side dish or dessert. Gossip and laughter drifted through the cold evening air. Conspicuously missing were Oliver Burke and Dave Underwood. The sheriff's election was coming up, and no one doubted that Cal would win by a landslide. I assumed the new sheriff's first order of business would be to send Burke on his way.

Jesse wandered about, snapping pictures of the celebration. I didn't have to wonder what would fill the front page of his next edition. Paula, I noticed, was sticking close by his side, chatting away. Was a romance brewing there? I sighed. Probably not. They'd make a neat couple, but Paula still had trust issues to resolve when it came to men.

Shivering in my old nylon windbreaker, I huddled next to the largest of the three barbecue pits, turning around to warm first my hands, then my posterior. Dorothy had brought a huge tub of her Rattlesnake Cider, and I was drinking it by the gallon, but its warming effects wore off entirely too soon.

Faith, wrapped in enough fake fur to carpet a small state, shook her head at me. "Taylor, you simply must buy a real coat!"

"I know," I said miserably. "I keep intending to, but..."

"You're too busy with other things," Keron finished, her eyes twinkling. "Like proving sweet old ladies innocent of murder."

"Sweet old lady, am I?" Bo growled. "Wait'll you get to know me, kid. I've been off my oats the past week or so, but now I'm back to normal and meaner than ever." Her craggy face eased into a smile as she looked at me. "I do thank you, though, Taylor."

"For the fiftieth time," I said. "Enough, already. You may have to do the same for me someday."

"I wouldn't rule it out," Cal agreed. "She's a trouble magnet."

"Well, if that time ever comes, ol' Bo'll be square in your corner, but 'til then..." She pulled a large, gift-wrapped box from beneath one of the picnic tables. "Just a little somethin' I picked up in Lubbock."

My fingers were too numb to manage the wrapping, so Keron and

Faith ripped the bows and paper loose. Inside, swaddled in tissue paper, was a thick, down-filled jacket with matching emerald green gloves.

"Oh," I murmured. "Bo, it's beautiful."

Cal helped me pull the jacket on and its warmth stopped my shivering almost instantly.

"Don't you dare thank me," Bo ordered. "I owe you so much more. Speaking of which, do you still want that old desk?"

I'd forgotten all about the desk.

"I sure hope so," she went on before I could answer. "'Cause I hired a couple of teenaged boys to lug it over to your house. By the time you get home, it'll be all set up for you, with that dag-nabbed computer of yours plugged in and everything."

"I loaned 'em my key," Cal whispered to me.

"Good grief," I said. "Bo, you don't have to pay me for helping a friend...that's not how things work."

"Not payment, darlin', just appreciation." She put an arm around Faith. "Not only for keepin' me out of jail, but for bringin' my daughter back to me. I'll sure hate to see her go back to Boston."

"I have to check on the gallery, Mama," Faith said. "But Harvey's trial is set for next February, so I'll be coming back then to testify."

"Danged trial better be over by festival time," Dorothy muttered. "That awful man has messed up enough lives in this town without ruinin' our tourist season, too."

"I don't think it'll be a long trial," Cal assured her.

"Y'all need to come to the festival," Bo told her daughter and granddaughter.

Faith smiled. "Keron might get a kick out of that. Meanwhile, I'm hoping you'll fly to Boston and join us for Christmas."

"Boston for Christmas? Sounds cold and god-awful boring," Bo said. "How 'bout if we all meet in Vegas?"

"Way to go, Grandma!" Keron cried.

"Will your husband be coming along?" Bo asked Faith, who blushed and cast a glance at Lewis. The town recluse was flipping hamburgers at one of the smaller grills and was surrounded by children who all wanted another ride on the back of his wheelchair.

"Alex and I have been divorced in our hearts since about five minutes after we said 'I do.' I think—and Keron agrees—it would be healthier for both of us to make it official."

"Really?" Bo pretended surprise. "I don't suppose your decision has anything to do with the fact that Lewis Tucker is moving to

Boston, does it?"

"Lewis has decided to enroll at Boston University," Faith said with a touch of her old primness. "Although he feels he's too old to begin an eight-year DVM program, he'd like to take some courses in animal psychology."

"Seems like he could do that at Texas A&M and not have to move clear across the country," Bo said solemnly, then broke into a grin. "I'm just foolin' you, honey. I think it's great."

"Here, here!" I thumped the table. "I'm just so glad he wasn't really Ralph's murderer. I liked him from the start."

Cal pulled me aside. "I've been debatin' whether to burst your bubble," he muttered, "but it'll dawn on you sooner or later anyway. If you'd told me you suspected Lewis, I could've let him off the hook right away. I knew he wasn't the killer."

I stared at him. "You did not! How?"

"Because of Ralph's truck. Don't you remember, Taylor? It was found in the church parking lot the day after he disappeared. Now, Bo heard that ol' truck engine comin' up the road the night before, and knew Ralph was out at the cottage, so—"

"So," I concluded, feeling suddenly foolish, "whoever killed Ralph drove his truck back to Perdue. And it couldn't have been Lewis because he wrecked his own car on the way back to town. Damn! Why didn't I think of that?"

"I'm sorta glad you didn't," Lewis put in. He'd rolled silently up behind us. "If you and Faith hadn't shown up at my apartment when you did, I'm real sure Harvey would've killed me. I mean, I'm sorry y'all were in danger too, but—"

"I'm glad we were there, too, Lewis. You have a lot to live for." I smiled at Faith as she walked over and took Lewis's hand. "So do I, for that matter," I added, resting my head on Cal's shoulder.

Dorothy's Hot Rattlesnake Cider

1/2 cup brown sugar
1/4 tsp salt
2 quarts of cider
1 tsp allspice
1 tsp whole cloves
3" cinnamon sticks
dash of nutmeg

Combine brown sugar, salt, and cider. Tie spices in a small piece of cheesecloth, and add to cider. Slowly bring to boil. Cover and simmer for 20 minutes. Remove spice bag, and float thin slices of orange on top. Place a cinnamon stick in each serving mug.

Elizabeth Dearl

Elizabeth Dearl is a former Texas police officer who also owned a small bookstore for several years. Her short mysteries have appeared in many magazines and anthologies. Her story "The Way to a Man's Heart" won a Derringer Award, and "The Goodbye Ghoul" has been optioned for a short film (for which Elizabeth is writing the screenplay).

Elizabeth's mystery novels, DIAMONDBACK (an EPPIE Award finalist which has recently been optioned for a feature film), TWICE DEAD (2002 EPPIE Award winner for "best mystery"), and TRIPLE THREAT (2004 EPPIE Award winner) are set in West Texas and feature amateur sleuth Taylor Madison, who is assisted in crime-solving by her ferret, Hazel. "Buyer's Remorse," a novella which also stars Taylor Madison, in included in the print version of TRIPLE THREAT, and was also included in BLOOD, THREAT and FEARS: Four Tales of Murder and Suspense (2002 EPPIE Award winner for "best anthology"). MALICIOUS INTENT (DiskUs Publishing) is a collection of Elizabeth's mystery/horror short stories.

Elizabeth is a member of Sisters in Crime and The Short Mystery Fiction Society, and is an instructor for Writer's Digest School's Writers Online Workshops. She lives in the Houston area with her husband, a fraud investigator, and two fur-children of the canine variety.

Website: http://www.elizabethdearl.com
Email: elizabethdearl@mail.com

More Taylor Madison Mysteries

DIAMONDBACK

When novelist Taylor Madison discovers a mysterious letter among her late mother's effects, she heads for West Texas in search of her father's identity. But small, sleepy towns don't appreciate rude awakenings and Taylor soon finds herself up to her neck in rattlesnakes and long-kept secrets—a deadly combination.

TRIPLE THREAT

Triplets, a tornado, and twisted lies add up to trouble for Taylor Madison as Perdue's townfolk gather for Hank Barton's funeral. Why do the three identical sisters dislike each other so much? Why did Hank put such an odd codicil in his will? Throw in swaggering new deputy, a citizen's police academy, and an amateur tornado hunter, and Taylor finds herself longing for the comparative peace of big city life!

Printed in the United States
87563LV00001B/84/A